"Where did you get that?"

Though he was several feet away from the cabin, Rob heard Valerie's sharp tone, and it surprised him. No one answered, which surprised him even more.

"Ginny, where did you get it?" Hearing the urgency in her voice, he headed toward the cabin. Behind him, around him, and inside the building there was only silence.

After a long pause, Rob heard his daughter say, "At home."

"And who does it belong to?"

Rob couldn't hear that answer, even though he now stood right outside the cabin. He put his hand on the screen door handle just as Valerie spoke again.

"Ginny," she said gently. "Ginny, give me the gun."

Dear Reader,

I suppose writing a story based on my eighteen years of experience with the Girl Scouts was inevitable. I have nothing but admiration for the goals and values that guided us in our time together. The girls I knew as children have matured into self-reliant, capable young women.

In my new book, *Single with Kids*, self-reliance is just what Rob Warren wants for his daughter, Ginny, challenged as she is by cerebral palsy. Valerie Manion prides herself on her own independence and her ability to take care of herself and her children without assistance. But Rob and Valerie must discover that life is at its sweetest when we can share the good times and the bad with someone we love. Their teachers for this lesson will be none other than their own offspring.

I've smiled a great deal while writing *Single with Kids*, and I hope you smile as you read. Thanks so much for spending time with me and my story—if you'd like to contact me, I'll be delighted to hear from you.

As ever,

Lynnette Kent
PMB 304
Westwood Shopping Center
Fayetteville, NC 28314
www.lynnettekent.com

Single with Kids
Lynnette Kent

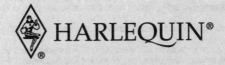

HARLEQUIN®

TORONTO • NEW YORK • LONDON
AMSTERDAM • PARIS • SYDNEY • HAMBURG
STOCKHOLM • ATHENS • TOKYO • MILAN • MADRID
PRAGUE • WARSAW • BUDAPEST • AUCKLAND

ISBN 0-373-71229-4

SINGLE WITH KIDS

Copyright © 2004 by Cheryl B. Bacon.

This edition published by arrangement with Harlequin Books S.A.

® and TM are trademarks of the publisher. Trademarks indicated with ® are registered in the United States Patent and Trademark Office, the Canadian Trade Marks Office and in other countries.

www.eHarlequin.com

Printed in U.S.A.

This book was written with fond memories of all the girls
from whom I had the chance to learn during my
years with the Girl Scouts.

Many thanks go to the women who worked with me—
especially Susan, Ruth, Karen, Ann and Terri. We met
our responsibilities...and we had a whole lot of fun.

Finally, to Elizabeth and Rebecca, the young women
who continue to inspire me and who make every
effort worthwhile... Love, always.

Acknowledgments:

My Girls Outdoors! group is strictly fictional, based
very loosely on the scouting program in the United States.
Any mistakes or misinterpretations are mine
alone and do not reflect the policy, procedure or
personnel of any existing organization.

Books by Lynnette Kent

HARLEQUIN SUPERROMANCE
765—ONE MORE RODEO
793—WHEN SPARKS FLY
824—WHAT A MAN'S GOT TO DO
868—EXPECTING THE BEST
901—LUKE'S DAUGHTERS
938—MATT'S FAMILY
988—NOW THAT YOU'RE HERE
1002—MARRIED IN MONTANA
1024—SHENANDOAH CHRISTMAS
1080—THE THIRD MRS. MITCHELL
1118—THE BALLAD OF DIXON BELL
1147—THE LAST HONEST MAN
1177—THE FAKE HUSBAND

CHAPTER ONE

"I WANT TO BE a troop leader."

At the sound of those beautiful words, Valerie Manion looked up from her paperwork with a relieved and grateful smile. Only as she focused on the person standing in front of the registration table did she acknowledge that the voice volunteering to help her belonged to a male. A tall, lean, corn-silk blond male with a twinkle in his blue eyes and a sweet curve to his mouth.

She blinked at him. "I beg your pardon?"

He grinned at her disbelief. "I signed my daughter up for your Girls Outdoors! program. You said in the parent meeting a few minutes ago that you need volunteers." A glance around the school cafeteria showed them to be the only adults remaining. "Looks like I'm it."

"Um…yes. I did. I do." She was still having trouble with the concept. A *dad* wanted to help out with the troop? "Tell me your name again."

"Rob Warren. My daughter is Ginny." He tilted his head toward the windows where a thin, chestnut-haired girl stood propped on crutches.

"Hi, Ginny," Valerie called. "We're glad to have you."

Ginny's mouth kinked into a half smile, but she made no effort to come closer or respond in kind.

Valerie picked up the stack of registration papers she'd just collected and paged through them. "Here we go. Virginia Warren, third grade."

Mr. Warren had meticulously filled in the blanks on the form with small, neat letters. He gave his work address as Warren and Sons Locksmiths, and provided names and numbers for a doctor and a dentist. He listed Carolyn Warren, identified as "Grandmother," as an emergency contact.

In the space for Ginny's mother's name, he'd carefully written "Deceased." Valerie bit back a small moan of sympathy.

As if that weren't tragedy enough, the explanation for those crutches came farther down the sheet. In answer to "List any special physical conditions," her father had written, "cerebral palsy."

With another glance at the girl by the window, Valerie noticed the braces on the girl's spindly lower legs. Then she looked up—a long way up—into Rob Warren's handsome face. "Ginny wants to be in GO! and you would like to work with the troop. That's terrific. Why don't you sit down, Mr. Warren, so we can talk? I'm getting a severe crick in my neck, staring up at you like this."

"Good idea." He pulled out a chair and folded himself into it. "The name's Rob."

"And I'm Valerie. Have you ever worked with a troop before?"

"I was a Boy Scout, if that counts. Got my Eagle award."

She nodded. "Are you familiar with the GO! program?"

"Only with what you've said this afternoon, and what was in the brochure that came to the house. And I did a little checking on the Internet."

"What is it about the program that Ginny particularly likes?"

Rob hitched his chair closer to the table. "To be honest, the whole thing is pretty much my idea. I think Ginny needs a chance to be with other girls, involved in a group like this. I want her to have these kinds of experiences, even though she's disabled."

That was a warning sign if Valerie had ever seen one. "There's no question that girls of all ability levels are welcome to join the troop. But they have to bring the right attitude with them."

"I understand. But you have to realize how hard it is for a girl like Ginny to fit in." Leaning forward, he rested his clasped hands on the table—strong, graceful hands with long fingers. "As a result, she's shy, a little withdrawn. I'm thinking that once she gets comfortable, she'll start to enjoy herself and be as enthusiastic as you could ask for."

"You realize this is an active program? We hike, swim, fish, sail…"

He nodded. "I do understand. And I know Ginny won't be able to participate in every activity to the fullest. But if I'm there, I can help her get the most out of what y'all do and contribute as much as possible to the group."

Valerie's misgivings only increased. A leader should

be responsible for *all* the girls. Chances were good that Rob would focus on his daughter and her needs, leaving Valerie to cope with the rest of the troop.

Without another leader besides herself, however, the troop wouldn't exist at all. Given the dearth of volunteers, she had no choice.

"Well, Rob, you've got yourself a job. No pay, no benefits, lots of overtime." She grinned at him and offered a handshake. "And lots of fun."

"I'll take it." He extended his hand to take hers. The warmth of his skin left Valerie feeling breathless. Tingly, even. She pulled back as soon as she could manage without appearing to be rude.

To hide her burning face, she bent to the file box beside her chair and began pulling out papers. "You'll need to complete these forms. GO! rules mandate that a male can only be an assistant—the troop leader must be female. Since no one else has volunteered, I'm the consolation prize. Are you okay with that?"

When she sneaked a look him, she found him frowning down at her. "You're a good deal more than a consolation prize, Ms. Manion. Myself, I'd say I'm lucky to have you."

The last thing she expected—or wanted—was a compliment. "Well…well, thanks. I hope we can work together to give the girls a great year in the outdoors."

"I'm sure of it," he said, just as a red-headed whirlwind blew into the room, chased by a poster-perfect Girls Outdoors! member in khaki shorts and a vest.

"Connor!" the girl yelled. "Connor, you little twerp, give it back right this minute."

Her shrill command only made things worse. Connor, a seven-year-old with a freckled face and the devil in his grin, ran up and down the long room holding a bright pink book over his head, always just out of the reach of the girl on his heels.

"Mom," Grace wailed. "Make him give it back."

"Excuse me, Rob. My children always pick the worst times." Valerie sighed and got to her feet. "Connor Mc-Nair Manion. Stop. Now."

Connor stopped running, but twisted his body around the book so Grace, leaning over him, couldn't get hold. Valerie went to stand in front of him with her hand held out. "I'll take the book."

"It's mine." Grace kept trying to reach over his shoulder for her property, which Valerie recognized as the diary she'd received from her father for her birthday back in June. He'd stopped by for fifteen minutes to deliver the gift, and they hadn't heard from him since.

"Yes, I know it's yours. Connor, give me the book."

"When she gets off me."

Once Grace had backed away, Connor looked over his shoulder, straightened up and handed over the diary.

"Thank you. Now, go sit in that chair and don't move until I tell you to."

Head down, shoulders slumped, her son went to the table and plopped into the chair she had used. As Valerie watched, Rob Warren grinned at him, but Connor stuck his lower lip out as far as it would go and turned his head away. Typical behavior these days from the little boy who had once been all smiles.

"Grace, have you met Ginny?" Valerie gave her daughter the recovered diary and then led her to the window. "Ginny's going to join the troop. And her dad will be the assistant leader."

Grace's eyes went round. "A man leader?"

"A dad. It'll be great—he was an Eagle Scout, so there's lots he can teach us. Why don't you two get to know each other while we finish up here?"

As Rob worked his way through the required forms, Valerie packed up her supplies, keeping one eye on Connor, sulking at the table, and one eye on Ginny and Grace, who didn't say a word to each other. She supposed she couldn't expect much else from a shy, disabled girl and the new kid in the class, though she'd have liked to see something go easily, for a change. Her recent move to North Carolina had been nothing but hassles so far.

Finally, Rob stacked his pages together and got to his feet. "Here you go—I think these tell more about me than even my parents know." He grinned without malice or sarcasm, and Valerie couldn't help smiling in response.

"Blame the lawyers," she told him. "They make the rules. And break them when they want to." Her own bitterness slipped out before she could stop it.

"That they do." The look Rob gave her offered sympathy without intruding. His longish hair and slow, sweet drawl made her think of Ashley Wilkes in *Gone With The Wind*. She'd read the book in the sixth grade and built her dreams of romance on Margaret Mitchell's foundation.

Then she'd grown up to discover that chivalry, like the antebellum South, was a thing of the past.

Rob was gazing at her with an eyebrow raised in question, and Valerie realized she'd dropped the conversational ball.

"Right. I'll turn these papers in and we'll get the troop going." Flushing, she bent to the plastic box of supplies beside the table and started pulling out the books he would need. "Here's the handbook, the activities book, the leader's guide, the safety manual and the regulation notebook."

"You want to hand me the IRS code while you're at it?"

She looked up, knowing she would find that warm grin again. "You volunteered. And I'm not letting you back out now."

"I wouldn't dream of backing out, Ms. Manion. You're stuck with me…with us." He glanced at the girls, silent by the window. "And I'm sure everything will turn out just fine."

For the first time, his smile was a little doubtful. As she stared up at him, Valerie had to wonder why Rob Warren worried about his daughter getting along in the troop. And how much trouble his worry predicted for her in the long run.

"Of course it will," she found herself assuring him. "We'll have a great year." She bent to pick up the box. "Our first meeting is next Wednesday. We'll have to get together to do some planning before then."

"Let me take that," Rob said, slipping his hands under the front corners of the container.

"I've got it." Valerie backed up, looking over her shoulder for her daughter. "Grace, could you get the other box? And Connor, bring that bag, please."

But Rob still hadn't let go of the box she held. "I'll get this one."

"No, thanks. I can do it."

"But you don't have to." He took a step forward.

"I want to." She grinned at him. "Are we going to dance around the room with this between us? Or can I just carry it to my car?"

Shaking his head and frowning, he backed away with his hands held up in a gesture of surrender. "You are one headstrong woman, Valerie Manion. Your husband's a patient man."

"I'm divorced." She said it quickly, flatly. "It's just me and the kids."

He gazed at her for a moment with a somber expression. "I'm sorry."

"Not your problem." She glanced around the room, double-checking for stray papers, then headed for the door.

Rob followed. "But I'm gonna be working with you. Should I be relieved or worried about this stubbornness of yours?"

"Both. Because I'm committed to making our troop the best it can be. And…" Balancing the box on her knee, she pulled her keys out of her shorts pocket and hit the button to unlock the doors on her van. "And I always get my way."

Even though he waited for Ginny to leave the building ahead of him, Rob somehow crossed the parking lot ahead of Valerie to open the van's rear door before she could.

"Always?" He reached out one more time for the box.

"Always," Valerie affirmed, sidestepping to put the container into the back of the van by herself.

"We'll have to see about that." He took Grace's load and stowed it next to other box.

Valerie managed to capture the bag Connor carried. "I win," she said, putting the sack next to the boxes.

But Rob beat her to shutting the door. "Whatever you say, ma'am."

Valerie rolled her eyes. "You're impossible. Should I be glad or worried?"

He winked at her. "Both."

WITH ROB'S FRIENDLINESS to think back on, Valerie found herself feeling more cheerful than usual as she made dinner. After cleaning up, Grace and Connor settled down in front of the TV with a movie while she completed GO! paperwork at the dining room table. The only part she didn't like about the program was the never-ending reports to be made. Tonight, though, she kept remembering her new assistant leader's IRS comment and his good-natured teasing about the forms, and the work went quickly.

The phone rang while she took a break with a cup of coffee in the kitchen.

"Good evening, Valerie." Connor Manion Sr., attorney to New York's new money, had taken speech lessons to smooth Brooklyn out of his voice.

"Con." She turned her back to the kitchen door, hoping the kids wouldn't hear. "What's wrong?"

"Why should there be something wrong? I called to check on my children."

"For the first time in three months."

"I've been in Europe on a case."

"How nice for you."

"Much nicer than Ohio or—where are you now?— Hicksville, North Carolina."

"What do you want, Con?"

"You should've stuck with the sure thing, Val. You could have been in Paris this summer, too. Great clothes in Paris, and I remember how you like clothes."

She chose to say nothing and, as usual, silence goaded her ex-husband into some fast talking.

"Anyway, I want to chat with the kids. But first I thought I'd let you know that the check's coming."

"In the mail, no doubt."

"Monday, at the latest."

"Is this July's check, or August's?"

The veneer cracked. "What the hell are you talking about? I sent money all summer."

"No, you didn't."

After a seething few seconds, he recovered. "My secretary must've scr…missed some paperwork. I'm sure I directed her to send those checks."

"That's what you'd like the court to think, anyway. Don't worry, Con. I haven't reported you. Yet."

"Don't sound so superior, damn you. You need the money, I know you do."

"The kids need your money. All I need from you I

have in them. Hold on and I'll bring Grace to the phone."

The excitement that Con's phone call produced in her children was depressing, but Val managed to maintain a cheerful expression until they went to bed. Worn out by the effort, she got into her own bed a half hour earlier than usual. Lying on her side, she rested her cheek on her right palm, and then remembered shaking hands with Rob Warren. The thought made her smile.

Maybe tonight, she could look forward to her dreams.

"THERE YOU GO," Rob told his daughter once they were in their van and headed home. "Sounds like fun, doesn't it?"

Ginny shrugged a thin shoulder. "I guess."

"Aw, come on. You like being outdoors, right? We can go camping and fishing and all sorts of things."

"We could do that anyway. We don't need a bunch of girls to go with us."

"Yeah, but I bet you'll have fun with those other girls. Grace seems really nice."

"She talks funny."

He chuckled. "She has a New York accent, like her mom. Definitely different from Southern English."

"And her little brother is a pest."

"That's what little brothers are for. So big sisters don't get too comfortable."

A spark of real interest flared in her gray eyes. "You treated Aunt Jen that way?"

"I'm sure I did. You can ask her tonight."

Ginny nodded. "I will."

She got her chance when his sister Jenny came through the back door, just as they finished cleaning up after dinner.

Jen stopped in her tracks, pretending to be surprised. "You didn't save me any?"

"You hate macaroni and cheese, Aunt Jen." Ginny gave her a hug. "Was Daddy really a pest when he was little?"

"The worst." Jen sat at the table and pulled Ginny close to her side. Mat the Cat jumped onto her lap and settled with a purr as Ginny rubbed his ears. "I could never get rid of him. And he would take my stuff and hide it. I still haven't found my favorite Barbie doll—the one I painted to look like a Shoshone warrior."

Rob leaned his hips back against the counter, tapping one finger against his temple, as if thinking hard. "Oh, yeah. Where did I put that?" He shook his head. "Nope, can't remember. It's gone forever. Ready for your bath, Gin?"

She heaved a huge sigh. "I guess so."

"Don't sound so put-upon." Jen got to her feet, pulling her shoulder-length, silvery blond hair into a ponytail with a band on her wrist. "I brought new bath lotion—bubblegum scent."

"Cool." Ginny led the way out of the kitchen. In a few minutes, her giggles floated down the hallway on the sound of water flowing into the tub.

As Rob folded the dish towel and turned out the kitchen light, Jen stuck her head around the doorframe. "You okay?"

He straightened his shoulders. "Sure."

"You look…tired."

"Long day." Weren't they all?

"Another argument with Dad?"

"Among other things. How about you?"

Her face dropped its smiling mask. "Sure. I'm okay." Sadness clouded her eyes, but then she shook her head. "We'll be done in a while. I'll go through her exercises with her tonight. You take it easy."

"Thanks, Jen. I'll be outside." Rob pulled a beer out of the fridge and carried it to the back porch, shutting the door behind him to keep the cool air in and the hot evening out. Despite the high cost of air-conditioning, he wouldn't think about turning the thermostat up. Ginny couldn't sleep if the house got hot. And they both needed her sleep.

As he shook off the disloyal thought, he heard a car door slam out in front of the house. The side gate creaked open, and his friend, Pete Mitchell, came into the yard.

"'Evening," Rob said, lifting his beer in a toast. "Want one?"

"Sounds great."

When Rob left the house this time, Mat the Cat came with him. The orange tiger started to rub up against Pete's leg, then took a sniff and darted down the steps into the grass. "I guess he smells Miss Dixie on my jeans." Sitting on the step beside Rob, Pete took the beer and cracked open the top. "I stopped to feed her before I came over."

"Yeah, Mat's not real fond of the canine club. No

classes tonight?" The state trooper organized and managed a nightly school program for teenagers who'd run afoul of the law.

"Friday night doesn't draw enough kids to make the effort worthwhile. Jen's inside with Ginny? How's she holding up?" Pete had been part of the law enforcement procession during the funeral of Jenny's fiancé, killed in the line of duty back in June.

"She says okay. What else can she say?" Rob took a draw on his beer. "Where's your better half? And your half pint?"

"There's a wedding shower for Jacquie Archer at Dixon Bell's house, so I'm on my own. Mary Rose took Joey with her. I guess babies and weddings kinda go together, don't they?" Pete leaned back against the step behind him.

"That's the best way, so I hear."

"I ate supper down at the diner with DeVries and Bell—both of them making do without wives tonight, like me. But, man, I hate being a bachelor again. Just doesn't feel right." After a swig of his beer, Pete threw him a sidelong glance. "That was a dumb thing to say. Sorry."

"No problem." Although Rob had been one of the first in their high school class to walk down the aisle, his three best friends and basketball buddies had caught up with him in the last couple of years. Along with Pete, Dixon Bell and Adam DeVries had each found a woman to share their lives with. Now Jacquie Archer, another friend of theirs from high school, had a wedding in the works. "I guess love is in the air these days in New Skye."

"So it's your turn." His friend punched him in the shoulder. "We need to find you a nice woman of your own."

Rob snorted. "Yeah, right. It's not that big a town, Pete. I already know every eligible woman—grew up with most of them—and the prospects aren't good. Besides…" He finished his beer. "I've got responsibilities nobody else can take on."

"Ginny doing well?"

"Sure. We enrolled in the Girls Outdoors! troop at school this afternoon. I'm gonna be assistant leader."

"Girls Outdoors?"

"Like the Scouts. Camping, hiking, all that jazz."

"With a bunch of little girls?" Pete shook his head. "Man, that's gotta be crazy."

They sat for a long time, talking a little now and then as the August twilight deepened and the air cooled. Just before dark, the door behind them opened and Ginny came out slowly, using her crutches without leg braces.

"Hi, Uncle Pete."

She couldn't sit easily beside him, so he gently hugged her around the hips. "Don't you smell good? Like bubblegum. Be careful—somebody's gonna chew you up."

Ginny giggled. "You're silly. Where's Joey?"

"His mom has him at a party, and I imagine he's being spoiled rotten as we speak." Pete got to his feet as Jen came outside. "So how's your first month on the EMT service going?"

She smiled, the mask firmly back in place. "Excellent, thanks. I'm sure it's the right thing for me to do."

"That's all well and good, but we sure do miss you in the shop," Rob said. "You don't even want to know what your files look like at this point."

She squeezed her eyes shut for a second. "I can imagine. Dad takes 'em out of the drawer and just piles them on the desk when he's done. I guess he expects the file fairy to come in overnight and put everything back. I'm off this weekend—I'll take a few hours and straighten up the mess."

Rob nodded. "That would be a godsend. I'm getting so many calls these days I don't have time for paperwork except at night. I hate having those files piled high and getting mixed up or, worse, lost."

Jenny put her hand on his arm. "It's okay, bro. You don't have to do everything."

"Amazing how many people get locked out of their houses or cars, isn't it?" Pete shook his head. "I did it myself just after Joey was born. Walked out the door to visit the hospital and left the house keys inside."

Rob thought back seven months or so. "I don't remember getting a call from you."

"I climbed in through a window." The state trooper winked at Rob. "And you don't need to tell me about home security, or being sure your windows are shut and locked. That's my line. I am thinking about an alarm system, though. That way, I'll feel better about Mary Rose and Joey at home without me. Can you give me a good deal?"

"Don't I wish. I keep nudging Dad toward the security business—electronic locks and alarm systems. But he digs in his heels every time. 'Three generations of

Warrens have made locksmith work their life.'" Rob imitated his dad's gruff tone. "'It was good enough for my daddy, it's good enough for me. Why the—'" He glanced at Ginny and changed his words. "'Why in the world ain't it good enough for you?'"

"Too bad." Pete stirred, stood up and stepped off the porch. "I guess I'll get myself home again. I'm a grown man—I ought to be able to survive an hour or two on my own." But still he hesitated, a lost look on his face. "How long can a wedding shower last, anyway?"

When Pete had gone, Rob turned to Ginny. "You ready for bed, sweetheart? If you want to go on inside, I'll say good-night to Aunt Jen and be there to tuck you in shortly."

Ginny frowned. "Do I have to go to bed? It's Friday night, and there's no school tomorrow. We could watch a movie, right?"

The tired ache in his shoulders felt like a boulder sitting on his neck. "I'm pretty much worn out, Gin— I don't think I'll make it through a movie, starting this late. How about we plan to watch a movie tomorrow night?"

"I'm not tired." The crossness in her voice belied her words. "I want a movie tonight."

Jen stepped up and put an arm around Ginny's shoulders. "Come on, Gin-Gin, I'll tuck you in. We can read abou—"

"No." Ginny couldn't stomp her foot, so she banged her crutch on the porch floor, scaring Mat the Cat back into the grass. "Other kids get to stay up late on Fridays and watch movies and eat pizza and candy. I never get to do fun stuff like that."

Rob put up a hand. "Ginny, that's not true."

"Yes, it is. I get boring dinners and a bedtime like I was a baby. Joey's not in bed yet and he's only seven months old. He's at a party!" She maneuvered around to face the door and fumbled with the door handle. When Jen reached out to help, Ginny slapped her aunt's arm away. "I can get it myself. I'm not a total freak. I can open a door."

Jen stepped back. "I was just trying to help."

Ginny was past noticing anybody else's feelings. "I don't need help. I need a real life." She got the door open, propelled herself into the kitchen and then managed to slam the panel behind her. Rob chuckled as he heard the lock click.

Jen looked at him, her eyes round. "She locked you out?"

He shoved his hands into the pockets of his jeans. "She does, every once in a while."

"But—"

"It's okay. After the first time, I made sure never to leave the house without my keys, even to take out the garbage." Putting his arm around her shoulders, he gave her a hug. "Thanks for helping out tonight. Sorry you got such lousy feedback."

She shook her head and started down the steps. "You know I love being with Ginny—even when she's throwing a tantrum. Mom said to tell you she'd be over tomorrow night as usual."

"I might call and ask if she can make it earlier, so we can have this movie night Ginny wants."

"I'm sure that'll work. 'Night, Rob." She crossed the

backyard to the stand of yellow oak trees they'd planted between his house and hers. "Get some sleep yourself."

"I will." He raised his hand in return to Jen's wave, until she disappeared into the shadows under the leaves.

After another minute of peace and quiet, Rob dug his keys out and unlocked the kitchen door. Inside the house, the television was defiantly loud. A ghostly flicker filled the living room. Ginny had put on her movie.

His little girl lay in front of the TV on top of her big soft floor pillows, with her crutches discarded nearby. Her eyes were open, but she pretended to ignore his presence, punishing him for the treachery of exhaustion.

With a sigh, Rob sat in the recliner in the corner. The cool leather embraced him, molded to his body by years of use. He'd slept in this chair many an hour, holding his daughter through a long, disturbed night. He could do it again. Even with loud cartoon voices and sound effects in his ears.

Along about midnight, though, when the movie had ended and the videotape had rewound, and when Ginny had fallen fast asleep, he got up and knelt to lift her from the floor. She hardly weighed a hundred pounds, no burden at all for him to carry. He set her gently down on the bed in her room and pulled the covers close— she would be chilled if she didn't use the blankets. After a return trip to the living room for the crutches, he stood for a little bit watching her sleep.

The daytime lines of effort and disappointment vanished from Ginny's face when she slept, so she appeared carefree in a way she never did when awake. He could see her mother in her thick reddish hair, the soft rose tint of her cheeks. Leah had been beautiful, enthusiastic, vibrant with life. If she had lived, she might have helped them discover the joy amidst all the compromises, limitations and accommodations. Rob knew they were lucky—Ginny's disabilities could have been much worse.

As things stood, though, Ginny and he had struggled from the very first time he'd heard the words "cerebral palsy" applied to his child. Rob had long since given up believing that one day the struggle would end.

In his own room, he dropped his jeans and shirt onto the floor and fell facedown on the bed. He was on call for the shop tomorrow, which would keep him tied to his pager and cell phone all day long. And he had a basketball game at 7:30 a.m. Getting some more sleep tonight would be a really good idea…

Only minutes later—or so it seemed—a small fist pounded at his shoulder. "Daddy? Daddy, wake up. It's the phone." Ginny stood by his bed. "I let it ring a thousand times."

Rob ran a hand over his face and realized it was daylight. "Man. I didn't know I was asleep. Sorry." He picked up the phone Ginny had dropped on the bed. "'Lo?"

"Rob? This is Valerie Manion."

With an effort, he pulled himself together and sat up in bed. "Hey, Valerie. How are you?"

"I've been better, actually." Her Yankee accent seemed sharper than he remembered. "I hate to bother you so early, but I need a locksmith as soon as possible."

He glanced at the clock. *Damn.* He'd slept through the basketball game. "What's the problem? Keys locked in the car?"

"Nothing so simple. I need to have all the locks changed today. According to the police, this house was previously used as a dope distribution center. The Realtor didn't tell me that, of course—just fixed the place up and sold it for a good price."

"You talked to the police?"

The deep breath she drew definitely sounded shaky. "I called them last night when someone tried to break into the house."

CHAPTER TWO

"ARE YOU OKAY?" Rob said. "Are your kids all right?"

Hearing the concern in his voice, Valerie felt the tension inside her relax a little. "We're fine. The police arrived while the guy was still trying to jimmy the back door lock, so they caught and arrested him on the spot."

"Thank God. You spent the rest of the night with a neighbor, right?"

"Um…no. We don't really know our neighbors yet—we only moved in last week."

"You went to a motel?"

"We stayed here, and I pushed a couple of pieces of furniture in front of the doors." Valerie thought back to the struggle of sliding the kitchen cupboard across the floor. "Heavy furniture."

By his stunned silence, she could tell Rob thought her choice a poor one. Who made him the expert, anyway? She could take care of herself and her kids without a man's input.

After a moment, he cleared his throat. "Well, you're right about one thing—you do need your locks changed this morning. That's no problem—I'll be there within the hour."

"Thanks." She set the phone down, propped her chin on her knuckles and closed her eyes. Grace and Connor were still asleep in her bed, where they'd all cuddled once the police had left and the doors were blocked. Valerie had stayed awake, listening to the multitude of night sounds and wondering about the windows, which were locked but vulnerable nonetheless. She'd never been quite so glad to see a sunrise as she was this morning.

Before she could give in to the need for a nap, the black van Rob had driven yesterday pulled into her drive. Blue and white lettering on the side advertised Warren and Sons Locksmiths. Somewhere in the middle of last night's terse police questions and frantic children's tears, her brain had latched on to a fact she'd only skimmed yesterday afternoon—Rob Warren was a locksmith. His phone number on Ginny's information sheet had relieved at least one of her worries.

With a strength that seemed to come out of nowhere, she pushed the TV cabinet away from the front door. "I'm so glad to see you," she called as he and Ginny crossed the grass. "Thanks for coming out this early." Her pleasure in seeing him was totally out of proportion to the occasion. He was coming to do a job. Right?

Rob stopped at the foot of the porch steps and grinned at her. "You're more than welcome. I'd have come last night, if you'd called. I hate to think of y'all barricaded behind furniture to stay safe." He looked the way a man should on a hot Saturday morning in August—relaxed and comfortable in a dark blue T-shirt and faded jeans that hung a little loose on his long legs, with his hair combed back and damp from a shower.

"Grace and Connor are still asleep," she said, willing her pulse to slow down. "But it's good to see you, Ginny. Come in and make yourself at home."

Ginny moved ahead of her dad, who waited behind her as she slowly climbed the steps—one crutch, then the other and then her braced legs. Her face was a frozen blank, as if she was trying to deny her own effort.

Valerie held the door open, then followed father and daughter inside. "I apologize for the place being such a wreck. We just moved in last week, and I'm still unpacking boxes at night after work. The kitchen's the neatest, Ginny, if you want to sit in there."

Unlike her dad, Ginny did not have a ready smile. "Whatever."

Rob glanced at her with lowered brows, but didn't comment. "Which locks did this guy mess with?"

"The front and back doors. He wasn't a pro, obviously, because he didn't get through either one, and started pounding away with something, trying just to break the door open. The police said he used a tire iron."

Nodding, Rob turned back to the front door and squatted down to examine the deformed dead bolt and splintered wood around it. His long fingers moved lightly across the different surfaces. He clicked his tongue. "This lock was no great shakes to begin with. But he's pretty much destroyed your door." In a clean, easy motion, he straightened to his full height. "How about the back?"

"This way." She led him through to the kitchen and heard Ginny follow them across the wood floor with a thump of crutches.

"Oops, I haven't moved that cupboard yet."

"Excuse me." His warm hand on her shoulder gently set her aside.

Valerie made sure Ginny took a chair at the kitchen table and then went to join him in pushing the big, heavy piece.

Rob shook his head. "I'll get this."

She put her hands on the oak frame. "I can move my own furniture."

"I see that. But you don't have to while I'm here. Just step back."

"All you have to add is 'little lady' and I'll believe you're John Wayne." She didn't smile as she said it.

His eyes widened and his mouth firmed into a straight line. "Well then, since I'm not the Duke, I guess we'll do it your way."

"I will admit," Valerie said when they'd shoved the cupboard against the wall, "that putting this thing in place again with you took a lot less time than moving it by myself."

Rob gave her a wink before turning to the back door. This time, he didn't need to bend over to see the damage. "Looks like he went at this one harder 'cause he didn't figure he'd be seen in back. This is another new door and lock. And the door frame's damaged, too. Before you can put in a decent lock, that'll need to be replaced."

Valerie dropped into a chair at the table. "So we really can't stay here another night. I know a carpenter won't come out on Saturday." On top of a sleepless night—and Con's phone call—the whole ordeal pressed down on her shoulders with the weight of a millstone. "I hate leaving our stuff at the mercy of whoever comes by. But—"

"Hold on a minute." Rob sat down across from her, with Ginny between them. "We can do better than that. I've hung a few doors in my time, but I've got a couple of friends who are professionals. Let me see what I can rustle up."

"You don't—"

He didn't wait for her protest, but whipped out his cell phone and punched in a number. "Hey, Adam. Yeah, I actually did. Sorry 'bout that. Listen, have you and Dixon got plans this morning? I have a lady in distress here, and I think you could help." After an explanation and a few quick words, he closed the phone. "There you go—they'll be here in about an hour. They were just sitting down to breakfast."

Valerie set aside her irritation at the "lady in distress" description and got to her feet. "Speaking of food, have you eaten anything, either of you?" She looked at Ginny, who pouted and shook her head. "Well, that's a problem I can solve right away."

Rob put up a hand. "Why don't I just go get some doughnuts, or—"

"Not a chance." She, too, could boss people around, including this smooth-talking, dictatorial Southern gentleman. "I've got a decent breakfast in the fridge and it won't take long to put together. Do you drink coffee?" she asked, with her head inside the refrigerator. "I try to avoid the stuff on the weekends because I live on it all week, but I can make a pot."

"I'm a tea drinker, myself."

"I have some tea bags." She pushed the refrigerator door closed with her hip. "I'll make you a cup."

"Well, actually—do you have any iced tea?"

She stopped in front of him, a carton of eggs in one hand and a jug of milk in the other. "Iced tea? At breakfast?"

"Lunch, dinner and bedtime, too." His eyes twinkled, reminding her of Connor at his most mischievous.

"I don't know how to make iced tea."

"I could show you."

"You make tea?"

"My daddy makes the best," Ginny put in. "He learned from my grandmama. When our family gets together for a picnic, everybody wants Daddy to make the tea."

Valerie gestured toward the pantry with the milk. "Well, clearly I'm in the presence of a master. Be my guest."

By the time she'd scrambled eggs and broiled bacon, Rob had produced a pitcher of tea and Grace stood at the door to the kitchen with Connor behind her, blinking at their early guests. "Mom? What's going on?"

"Good morning, sleepyheads. Come to the table. Mr. Warren and Ginny are here for breakfast, and then Mr. Warren is going to fix the locks on the doors."

Not budging a step farther, Grace glanced at the back door. "Did that man come back?"

"No. No, he won't come back. The police took him away, remember?"

"C'mon, dummy, move!" Connor pushed from be-hind and stomped past his stumbling sister into the kitchen. "I'm hungry." In the middle of the room, though, he stopped short and pointed at Ginny. "She's in my chair."

Valerie nodded at the space next to Rob. "We brought in a new chair for you. Grace, come sit beside me."

"I'm not sitting next to her." Connor walked around to his usual place. "Give me my chair."

Ginny stared at him with a challenge in her eyes. "No."

"Ginny—" Rob started.

"Mommy," Connor whined, "I want my chair."

She took his hand and led him to the other side of the table. "You will sit here. Or you won't eat." Her son slouched into the disputed seat. With his arms crossed over his chest, his cheeks puffed and lower lip stuck out, he resembled a grouchy frog.

Ignoring him, Valerie looked at her daughter. "Come sit down, Grace, before the food gets cold." After an-other moment of hesitation, Grace sidled in behind the table to sit next to her brother, who promptly blew a raspberry at her.

"Hey." Rob's hand closed over Connor's shoulder. "That's no fair."

Connor turned his freckled face toward Rob. "What do you mean?"

"You can't blow raspberries without a reason."

"Who says?"

"It's the rule."

"Whose rule?"

"Everybody knows raspberries don't count unless the other guy—or girl—did something to you first." With a shrug, Rob sat back in his seat. "That's the law of the land."

With eyebrows lowered and lips pursed, Connor stared at him for a long time. At last, he turned to Valerie. "Can I have some eggs now?"

"Please," she reminded him.

He rolled his eyes. "Can I please have some eggs now?"

"Good man," Rob told him with a grin.

Valerie watched as Connor started to smile back, then quickly reverted to his standard belligerent attitude. After a year of his moods, she'd begun to wonder if the cheerful little boy she'd once known would ever reappear. Thanks to Rob Warren, she now saw that he still lurked beneath the mask—daunted but not gone forever.

Once the kids cleared the table after breakfast, Ginny returned to her chair and Grace and Connor went to get dressed. Valerie attempted to load the dishwasher without Rob's help.

"I can do that," he insisted. "You cooked. I want to clean up."

"I will finish the kitchen," she said through gritted teeth. "Sit down and drink your tea or go for a walk around the block. But don't stand here in my way."

A knock at the front door forestalled his answer. She started to leave the kitchen, then turned back. "Don't touch the dishwasher," she warned. "Or heads will roll."

He put up his hands in a gesture of surrender. "Ginny and I will come along so you can keep an eye on me."

"Good idea." When she reached the door, she found two good-looking guys in shorts, T-shirts and sneakers standing on the porch.

The taller one spoke first. "Ms. Manion? I'm Dixon Bell, and this is Adam DeVries. Rob Warren gave us a call about your doors?"

Rob stepped up behind her. "About time y'all showed up. I was beginning to think I'd have to hang these doors by myself."

"God f-forbid," Adam DeVries said. "You'd never get them square."

"Wait a minute." Valerie shook her head. "I thought I read in the paper…saw somewhere…that the name of the mayor is DeVries."

The dark-haired man smiled at her. "That's me. And on b-behalf of New Skye, I'd like to w-welcome you and your f-family to the city. We're glad to h-have you." His gaze dropped to the doorknob and he scowled. "Although this is not at all the kind of reception you should have gotten. I'll be talking to the police chief."

"Adam owns a construction business," Rob said over her shoulder. "And when he's not putting down other people's best efforts, he does a good job. Dixon has done a lot of restoration work on his own house, so he's another one you can trust to get your doors hung right."

She felt as if she was being swept along by a river of masculinity. "I really don't want to bother you—"

"It's no bother." Dixon smiled, and she realized he was nearly as handsome as Rob, with a moonlight-and-magnolias accent all his own. "We're glad to help a new neighbor."

Adam pulled a tape measure out of his pocket and reached to the top of her door. "All we have to do is m-measure, then we can get the right-size d-doors and get on with the j-job." The mayor seemed quieter than his friends, but his steady gaze was reassuring. Valerie decided he had her vote.

"We'll need to measure the back door and check out the frame," Rob warned. "That's got to be replaced, too."

The men were soon deep into a cryptic conversation involving tools, wood and screws. Valerie stood her ground, trying to understand, hoping to remain an active part of the process. In the end, however, she assured Rob that Ginny was welcome to stay with her while he went for supplies and then watched helplessly from the front porch as the three of them got into a white pickup truck and drove off.

When she turned back into the house, Ginny stood nearby. "What am I supposed to do now?"

Valerie called up her most encouraging smile. "Well, let's go find out what Grace is up to." She led Ginny down the hallway to Grace's bedroom, only to find the door closed. "Grace, are you okay?"

Her daughter opened the door to create a narrow crack she could peer through. "Yes." Her glance flicked to Ginny and then away.

"Ginny's here while her dad has gone to get the new doors. I thought the two of your might find something to do together."

The hesitation in Grace's face was easy to read, and Valerie felt sure Ginny saw it. But after a long moment, the door opened all the way.

"Sure," her daughter said, with a marked lack of enthusiasm. "Come in."

Valerie stepped to the side, giving Ginny room to pass. She could practically feel the temperature drop below freezing. "I'm going to help Connor unpack his room," she told them. "He's been waiting all week. So, you two…um…have fun."

The two girls stared at her, their expressions a similar mix of impatience, resentment and uncertainty. Valerie turned her back and escaped to the simple world of the seven-year-old male. Maybe there she could establish a position of authority.

As she reached Connor's door, a foam missile hit her in the face.

Then again, maybe not.

GRACE RETREATED to her bed, leaving the other girl the rest of the room. After a couple of minutes, the girl came in—you couldn't call it walking, exactly, with the crutches. She stopped in the middle of the rug, looked around but didn't say anything.

"What do you want to play?" Grace said at last, just to end the silence.

"I don't care," the girl said without looking at Grace.

"Do you like dolls?"

"Dolls are for babies."

Grace glanced at her favorites, all lined up on the bed. She hoped they hadn't heard. "Um…I have puzzles."

"Boring."

She didn't see how they could play dress up. And she didn't want to play dress up with the girl, anyway. "We could build with Lego's. Or play Life."

The girl sighed, went to the chair at the desk and sat down. Grace gasped when she remembered that she'd left her diary there, open. She started to jump up and grab it out from under the girl's face.

But the girl didn't seem to notice the diary. "So what happened last night? Did some guy really try to break down your door?"

"Yes." She shivered when she thought about it.

"Did he make a lot of noise?"

"N-not at first. It got louder, the more he tried."

"Were you awake the whole time?" The girl seemed really excited. She hadn't said this much in the entire first week of school.

"I don't think so. Mom came to get us and took us to her room, then called the police."

"And you just sat and listened until they came?"

Grace nodded, then swallowed the lump in her throat at the memory.

"Scary, huh? What were you going to do if he got in before the cops came?"

"My mother—" She remembered just in time. *Tell nobody. Absolutely no one.* "I don't know."

But the girl didn't believe her. "What were you going to say? Your mother…?"

"My mother locked the bedroom door. We were safe enough until the police came."

The girl's pale eyes narrowed. "I don't think that's

what you meant. I think you were going to say something else."

She gripped her bedspread with both hands. "No, I wasn't. That's all."

Now the girl did turn to the desk, and she picked up the diary. "I could keep this and give it to your little brother."

Grace jumped to her feet. "You can't do that. It's mine."

"And if you try to take it away, I'll tell your mother you were hitting me." The girl gave a fake smile. "Nobody likes it when you beat up on a cripple."

"Please, give it back."

"Tell me what you started to say."

"I—I can't. I promised not to."

"Okay." She shrugged and then wiggled to her feet, with the diary caught in her hand next to the crutch. "I'll go see your little brother."

"Wait. Stop." Grace took a deep breath. It wouldn't hurt to tell *what*. She wouldn't say *where*. "I'll tell you."

"I'm listening."

"I—" She glanced at the door, as if her mother could hear.

"Well?"

"My mother has a gun." Grace dragged in a deep breath. "We sat on the bed facing the door, and she loaded and cocked the gun. If the guy had come in, she was going to blow his head off."

"Could she do that?"

"She took shooting lessons. I think she could."

"Wow." The girl set the diary on the desk. "That's cool."

Grace reached out and grabbed the little book, hugging it close to her chest and ran back to her bed.

"But she didn't get to shoot him, did she?"

"No." She finished stuffing the book under the mattress, then turned and sat down on top of it. "The police came."

"Can I see it? The gun?"

"No."

"Why not?"

This time, she had an answer ready. "My mom hides it. I don't know where she keeps it."

"We could look for it."

"She'd figure out pretty fast what we were looking for. And then we'd get in trouble." Major trouble, since Grace wasn't supposed to have said anything in the first place.

"Too bad." The girl sighed. "That would have been fun." They both sat and did nothing for a few minutes. "Does your boom box work?"

"Of course."

"Do you have any decent music?"

"What do you think is decent?"

"Canned Tin?"

Grace couldn't help releasing a smile of relief. "Have you heard their latest CD? It's awesome."

"I know. And my dad won't get me the disk—he says it's not good music."

"Your dad's crazy out of his mind." She expected to be slapped for the words.

But the girl smiled again—a real smile, this time. "I know."

DIXON AND ADAM got the doors hung around midafter-noon, and shared a glass of iced tea and a plate of choc-olate chip cookies with Valerie and the kids before going back to their own families. Then Rob went to work on the locks.

After only a few minutes, he felt eyes boring into the back of his head. A glance to the rear showed Connor standing behind him. "Hey. Want to watch?"

"No."

"Okay." Rob turned back to his work, but the sensa-tion of being observed didn't go away. "Since the other door was about twenty years old," he said conversation-ally, "the lock hole on a new door wouldn't have been in the right place. So we got a door without a pre-drilled hole and I'm gonna make one that matches the old door." He picked up his router and set the point on the door. "This'll be loud." The high-pitched roar of the tool took over for a few minutes.

With the hole drilled, Rob popped out the plug of wood. "That's all there is to it." He set the plug to his side and a little behind him, where a small hand promptly snatched it up. "Now I need another, smaller hole for the tongue to go through."

Step by step, he talked his way through the dead-bolt installation, without ever seeing Connor face-to-face. "All that's left is to tighten these screws." He suited ac-tions to words, then stepped back. "Now there's a good strong bolt on this door, at least." With the door shut, he locked both the dead bolt and the knob. "I bet no-body's gonna get that door open without a key any time soon." Gathering up his tools, he headed for the kitchen without a glance around.

But he paused in the dining room and grinned as he heard the distinct sound of a little boy rattling a doorknob.

By dinnertime, both the front and back doors of the Manion house boasted state-of-the art brass doorknobs, plus heavy-duty dead bolts.

"That's a start." Rob surveyed the finished back door from inside the kitchen. "No junkie's gonna get through steel and brass before the cops get here."

"Fantastic." Valerie stood beside him, her dark, curly hair barely level with his shoulder. "I miss the windows in the door, though. I liked looking out onto the backyard while the kids played."

"You still can—that's why we've got the storm door, here." He reached around her shoulder to open the inner panel. "When you're home, you can leave the door open and look through the glass. Come nighttime, or when you're away, this thick metal door will keep you safe."

He followed Valerie out onto the deck, where Ginny sat with a book. Connor and Grace were climbing on the play set in the shade underneath a grove of pines, but Rob didn't like Ginny using a swing unless he was nearby.

"What I really need is a security system, with all the doors and windows wired." Valerie rubbed her hands up and down her arms, though the evening was far from cool. "My last two houses had one. Does your company install alarms?"

Rob blew out a deep, frustrated breath. Another potential sale he had to turn down. "No, we don't. I can send you to a couple of good companies up in Raleigh. But there's nobody local who installs and monitors alarms yet. I'm pushing my dad, but…" He shrugged. "Mike's a little set in his ways."

Valerie looked at him curiously. "Do you like working with your family?"

"Has its ups and downs." Mostly downs, lately.

"I know I couldn't work with my dad. He still can't believe I actually read the financial pages and run whole departments in big companies. And whenever we go home, he tries to tell me how to parent my kids." She made a wry face. "I don't go home very often."

"The grandparents think they know best, don't they?"

"Of course. And it's worse since the divorce. He's sure I don't know what I'm doing with Connor." It was her turn to sigh. "Unfortunately, half the time I think he's right."

"Don't give up yet. I imagine it's hard on a kid, losing his dad. Does he get to see your ex often?"

She turned away to fiddle with the leaf of a potted plant. "No. Con Sr. doesn't do kids anymore."

Rob had a word for men like that, but he kept it to himself. The sun had dropped behind the treetops, leaving the deck and the entire backyard in shadow. Valerie lifted a hand to the nape of her neck and massaged the muscles there. He knew she had a headache, from the tiny line between her brows.

"You must be tired," he said. "I doubt you got much sleep last night."

"None." She looked up, smiling. "But tonight I can sleep safe behind my strong new doors."

That smile was a killer—sweet and saucy, with the dimple, and yet a little shy. He got hit by the strangest need to trace the shape of her mouth with his fingertip. Or to sample the taste of a kiss.

In his head, bells clanged and a siren screamed. Rob backed all the way to the rail of the deck. "I…think Ginny and I had better be getting home. Leave y'all in peace." Even an argument with his daughter would be preferable to the wild ideas currently racing through his brain. "Ginny, time to go."

"I really appreciate all you've done." Valerie followed as he wrangled a protesting Ginny to the front door. "I expect a bill for your time and all the materials."

"You'll get one," he promised. "Or my dad'll be on my back." He reached the car without further temptation. "'Night," he said, as Valerie stood by his open window. He pressed the brake and shifted gears, almost escaped.

Then she placed her hand on the door—a capable hand, with well-tended nails and soft-looking skin. "Rob, we need to get together to talk about the first GO! meeting. I've got a general plan, but I want you to contribute. When are you free?"

He'd forgotten GO!. "Anytime," he said, relaxing in the seat, accepting his fate.

"How's tomorrow afternoon? Around two?"

"Fine. Shall I come here?"

"That's good."

"Okay, then. Y'all have a peaceful night." He couldn't help adding, "And call me if you need help this time."

"Sure." That reassuring smile meant *Not a chance.*

"Promise." He glared at her. "Let me hear you say it."

Valerie put her hand over her heart. "Okay. I promise."

Rob nodded. "Right." She stepped back and he made his getaway. Only for a brief reprieve, though. Tomorrow, he would come back…to a woman who inspired ideas he hadn't allowed inside his brain for years.

Maybe by tomorrow, he'd have recovered from this temporary insanity. Tomorrow, she'd look like every other woman he'd met in the last eight years. Nice. Ordinary. Right?

Yeah, right. Sunday afternoon, Valerie met him at her new front door, wearing a light-blue sundress. Her shoulders were bare and tan, as were her long, smooth legs.

At the sudden spike in his heart rate, Rob acknowledged the fact that this woman might turn out to be the exact opposite from nice and ordinary, after all.

CHAPTER THREE

VALERIE LOOKED BEYOND him as he stepped onto her porch. "Where's Ginny?"

Before he could answer, though, she gasped. "What a gorgeous car! Is it yours?" Leaving the front door wide open, she rushed out to the driveway. "A '55 Thunderbird, right? I love the turquoise and white. Oh, and it's a manual transmission. How cool is that? Aren't those whitewalls just to die for?"

"Uh…yes." Rob grinned and leaned a shoulder against the porch post while she circled around his car, making little noises of pleasure. He'd hadn't seen a woman as cute as Valerie Manion in a long, long time. "Glad you like her."

She glanced up from her intense study of the taillights. "I know, I'm crazy. My granddad had one of these, and my dad dated my mom with that car. By the time I could drive, though, they'd retired the Thunderbird to a place of honor in the garage. Never took it out, just kept it polished for nostalgia's sake." Shaking her head, she backed away. "I used to sit behind the wheel and pretend to drive. But I never got the chance."

A pretty woman in a sexy sundress, driving his pre-

cious 'Bird on a sunny summer day...not an offer a guy
could be expected to pass up. He pulled the keys out of
his pocket and twirled them around his finger. "Well,
then, let's go. It's a nice afternoon."

For a second, her face brightened. "Could we?"

Then a kid's voice called out something from the
backyard, and Valerie shook her head. "No, with only
two seats there's not enough room for Grace and Connor, and I can't leave them home by themselves. Another time, maybe?" Her hopeful expression convinced
him she really meant it.

"Sure. We can park your kids with Ginny at my parents' house, and take off for a couple of hours. Just say
the word."

She came back to the porch and opened the door
again. "I'll do that. Meanwhile, come in."

The moving boxes stacked in the living room yesterday had disappeared overnight. Books and pottery and
candles filled the shelves on either side of the fireplace,
a nice rug covered the floor, and the blank walls displayed photographs of Connor and Grace, along with
a couple of signed and numbered prints.

"This looks great," Rob commented, studying the
framed landscape hanging above the couch, as an alter-
native to staring at Valerie. "Is this one by Stephen
Lyman? That's Half Dome mountain in Yosemite Park,
right?"

She came to stand beside him, which defeated the
whole exercise. "You know his work?"

How long had it been since he noticed a woman's
scent? Valerie, he'd just discovered, smelled like fresh

summer grass. He shifted his weight to put more distance between them. "I was really into the outdoor life when I was in high school. A friend and I had this goal to head out to California on motorcycles and spend a summer camping. I guess I came across one of Lyman's pictures somewhere and incorporated him into the plan. Those images of firelight in the dark wilderness always appealed to me."

"And did you get to California?"

"Nope. The friend took off before graduation, I got married and settled down. Have you been out there?"

"We spent our honeymoon in San Francisco." To his relief, she went to sit in the armchair beside the couch. "My ex-husband wasn't a camper, but he did agree to spend a couple of days in Yosemite on a driving tour. So I've seen it, at least."

Rob dropped onto the end of the couch nearest her chair—too close for comfort, but he didn't want to be rude. "Maybe we'll have to get this troop experienced enough so that we can all go out to Yosemite together."

"Definitely. Older GO! girls are encouraged to set their sights on a big project like that, develop a plan for earning the money and then follow through on the arrangements. It's a great learning tool."

Her smile brought the dimple into play. "In the third grade, though, we're not quite so ambitious. Have you had a chance to look at the books I gave you? There's some information about the general organization of a meeting." She pulled out a clipboard and balanced it on her knee...after crossing her legs with a smooth motion that raised his blood pressure ten points.

"I…uh…paged through last night. Sad to say, I fell asleep over the chapter on Safety At The Meeting Place."

To his relief, she laughed. "I'm not surprised. It's all pretty basic, commonsense stuff. Let me tell you about some of the ideas I've been working on for this first meeting."

In the next hour, they created a detailed meeting agenda and a rough outline of the first three months' activities. As they talked, Valerie realized that Rob consistently understated his talents and his preparation for the role he'd assumed as assistant leader. She didn't have to explain why she made certain choices of activities—he understood what she wanted to do, and his suggestions improved her plans.

"This looks great," she said, surveying her notes. "A couple of hikes, two cookouts and then the overnight camp before the weather gets too chilly. When the weather changes, we can switch to more indoor activities."

A glance at the empty coffee table in front of them reminded her that she hadn't even offered him a cup of coffee. "You must think I've got the manners of a carpetbagger. I didn't ask you if you were thirsty or hungry. I've still got some cookies…"

Rob shook his head as he stretched to his feet. "No problem. My mom makes a big Sunday lunch, so I've had plenty to eat and drink."

"I'm well aware of the Southern tradition of hospitality, not to mention great food. I hope it's contagious."

Rob chuckled. "I think we figure if somebody's

stuffing their face, they can't be disputing what we're trying to say." He accentuated the drawl, and then gave her a wink. "Pretty wily, us Southerners."

"Outrageous might be a better word." She followed him onto the porch. Her new neighborhood wasn't quite the peaceful setting she'd hoped for—there seemed to be a lot of engine noise in the air, and more traffic than she liked in front of her house. "I guess it's a good thing the backyard is fenced," she said, as a car drove by at a speed considerably over the limit. "Connor would be out in the street with his ball before I could sneeze."

"Yeah, this isn't the neighborhood I would've steered a single mother and her kids to, if they had other options." He winced as a pair of Harleys roared past. "Or maybe I'm just used to my part of town, where it's quiet and a lot less hectic. My sister, Jenny, and I bought a big lot that stretches from one street to the next, and put a house for me and Ginny on one end and a house for Jen on the other, with a nice stand of trees between the backyards. Works really well."

"Your wife didn't live there with you?" The question was out before she realized what she'd said. "I'm sorry, Rob. It's none of my business."

He held up a hand. "It's okay. I don't mind telling you. Leah and I had an apartment across town. I didn't want to live there after…" He swallowed hard. "Her labor didn't go well, and Ginny had the cord wrapped around her neck. Just real bad luck altogether."

She put a hand on his wrist. "You must have been devastated."

"I didn't get to think about that aspect of things too

much. Babies take a lot of time and attention. I was pretty busy."

"My husband left on a business trip two weeks after Connor was born. I know exactly what you mean."

"We're a pair then, aren't we?" His gaze held hers, and his arm turned under her fingers until their hands closed upon each other, palm to palm. Not a simple handshake, but a deeper, warmer connection. She felt the texture of his skin, felt the strong dome of muscle at the base of his thumb, the deep valley over his life line. They held each other so tightly, a single pulse beat through both of them…or so it seemed.

In another instant, though, he had released her and dropped off the porch steps into the grass. "If you think of anything else you need before Wednesday, just call me," he instructed, walking backward toward the driveway. "And be sure you use those new locks."

"I will. Thanks for everything." She waved to him as he pulled out of the drive, and should have gone inside at that point. Instead, she stayed on the porch, watching the Thunderbird drive down the street until it was lost from sight.

A very nice guy, she thought. A good friend, a great father.

And the sexiest man she'd met in…well, ever. She'd thought she preferred dark, compact professional men, until Rob. Now, tall and blond and lean was her idea of perfect. Forget the business suits and ties—give her a guy in a baseball cap, a black T-shirt and jeans faded to nearly white, with a rip across the knee and frayed hems. Let him drive a 1955 Thunderbird, turquoise and white. Her heart pounded just remembering how great he looked in that car.

Grace joined her on the porch. "Mr. Warren's nice, isn't he?"

"Mmm-hmm."

"You could go on a date with him. Ginny said her mom died a long time ago."

"I don't think Mr. Warren and I will be dating, Gracie."

"Why not?"

"Because—" She gave in to a moment of temptation and imagined Rob with her on a date. Specifically, the end of the date, where he would reach across that white leather seat, take her in his arms and lift her chin up, then press his mouth to hers…

"We work together, and that's all. For the troop. There can't be any other complications." She shooed Grace into the house and followed close behind, hoping she could heed her own sensible advice.

Otherwise, she had absolutely no doubt that indulging her attraction to Rob Warren would qualify as the most colossal complication of them all.

AS SOON AS HE opened the shop door on Monday morning, Rob heard his dad's voice rumbling in a constant stream of complaints. When he looked in the doorway of the office, he found Mike Warren standing in front of the file cabinets with half the drawers already open. A pile of folders and a messy stack of loose papers on top of the desk reversed all the progress Jen had made during the weekend.

"What's going on, Dad?" Rob stepped into the small room and noticed—again—the dusty window and blinds, the worn paint on the walls, the outdated calendar. The place needed a serious face-lift. If only he had the time...

"I was lookin' for the invoice from that latest order we placed for lock sets. I know I laid it on the desk here last week, but I'm damned if the whole place wasn't straightened up, so this morning I can't find a damn pencil, let alone the papers I need." Mike paged through one folder, pushed it aside and started on another as the papers in the first folder slid toward the edge of the desk and then the floor.

"Jen came in to do some organizing." Rob caught the papers just before they fell, stacked them together and put them back into the folder. "Maybe what you're looking for is in a file."

"Yeah, well, why do you think I've got this stuff out on the desk?" His dad made a helpless gesture with his hands. "But the only folder I can find with the company name on it is catalogs. I don't need the catalog, I need the damn invoice."

Rob went to the far right file cabinet and pulled out the top drawer. "As I recall, she files the year's invoices by month received, and month paid. We got that shipment...what? Two months ago?" He checked the June folder, then July. "Here it is. Those locks came in at the beginning of July."

"Well, thank God you had some idea of where to look. This whole system is just a mess." His dad tugged the paper of out Rob's hands. "How'm I supposed to remember what month the damn locks came in?"

"There's a logbook, Dad." Rob took the journal from the left drawer of the desk. "We record the deliveries." He didn't mention that his sister simply did what their dad had told her to with regard to the paperwork. Mike wouldn't want to hear that the system he despised this morning was his own invention. "So what's the problem with the invoice, anyway?"

"I keep taking down locks that don't work right." His dad left the office and went into the workshop. On his bench was a stack of six boxes containing brand-new locks. "Gotta send 'em back."

"That's a good company. It's hard to believe they'd distribute defective merchandise. Have you tested every lock in the shipment?"

"That's your job today." Without so much as a glance in Rob's direction, his dad started checking over his toolbox, getting ready for the day's work.

Rob stood still for a minute, unwilling even to breathe for fear his temper would get the best of him. "My job?" he said, finally. "You want me to test five hundred locks?"

Mike nodded. "That's right."

"And I get this job because…?"

"Who else? Trent's on call today. Smith is working on that office building project, which leaves you."

"I'll take call again. Let Trent test the locks." He sounded like a whiny teenager. But he wasn't an errand boy or an apprentice. "Or let Smith stay here and work with the locks. I should be doing the office project, anyway."

"You weren't able to stay until six in the afternoons,

like they needed. So Smith took the job. And you test the locks."

"Why don't you test the locks?" Absolutely the worst thing he could've said.

Mike looked at him, then—Rob felt like he was staring at his older self in a mirror—and straightened up to his full height. "I run this business. I make the decisions and I assign the jobs. Nobody argues. That's the way it is."

And I quit, Rob said, but only in his mind. He'd had the thought a thousand times in the last fourteen years, and never acted on the impulse. Quitting his job would cause havoc in the family. More importantly, the insurance he carried through the business handled Ginny's medical bills. He couldn't afford to give up the insurance unless he had a better policy to replace it with. And these days, getting new insurance for a child with a preexisting condition was about as easy as changing his dad's mind.

So he swallowed the words, along with a few choice phrases he would like to have used. "Yes, sir." He headed toward the storeroom and the boxes of locks. "Whatever you say."

WHEN HER OFFICE INTERCOM buzzed during her Monday morning staff meeting, Valerie could have sworn in frustration. "Excuse me, gentlemen."

The other department heads relaxed in their chairs as she crossed the room to pick up the phone on her desk. She turned her back to the conference table before she spoke. "Terri, I asked you not to disturb me during the meeting."

"I know, Ms. Manion. But it's your children's school calling. I thought you'd want to know if someone was sick or hurt." Her secretary had three children of her own, their pictures proudly displayed on her desk.

"Yes, of course." Valerie sighed, sweeping her fingertips across her own bare work surface. "Put me through."

After a click, a man's voice said, "Hello?"

"This is Valerie Manion."

"Ah, Mrs. Manion. This is Charles Randleman, the principal at Crawford Elementary School. I need to speak with you about your son, Connor."

"Is he hurt? Sick?"

"Uh, no. Connor is fine. But he's been causing us a great deal of trouble, and I think it's time I involve you in the situation."

Oh, Connor. Not again. "Has he hurt somebody?"

"No, no, not really. But—"

"Is the school building still standing?"

"Yes, of course. But, Mrs. Manion—"

His use of "Mrs." set her teeth on edge. "Then I'll have to call you back, Mr. Randleman. I'm in a meeting and I really can't talk right now."

"But this is your son, Mrs. Manion. Surely, he's your first priority."

"Yes, and if I don't work, he doesn't eat, which is a priority for both of us. So I'll call you when I'm free and we'll set up a time to talk. Thanks for letting me know there's a problem." She hung up on the principal's bluster, took two seconds to master her worry and then turned to smile at the four men waiting for her. "Now, we were reviewing those production figures for the last quarter, weren't we? Do we have a good reason for the six-percent drop?"

An hour later, she finally had her office to herself. As she put together the reports she'd received, Terri knocked on the door. "Here's your lunch, Ms. Manion." She set a tray on the conference table. "Is there anything else?"

Valerie didn't glance at the food. "Terri, we need to get something settled. I'm going to notify the school that you are authorized to receive any emergency information about Grace and Connor that needs to be delivered. I don't want to be interrupted in a meeting unless there's a really good reason. This morning's chat with the principal was not a good reason."

Terri's pale blue eyes went round with shock. "You want me to…to…to brush off a principal?"

Valerie grinned. "Haven't you always wanted to?"

But Terri didn't smile back. "N-No. I haven't."

"Oh. Well, yes, I want you to tell the principal that if no one's life or health is at stake, I will call him when I have a chance."

"But you're their mother. You have to care about what's wrong."

"I do care. But I care about my work, as well. Do the other vice presidents take personal calls from the school during meetings?"

"I—I don't know…"

"I've been working in management for ten years now, and I've never seen it happen."

Terri couldn't seem to grasp the concept. She wrung her hands. "Their f-father isn't—"

"No, he isn't. And he didn't take calls when he was. I'm not saying I want to ignore a serious problem, Terri. If Connor's sick, I want them to tell you and I'll leave as soon as possible to take him home. I just need to be able to prioritize. That means only bona fide emergencies during the workday. Okay?"

"O-Okay."

Still looking confused, the secretary went back to her desk. Valerie sat down in front of her salad and crackers, with the production reports in front of her. Work time was for working, or else she'd never get everything done.

The intercom buzzed again before she'd had time for more than a forkful of lettuce. "Yes?"

"Ms. Manion, I'm sorry. But it's the school again."

"I—" No, she wouldn't complain. Her authorization wasn't in place yet. "Let me speak to them."

Another click on the line. "Mrs. Manion, this is Principal Randleman. I'm afraid we do have a serious problem this time."

Valerie waited, expecting to hear about some wrestling match in the library.

"Connor punched his fist through a window," Randleman said. "We had him taken to the hospital in an ambulance."

ROB ARRIVED AT the elementary school thirty minutes before the end of class on Wednesday. As early as he was, though, he found Valerie there ahead of him, with her boxes of papers, books and supplies already unloaded and sitting on a cafeteria table.

"You are one organized lady," he told her, noticing the precut craft supplies, the cookies and juice for snacks already prepared. "I'd have to be a real early bird to get the worm before you do."

She smiled, but he thought her eyes looked strained. "I like knowing everything is ready ahead of time. Surprises make me nervous."

"I understand." He held out the bag he carried. "Twenty-five compasses, donated by Moore's Outdoor Store."

"Donated? Really?" She gazed into the bag, then looked up in amazement. "How did you get them to do that?"

"Hank Moore's a friend of mine from high school. I asked and he said he'd be glad to contribute."

"That's terrific. We can do the orienteering activity we talked about." Valerie set the bag beside her other materials. "I came up with another game to have in its place, but I'd much rather work with the compasses."

Irritation flickered inside him. "I told you I'd get them. You didn't need to waste time worrying about another activity."

She turned away. "Well, yes, but sometimes people don't get around to doing what they say they will, so it's best to be prepared."

He caught her wrist between his fingers and tugged her back around. "Listen, Valerie. When I say I'll do something, you can count on it getting done. No excuses, no second thoughts." She still hadn't looked at him, so he lifted her chin with his other hand. "Got that?"

"Got it," she said, breathlessly, her brown eyes wide. Rob realized suddenly how close he'd brought her—close enough for a kiss, if he bent his head. Just a touch of his mouth to hers…

The loud jangle of a nearby bell announced the end of school. Before the vibrations had died away, he and Valerie stood a table's length apart. In the next moment, little girls started pouring into the room, which effectively doused any adult inclinations he might entertain.

In time, Rob supposed, he would learn all their names, but to begin with there seemed to be a hundred of them, all about the same size and shape, all dressed in khaki shorts and vests and dark blue shirts, all running and chattering and in general creating chaos. Talk about safety in the meeting place! Ginny came in last of all, wearing the same outfit but easily distinguished by her crutches.

He met her in the center of the cafeteria. "Hey, sweetheart. How was your day?"

"Okay." She looked tired, as she always did after school. "This is really crazy." As she spoke, a redhead with pigtails flashed by Rob, headed at top speed across the room. Next thing he knew, Ginny cried out and both girls went down in a jumble of legs, arms, and stainless steel.

"Oh, man." He knelt by his daughter, who was thrashing around. "Settle down, Ginny." He put his hand on her shoulder. "You're okay."

"I am not. She hurt me!"

The redhead was crying, too. "Oww. My arm hurts."

Valerie knelt on the other side. "Sit up, sweetie.

There you go. Let me see your arm." Rob helped Ginny sit up, and they got the two bodies separated. The four of them were now the center of a circle formed by wide-eyed little girls.

"That was a stupid thing to do." Ginny had shifted into a high-gear tantrum. "You don't run around people with crutches—you might hurt them. Can't you see where you're going?"

"Hush," Rob told her. "It was an accident."

"I think you're okay," Valerie told the other girl. "You just fell hard on your hand." She looked around the circle. "Why don't we start the meeting? Girls, get your books from your backpacks and sit down here. Grace, would you bring my books over? And where's Connor?"

"He went outside to the playground," Grace said as she handed her mother the materials.

"He can't play outside with his hand in a bandage. Go get him, please, and tell him to come inside."

"He won't come if I say so."

"Tell him I'd better see him in here in one minute or he'll be missing TV for the rest of the week."

Grace heaved a big sigh and went toward the door. Rob could sympathize—he had it on Jen's authority that it wasn't fun, keeping track of a little brother all the time when you'd rather be participating in your own activities.

Thanks to the planning session on Sunday, he'd brought along Ginny's floor chair so she could sit with the other girls. By the time he'd gotten her settled, Grace was back with a disgusted Connor. The boy's hand was bandaged from fingertips to elbow.

"Did you get in a fight with a bobcat?" Rob winked at him. "They're mean critters, aren't they?"

Connor narrowed his eyes. "There are bobcats around here?"

"Not really. What did you do to your hand?"

But Connor wasn't volunteering an answer. He turned his head away, just as Valerie officially started the meeting.

"I'm glad to see all of you at our first Girls Outdoors! meeting. I'm Ms. Manion, your leader, and this is Mr. Warren. He'll be my assistant leader."

"I didn't know men could be leaders," said a little blonde across the circle.

A dark-skinned girl spoke at almost the same time. "I didn't know men could be assistants."

Valerie grinned. "Well, according to the rules, men can be GO! assistant leaders. Mr. Warren was a Boy Scout and earned his Eagle award, so he knows lots of stuff about the outdoors he can share with us. Now, let's go around the circle so each one can tell us her name and one interesting outdoors fact about her. Grace, can you start?"

Rob saw Grace flush, and her eyes looked a little bright. But she knew what to do. "My name is Grace Manion and I like bird-watching."

Around the circle they went, learning names and hearing about girls who liked soccer or swimming or tennis, who camped with their families or sailed or spent a week at the beach. As the girls spoke, Connor started scooting away from the circle, pushing with his feet and sliding on his backside in an attempt to escape.

Rob watched with a smile as Valerie grabbed the leg of the boy's jeans just before he moved out of reach and pulled him back to sit beside her, all without even glancing in her son's direction.

Just then, Ginny's turn to talk arrived. "I'm Virginia Warren," she said. "I like to ride horses."

One of the girls on the other side of the circle said, "You ride horses? I don't believe it."

"I do ride." Ginny's face turned red. "I take lessons, too."

On Rob's left, Valerie nodded. "There are riding programs for people with all sorts of abilities. And there are GO! badges for horseback riding, among lots of other things. Open your books right now to page one hundred seventy—that's the HorseCare Badge. To earn that badge, you have to do six of the activities listed on these pages. And when you do them all, then I can give you a little circle which looks just like the picture. You sew your badges on your vest and everyone can see all the interesting things you've done when you wear your uniform."

She took them through the book as she had planned, pointing out the soccer badge, the swimming badge, the shell-collecting and bird-watching awards, plus cooking and camping and a myriad of other activities. "What you'll need to do is to look through and decide which badges appeal to you the most. Some you can earn on your own, and some we'll earn as a troop."

Valerie got to her feet. "As a matter of fact, we have a couple of badge activities to do this afternoon. On page one-thirty-nine is the hiking badge." She walked over to the table and took one of the compasses out of the bag. "Anybody know what this is?"

A couple of hands went up, including Grace's. Valerie called on a different girl. "That's a compass."

"Right. And what's it used for?"

Grace and several others raised their hands. "To find directions," someone said.

"And which of the badge requirements does using a compass satisfy?"

All heads bowed low over the handbooks, each girl trying to read fast and be the first to answer the question. Grace put up her hand a minute before anyone else. Ginny was next.

"Tell us, Ginny," Valerie said.

"We're supposed to use the compass to make a path from one place to another place."

"Right." Valerie smiled. "So let's all get up and Mr. Warren will start teaching us how to do just that."

Rob thought he'd planned out his twenty allotted minutes very carefully, but he hadn't counted on the silliness of third-grade girls. His time was up long before he'd gotten everyone to understand which way to point the compass, let alone how to change directions.

Valerie grinned at him as she raised her hand for quiet. "Looks like we're going to need more than one meeting to understand orienteering. For now, all of you can put your compasses back into the bag, and then sit down at the table for snacks." The girls stampeded toward Rob as he held the bag, then rushed to the table to jostle for their places. Grace and Ginny brought up the end.

"I understand," Grace said quietly. "My mom and I have worked with compasses before."

"I could tell," Rob told her with a smile. "I saw you trying to help the others. I appreciate the effort."

Her eyes shone at the praise. "You're welcome."

"Excuse me." Ginny's voice was at its most impatient. "I want some snacks before it's all gone." Grace stepped aside and went to sit at the end of the table.

Rob eyed his daughter with disapproval. "That was not polite."

"Was I supposed to wait forever?"

"You—" He swallowed the reprimand. "Have a seat so everybody can eat."

After snack came the craft segment, which had to do with making paper chains to represent the food chains in nature. Ginny's fingers didn't maneuver scissors well, so Rob spent most of his time cutting out the pictures she wanted from the pages of animals and plants Valerie had provided.

The meeting ended at four-thirty with another circle, standing up this time. "Link hands," Valerie said. "Like this." She crossed her arms and reached for the hands of the girls on either side of her. Everyone else followed suit…except Ginny, who couldn't hold her crutches and cross her arms.

"Just take my hand," Rob told her. "Don't worry about it." But he could tell by the set of her mouth that another storm was brewing.

As they all held hands, Valerie taught them a song about friendship. "This is how we'll close every meeting," she told them. "As friends and as a troop. Remember the GO! motto—All for one, and one for all!" At the words, she turned in place, uncrossing her arms as she did so. The girls—except for Ginny, and Rob—followed suit.

Then there were parents arriving to pick up their daughters, book bags to gather and chains to collect, and more excited chatter than Rob had ever imagined.

Finally, the room grew quiet, with only three children left to deal with. Ginny had made her way to a chair and sat there twirling her paper chain around her wrist. As Valerie packed up her supplies, Grace gathered trash from around the room and under the table where girls had let their scraps fall.

Connor had subsided onto the bench of a table and put his head down on his unbandaged arm. "What did happen to his arm?" Rob asked Valerie. "Is he okay?"

She put the last of the construction paper away. "He and another boy got into an argument at school on Monday. When the other boy teased him from behind a window, Connor…" She closed her eyes, then shook her head as if she still couldn't believe it. "Connor punched his fist through the window."

"Ouch." Rob winced. "That had to hurt really bad."

Valerie nodded. "He's winding down on the pain medicine now. He didn't damage anything badly, but he's got several cuts with stitches and lots of others that just burn."

"Did the other guy get hurt?"

"No, thank goodness. Then we'd be in an even bigger mess. As it is, they want me to take Connor to the doctor. The psychiatrist, actually." She pressed her fingertips to her eyes. "They say his behavior is unman-ageable. The school nurse suggested medication might help."

Rob glanced at the little boy. "Do you want to go that route?"

"Of course not. And he's not unmanageable to me. But I can't be with him every day, every minute. He's got to be able to control himself." Valerie sighed. "He's so angry."

"Does he have friends? Play sports?"

"Two weeks in town isn't long enough for friends." Her shoulders slumped. "And I haven't had time to in-vestigate sports programs. I imagine it's too late to join a team now."

"I don't know about that." Rob picked up the box she'd packed before she could. "What does he like to play?"

"Soccer, of course. Doesn't everybody?" Valerie reached out to take the box, but stopped when Rob frowned at her. "Fine. I'll let you carry that one. I've got several more."

"Why don't you just unlock the car and open the door and let me do the carrying?"

She went to the door of the cafeteria and pointed the remote lock control at the van across the parking lot. After a pointed glance in his direction, she went to pick up a different box of supplies. "You see—I can compro-mise."

"Stubborn," he muttered as he walked past her.

"Independent," she countered, following him.

The afternoon breeze carried a hint of autumn, and

Rob stood still for a second after they'd loaded the van, appreciating the difference. "Every so often we'll get a day like this, where the humidity is low and the shadows are crisp. Fall comes to this part of North Carolina, but it's slow." He looked at Valerie, noticing how the wind brushed her curls back from her pretty face. "I'll bet you're used to early autumns and cold winters."

"Ohio, the last place we lived, had its share of winter weather." She shook her head. "I won't miss shoveling snow in the least."

"We had a big storm here last winter—New Year's Day, to be exact. We got almost ten inches of the white stuff. But it didn't stay long."

"That sounds good to me." She shut the rear door of the van and turned back toward the school.

But Rob held his ground. He'd got her talking about herself, and he wasn't about to give up now. "You aren't from Ohio, right? Your accent says New York."

"Brooklyn, actually." She hesitated, as if unwilling to elaborate. "Before Ohio, though, we lived in Maryland for a couple of years."

He leaned back against her van and crossed his arms over his chest. "Why so many moves? If you don't mind telling me."

"Those two moves were both promotions within my company. Great opportunities that I couldn't turn down." Valerie looked at him out of the corners of her eyes. "And before you ask, I'll say that my husband refused to leave New York. Since he'd already moved out, there didn't seem to be much point in trying anymore, and we filed for a divorce."

"Ah. How long were you in Ohio?"

"Five years."

"And now you're in New Skye. Because…?"

"Because I got a job with a different company."

"Another offer you couldn't turn down?"

"Exactly." Hands propped on her hips, she faced him. "Why is that so hard to understand? If I were a man, nobody would question my desire to succeed, to excel. A man is supposed to take the chances that come along for a better job, more money, more authority. Just because I'm a woman doesn't mean I don't have the same ambitions."

Rob held up his hands in surrender. "I didn't say—"

"My husband, weasel lawyer that he is, managed to construct a settlement that benefited him while shafting me and his kids. I am our sole support. I'm going to be responsible for their college money. I'm responsible for my retirement income. And I have every right to be just as damn successful as I want to be."

"Valerie." He put his hands on her shoulders. "Hush." She opened her mouth to say something else, but he shook her slightly and she backed down. "I'm not attacking anything you've done. I admire your gumption and your achievements. So relax."

"That's not what it sounded like," she mumbled, staring down at the ground.

"You didn't listen—just went off half-cocked."

"Sorry." When she looked up at him, her big brown eyes had a suspicious shine to them, as if she'd fought back tears. "It's been a hard couple of weeks."

"I'm sure it has." He still held her shoulders, and he really liked the feeling of having her this close, which was as good a reason as any to let go. After a moment's struggle, he managed to step back, putting her out of reach. To be safe, he jammed his hands into the pockets of his jeans. "So I have a suggestion. How about dinner out tonight?"

Her eyes widened. "I..." She swallowed. "I don't think so, Rob. I mean, I don't have anything to do with the kids."

He grinned. "I like the way you think. But I'm suggesting we bring them with us."

"With us? You mean, to a restaurant?"

"Yeah. I know a place they'll really like."

She eyed him suspiciously. "I do not want to eat at some fast-food joint."

"Nope. Not fast, not a joint. Just the best place in New Skye for a laid-back, delicious dinner." Ginny had come to stand at the door to the school, no doubt wondering what could be keeping him so long. He called across to her. "What do you think, Ginny? Dinner at the Carolina Diner tonight?"

His daughter pumped her right arm in the air. "All right!"

Rob looked at Valerie. "See? What more testimony do you need?"

She smiled, setting those cute dimples on display. "Lead the way. I'm suddenly very hungry."

CHAPTER FOUR

VALERIE FOLLOWED Rob Warren's shiny black van out of the school parking lot, reflecting that she had a perfectly good jar of spaghetti sauce at home on the pantry shelf. There really was no need to make the effort to go out, though he'd promised her a restaurant with good food and a casual atmosphere for the kids. She had to admit, relaxed would be a welcome change of pace in her life.

"Where are we going?" Connor piped up from the back seat. "McDonald's?"

"I don't think so. Mr. Warren says this place is one of a kind."

"Do we have to go?" Grace sounded tired. "I've got a lot of homework."

Valerie glanced into the rearview mirror, but Grace avoided her eyes. "We need to eat. This won't take any longer than cooking our own dinner. And you can get to know Ginny a little better."

"Great." The one word was not enthusiastic.

"What's wrong?"

"She's in my class at school, Mom. And she's…hard to talk to."

"Her dad says she's shy."

"What's wrong with her, anyway?" Connor wasted no time on tact. "She crippled or something?"

"Cerebral palsy is a birth defect," Valerie explained. "Sometimes it happens when the baby is being born and doesn't get enough oxygen to breathe. That causes problems with their nerves and muscles."

"Can I catch it?"

"No, Connor. And I expect you to be polite while we're at dinner—don't stare, don't ask questions. I'm sure that in most ways, Ginny is just an ordinary kid, like the two of you."

She thought she heard Grace's *hmmph* from the back seat, but she decided to ignore it. This dinner really was a good idea—as the new kids in school, both Grace and Connor were still trying to adjust and make friends. If Grace and Ginny could connect, that would be a start.

At the high school, the blinker on Rob Warren's van signaled a right turn, and then an immediate left into the gravel parking lot of a bright yellow, concrete block building hung with a blue-and-white awning. The neon sign over the door identified Charlie's Carolina Diner.

Valerie left the car slowly, wondering what she'd gotten herself and her kids into. The place didn't look dangerous, exactly, but there were plenty of trucks and motorcycles in the parking lot. The proportion of cars seemed low for a family restaurant. What kind of people actually ate here? That twinkle in Rob's eyes led her to put more trust in him than she usually ventured, at least so soon. With the well-being of the GO! girls at stake, had she misjudged him?

"Hold my hand," she told Connor, who had a tendency to dash without looking for traffic.

"Aw…"

"Hold my hand. Stay close, Grace."

As she approached the black van, Rob stood at the passenger door to help Ginny down. "Careful," he warned his daughter as she made her way across the parking lot, setting the ends of her crutches between stones. "I'm gonna talk to Charlie about a sidewalk out here. It sure would be helpful."

Valerie moved to Ginny's other side, just in case. "You know the owner?"

"I've known him since I was Connor's age, I guess." He watched Ginny's progress, one hand held ready in case she needed help. "Charlie's has been here at least that long. Once kids get to high school, they spend a lot of their snack money over here. My friends and I did, and I haven't seen anything change in the last fourteen years."

They reached the front door. Rob blew out a short breath of relief and ushered them in with a gallant gesture. "Be my guests."

Connor, rambunctious as always, tried to slip inside first, just as Ginny went through the doorway. When Valerie bent to grab his arm, her shoulder bumped Ginny's crutch. The girl squeaked and started teetering. Heads at every table turned to look in their direction. Before Valerie could decide whether to let go of Connor or just get him out of the way, Dixon Bell came to the rescue, putting his hands securely on Ginny's shoulders to keep her upright.

"Whoa, there, sweetheart. You're okay." He grinned at Valerie. "Everybody else all right?"

She nodded, her hand tight around Connor's arm. "Thanks so much."

"No problem." He stepped back and looked at Ginny again. "Right?"

For this man, at least, Ginny had a smile. "Thanks, Mr. Dixon."

From behind Grace, Rob extended his hand. "Hey, Dixon, how's it going?"

"Just fine. You've brought a crowd with you tonight. Why don't I let you into the place to find a seat?"

As Dixon backed out of the way, Rob came up beside Ginny. "We'll do that. Is Kate here with you?"

"Nope. There's a final fitting for Jacquie Archer's wedding attendants at my house tonight." To Valerie, he said, "A good friend from high school is getting married in a couple of weeks. Males were not on the invitation list, so I'm here by myself."

Something about his easy charm inspired her to ask, "Can you join us?"

Before she could have second thoughts about the invitation, Rob said, "Good idea. Sit down with us, why don't you?"

Dixon nodded. "You know I'd be glad to. I wasn't enjoying eating alone at all. I'll bring my tea over."

They settled at the table with relatively little fuss. Valerie sat between Rob and Connor, with Dixon across from Rob. The girls sat next to Dixon and beside each other, but didn't appear to have much to say.

"This looks like a hungry crew." A strong, square

man with a military haircut put a platter of corn chips and a bowl of cheesy-looking dip on the table between the kids. "Thought I'd better get you started before you fall down from hunger."

"All right." Connor leaned across the table to dig in.

Grace looked at the dip suspiciously. "What is it?"

"White chili," Rob volunteered. "Terrific stuff. And this is Charlie Brannon, owner of the Carolina Diner. Charlie, meet Valerie Manion, Connor and Grace."

Charlie nodded. "Good to have y'all stop by. What can I get you to drink?"

Valerie chose soft drinks for the kids and coffee for herself. When Charlie left without waiting for Rob's order, she looked at him in surprise. "Don't you want something?"

Rob lounged back in his chair. "Charlie knows I'll have sweet tea and Ginny will have milk. You watch— he'll get it right."

In just a moment, Charlie Brannon returned with a tray and set down drinks in front of them all. "Take a few minutes to decide what you want to eat. I'll be right back." As he walked away this time, she noticed that he limped.

"Charlie is a Marine," Rob told her. "He was injured in Vietnam and came back to start the Carolina Diner with his wife."

"Does she do all the cooking?"

"Miss Abigail died the summer after we graduated from high school." Dixon picked up the story. "Charlie and his daughter, Abby, share the work these days."

"I heard my name," a woman said out of Valerie's

range of sight. When she came around the table, Abby proved to be plump and merry-looking, with dark auburn hair and laughing hazel eyes. "You'd better be saying something nice, Dixon Bell, or there'll be salt in your ice cream and vinegar in your gravy."

Dixon laughed at her. "Why would I say anything else? You make the best fried chicken in town—besides my wife's and my grandmother's—and I'm planning to enjoy it for dinner."

"That's better." She looked at Rob. "You brought us new customers. For that, you get an extra piece."

"I would have brought them even without the incentive," Rob said. "This is Valerie Manion, her daughter, Grace, and her son, Connor. They're new in town—Valerie works at the tire plant and is starting up the Girls Outdoors! troop that Ginny's joining."

Abby shook Valerie's hand and smiled at Grace and Connor. "Welcome to New Skye. Have you been here long?"

"Two weeks."

"Where did y'all come from?"

"Brooklyn by way of Frederick, Maryland and Columbus, Ohio."

Abby's jaw dropped. "Wow…y'all do get around." She glanced at Grace, kindly including her in the conversation. "You'll have to tell me about all the things you've seen. I've never been more than two hundred miles from New Skye in my entire life."

"It's good to have a home, though. You start feeling kind of rootless." Valerie still winced when she thought about Grace's tears over the move to North Carolina.

"Well, now you've got New Skye for a home. You'll have to settle in and stay for a good long while. What can I get y'all to eat?"

While the others placed their orders, Valerie considered the remote possibility that she would be in this pretty little town for more than a year or two. Advancing in management usually required a hopscotch approach—take on a new challenge with a new company, succeed brilliantly and then move on to the next. She wouldn't reach the top of the ladder unless she competed on equal footing with her male colleagues and displayed the same willingness to jump for the big prize.

Rob's touch on her shoulder startled her. "Earth to Valerie. What do you want for dinner?"

"Um…" She glanced at the menu, a long list of sandwiches, salads and full meals, plus desserts. "Connor will have a cheeseburger and fries. I'll have…whatever you're having."

"Good choice." He nodded at Abby. "Make that three all-white-meat chicken plates with mashed potatoes and fried okra."

"You got it."

As Abby hurried away, Valerie stared at Dixon, then Rob. "Fried okra? What in the world is fried okra?"

"Delicious," Rob assured her. "You'll love it."

"Is it anything like grits? We tried that in a restaurant in Maryland."

Dixon braced his crossed arms on the table edge. "You didn't enjoy the grits?"

Valerie gave a very real shudder. "Horrible. White and runny and…and gritty."

"What do they know about grits in Maryland?" Rob shook his head. "You try Abby's grits for breakfast some morning. Warm and rich and thick and buttery. One of God's perfect foods. Right, Dixon?"

"Without a doubt."

Before Valerie could clarify the okra issue further, the sound of a slap and a yell drew the attention of everyone in the restaurant to Connor. He sat holding his good hand in his injured one, working up to a loud crying fit.

"Mommy, she hit me," he complained. "Hard."

With an arm around her sobbing son, Valerie widened her eyes. "Grace? What in the world is going on?"

Grace stared at the table. "He…took the last chip."

A pulse started pounding in Valerie's temple, but she kept her voice low. "And are you starving? On the brink of death, that you have to fight your brother for a chip?"

Her daughter shrugged without answering.

"We'll talk about this later." Bending her head to Connor, she coaxed and soothed until he sat up in his chair again with just a sniffle. She knew he was manipulating the situation—he hadn't been hurt in the least, but merely wanted to score points over his sister.

Valerie, however, felt hardly able to look Rob and Dixon in the face. She'd been warned about how Southerners valued proper manners. They must be appalled to see such ugly behavior in her children.

The two gentlemen managed to ignore the incident and chatted genially about Southern specialties—hush puppies, butter beans and barbecue—until Abby returned carrying a tray of plates mounded with food. Connor immediately assaulted his sandwich, cut in half to be easier for one-handed eating. Grace had ordered spaghetti and seemed satisfied enough, though her eyes were suspiciously bright. Beside her, Ginny carefully arranged her fork in her left hand and began to eat her mashed potatoes. The slice of meat loaf on her plate had already been divided into smaller pieces, and the lettuce for the salad torn into manageable bites. Abby and Charlie really did look out for their customers.

Turning back to her own plate, she considered the familiar sight of golden-brown chicken breasts and fluffy mashed potatoes with a dot of butter on top. The okra, though…

Rob leaned closer, until his shoulder pressed against hers. "It's good. I promise."

She speared one small, green, crispy cylinder with her fork and held it up for closer inspection. "What's the coating?"

"Cornmeal," Dixon said. "Deep-fried."

"Close your eyes," Rob suggested. "The first time's the worst."

Why her mind took that suggestion in a completely different direction—a direction having nothing to do with food—Valerie couldn't have said. But her surprise at the sudden, tempting picture in her mind erased all fear of okra. Before she realized, she'd popped the little piece in her mouth and caught a delicious combination of crackly corn coating and tangy green vegetable.

"Oh, that is good!" Grinning, she stabbed several more pieces. "What an amazing taste!"

Rob sat back in his chair. "You'll like it better every time," he told her, pleased to see her enjoying herself. He wasn't sure Ms. Valerie Manion got much of a chance to relax and have fun. She shared some of her new discovery with both her kids, who agreed that the taste resembled popcorn, but better. The Manion clan appeared to have settled down. And Ginny…

Ginny sat pouting over her uneaten meat loaf. Her food preferences were limited, her dislikes many, and she never ate much at the best of times. He could usually count on a good meal at the diner, though.

"What's up, Ginny? Not hungry?"

Lower lip stuck out, she shook her head.

"Want some chicken? I've got extra."

"I want to go home," she declared, loudly. "I want to eat at home."

Rob swallowed his first impatient answer and then nodded. "Okay. We've got macaroni and cheese left over. We'll get you some when we get home."

"I'm hungry now."

Dixon nudged her gently with his elbow. "Sure you don't want some chicken? Abby could bring drumsticks—those are your favorite, right?"

Now well into her sulk, Ginny simply turned her head away without answering. Dixon threw a glance of apology in Rob's direction.

"Dessert?" Rob said, sounding more desperate than he'd meant to. Anything to keep her peaceful for just a few more minutes. "I see coconut cream pie in the pie case."

Like a butterfly exploding from its cocoon, Ginny started to struggle out of her place at the table, attempting to get a hold of her crutches, push the chair backward and stand up. When Dixon bent to help her with the crutches, she slapped his arm with both hands.

"No!" she yelled. "I can do it."

Good friend that he was, Dixon didn't react, but calmly proceeded to retrieve the crutches and steady them until Ginny could get to her feet. By that time, Rob had rounded the table to help her cross the room. He put a hand on Dixon's shoulder. "Sorry. I'll settle with you next time, okay?"

Dixon held up a hand. "No problem."

Then Rob looked at Valerie. "Kids," he offered, with an apologetic shrug. "I hate to cut out on you."

"That's okay. She's had a long day." He thought he read understanding in Valerie's bright brown gaze, but that might have been wishful thinking. "Have a good night."

"You, too. Stay safe." With an effort, he got to the door in time to open it for Ginny. He walked beside her to the van, but didn't say anything until they were inside and on the way home.

At the first red traffic light, Rob took a deep breath, preparing for battle. "I don't like the way you acted tonight."

"I didn't do anything wrong." Ginny's tone told him she knew the truth even as she denied it.

"You were rude, sweetheart. To my friends and yours."

"They aren't my friends."

"They would be, if you let them."

"Connor's a little creep. He barely left any chips for me. And he tattled on his sister."

"Hitting people—as you hit Dixon—doesn't solve problems."

"And Grace is…is…a baby. She can't do anything unless her mommy tells her to."

The bitterness in Ginny's voice hinted at more than just bad temper. Rob gentled his approach. "Are you jealous that Grace has a mother, and you don't?"

"No. That's stupid."

He let the silence speak for him.

"Besides," Ginny said after a while, "they don't have a dad. It's no different."

"Seems like that would give y'all something in common."

She rolled her eyes and didn't bother to answer. They rode the rest of the way home without speaking and pulled into their driveway just as the sun dropped behind the trees.

"It's getting dark earlier every night," Rob commented as he held the house door open for Ginny to pass through. "In another two weeks, autumn will officially arrive." When Ginny didn't answer, he remembered the macaroni and cheese. "Come into the kitchen and I'll warm up some of the leftovers for you."

His daughter sank onto the sofa and shoved her crutches away so they went clattering across the scarred coffee table. "I'm not hungry."

"You need something to eat, Ginny. You know your medicine works better on a full stomach." He hated the nights she wouldn't eat. She was too thin as it was.

"I don't care."

"Well, I do."

The ensuing argument was still in progress when Jenny came in from the kitchen. "Hi, guys. How was the GO! meeting?"

Ginny's *dumb* clashed with Rob's *fun*.

Jenny looked at each of them in turn. "Okay. Got it. Ready for a bath, Gin-Gin?" Not one to wait for an answer, she went down the hall and started water running in the tub. After a minute, Ginny struggled to her feet and, without looking at Rob, headed after her aunt.

Once again exhausted, Rob went to stand at the front window. The darkness bothered him for some reason, as if a threat lingered outside. Everybody was safe and sound in the house, of course...

Everybody but the Manions. Leaving the diner even later than he had, they would be going home to a dark house. If Valerie wasn't worried about somebody lurking in the bushes or hiding out in the backyard, she should be.

"I'll be back in a few minutes," he called to Jenny on his way out the door. If she answered, Rob was in too much of a hurry to hear.

PARKED IN HER own driveway, Valerie sat in the car for a minute after she cut the engine off, staring at the house. She and Grace and Connor had been on edge these last few days, though nothing worrisome had happened.

Still, coming home in the dark like this, with the lights off inside, spooked her a little.

Connor spoke up from the back seat. "Is somebody in there?"

"No, of course not." She swallowed hard. "But I'll check around to be sure. You two stay in here with the doors locked."

Just as she shut the car door behind her, a vehicle pulled up at the curb. The streetlamp flashed on blue and white lettering, and Rob rounded the front end of the black van.

"Hey, there." His smile gleamed white in the dark. "I thought maybe you'd like me to check the place out, make sure everything's still locked up tight. Coming home in the dark can be kinda nerve-racking."

The surge of relief she felt annoyed Valerie almost as much as his assumption that she couldn't take care of herself and her kids. "Where's Ginny?"

"At home." He sobered at the mention of his daughter. "My sister's with her."

He'd involved yet another person in this rescue attempt? Valerie clenched her jaw. "You shouldn't have bothered coming over. We're fine."

"Glad to hear it. But I'll feel better knowing those locks are holding and y'all are safe and sound. Just wait here for a little while."

No way was she standing out front like some helpless princess while he played knight-errant. "I'm sure everything's locked up," she said, following him around the side of the house. "You really don't have to do this."

"I want to." He winked at her over his shoulder. "I'll sleep better." His long-fingered hand brushed over the brick walls and the windows as he moved along the side of the house. "You should put a lock on this gate," he commented as he walked through the fence into the backyard. "And floodlights would be a great idea. Nothing deters a criminal faster than locks and lights."

For the first time, Valerie realized that the back of the house was, indeed, as dark as a cave. Tall pine trees loomed like walls of rock, while the sickle moon and faint stars offered no useful light. When Rob climbed the steps of the deck to check the back door, she scurried after him. He turned just as she reached him, and they bumped chests.

"Whoops." His hands closed over her shoulders. "Sorry. Everything's still locked up tight."

Valerie stared up at him, unnerved even more by his touch than by the night around them. "I—I didn't realize how scary it was out here."

Rob looked beyond her for a second, then his gaze came back to her face. His eyes were kind. "Yeah. You could have a great Halloween party—strings of orange lights between the trees and glow-in-the-dark decorations hanging from the branches."

The idea made her relax. "You're right, though Grace and Connor might be a little young yet for that kind of fun." She took a deep breath and shook her head. "Sorry. I usually don't mind the dark at all. I love camping."

He squeezed her shoulders gently. "You've got a reason to be worried right now. There are bad people hanging around. The woods always seemed safe to me, with just bears and snakes to look out for, compared with the lowlifes in town."

Valerie chuckled. "Humans—the most dangerous predator."

"Exactly." He didn't say anything else…and yet they didn't seem to be getting on with the inspection. They weren't even backing away from each other. Rob felt no inclination to move, in fact, unless moving meant drawing this woman closer, letting her warmth settle against him, then tilting her face to his and grazing her mouth with his own. The darkness pooled in her big eyes, so he couldn't read her face, but he felt tension between them, felt a need in Valerie which answered his own. He hadn't kissed a woman's mouth in nine years. Hadn't wanted to. But Valerie Manion had changed that way of thinking the first time he saw her smile.

An owl hooted in the trees nearby. At the sudden rush of wings over their heads, Valerie jerked out of Rob's grasp.

"Stupid bird," she sputtered, with a nervous laugh. "He's woken me up every night with his noise."

Rob swallowed his disappointment. Not wanting a woman in nine years had at least meant not being frustrated. "You won't have mice, anyway."

With no other concession to courtesy, he crossed the deck, skipped the three steps with a single stride to the ground, and resumed his self-appointed task. The rest of the house windows were secure, the front door locked tight. Valerie followed him at a safe distance, which both relieved and irritated the hell out of him.

She signaled her children to come in from the car as he crossed the grass to his van. "Thanks," she said in a constricted voice. "We'll sleep better tonight knowing you checked everything out."

Rob nodded. "You're welcome." He said it without turning around.

"You don't have to worry about us," she called. "I've been taking care of my kids by myself for quite a while now. I'm good at it."

"I'm sure you are." He reached the van and started around the hood.

"Anybody who wants to hurt us is risking their life."

He grinned to himself. "Are you a black belt?"

"I'm an experienced marksman with a .357 Magnum under my pillow."

He turned to look at her, his jaw hanging. "You have a gun?"

"I told you, I can take care of us."

"I guess you can." He ran a hand over his face. "Well, then. I won't worry."

"Thanks for dinner, by the way. The Carolina Diner is a great place."

"Charlie'll be glad to have you back whenever you're hungry." He was always willing to advertise for his friends.

Grace and Connor disappeared inside the house and lights popped on behind all the windows. Valerie glanced over her shoulder at the cozy picture and then looked toward him again through the dark. "Good night, Rob."

He raised his hand without trying to frame words.

"I'll call you about getting together to plan next week's meeting."

More torture. "Sure."

"Tell Ginny to sleep tight."

Such tolerance, after his daughter's behavior at dinner, left him truly speechless. He nodded, waved again and shut the van door. Without a backward look, he drove out of Valerie's vicinity as fast as the residential speed limit would allow.

How had something so simple gone so wrong so fast? He'd volunteered as a troop leader. He'd intended to give his daughter some fun, with himself along to keep her safe, and maybe do a good deed for a few other little girls while he was at it.

If he kept reacting to Valerie this way, though, the situation would soon enough become impossible. They couldn't work comfortably together with such tension between them. Sexual tension, of a kind he hadn't experienced since he was a teenager. The kind he'd relieved by marrying Leah.

He couldn't marry Valerie, of course. Her priorities centered on her career and her kids. From what she'd said—and even more from what she hadn't—he understood she didn't want another husband. But in a small town like New Skye, and with children in the picture, nothing else would work.

So he would just have to smother these unaccountable urges…the desire to stroke a finger along her soft, round cheek, to taste her lips or shape her curves—such tempting curves—with his palm. Surely he was strong enough to elevate willpower over libido.

After all, he'd spent a lifetime learning how to control his feelings. Ginny's lifetime. Since the day he stopped being a husband and became a father, his life had been about taking care of his little girl. Nothing had to change just because he'd met a woman who stirred his blood. He would simply have to keep his mind on troop business. And keep his hands strictly to himself.

When he came through the front door, Jenny looked up at him from the recliner and put a finger to her lips.

"She just now fell asleep," she whispered. Ginny was draped over her aunt's lap with *Goodnight Moon* beginning to slip from her loose fingers.

Rob eased the book away. "The old favorites always win out, don't they?"

"Especially when we're stressed. What happened tonight?"

Lifting Ginny and carrying her to bed, he didn't answer. But when he returned, Jenny refused to accept his evasion. "What happened?"

He sighed as he dropped down onto the couch. "Nothing major. We were at the diner with Dixon and the troop leader—Valerie Manion—and her two kids. Ginny decided she wanted to eat at home." He rubbed his hands over his face and through his hair. "You know how she does, just suddenly…"

"Feels threatened and starts to manipulate you," Jenny finished.

"Not at all." He glared at his sister. "Ginny doesn't think that way."

"Of course she does. All the time."

"Ginny has no reason to feel threatened."

"Being nine and handicapped might be reason

enough." When he started to protest, Jenny held up a hand and got out of the chair. "Let's not argue tonight, okay? You need some rest and I'm on duty this weekend. See you later."

"Thanks, Jen."

She shook her head as she went toward the kitchen. Rob slumped back on the couch and closed his eyes. If Ginny felt threatened, he must not being doing a good enough job. She had to know she could count on him for anything she needed, as long as he lived. That was his commitment. His responsibility. His life. Nothing and no one mattered as much as Ginny.

Which was why, tired as he was, he lay sleepless for hours that night, struggling to banish the thoughts of Valerie drifting like fumes of incense in his head.

CHAPTER FIVE

VALERIE DECIDED she and Grace and Connor deserved a night on the town, so to speak, so they caught the latest Harry Potter movie Saturday night. Afterward, they went on their own to the Carolina Diner to share a Super Duper Triple Scooper Banana Split. Using a straw as a wand, Connor tried turning the napkin holders into owls and lizards, while Grace propped her chin in her hand and gazed into the rainy darkness outside the window.

"Here you go." Abby Brannon set down a huge concoction of ice creams, sauces, nuts, bananas and whipped cream erected on a boat-shaped dish. "One of my better efforts, if I do say so myself."

"Awesome." Con discarded his wand and, kneeling on the seat of the booth, positioned his spoon. "I get all the butterscotch sauce."

"Mom," Grace protested immediately, "make him leave me some."

Con stuck out an ice-cream-coated tongue at his sister.

"Connor Manion, behave yourself." Valerie felt the blush creeping up her throat. How had her children become such hellions without her realizing it? "Sit down on the seat. Eat like a human being. And save your sister some butterscotch. Me, too." She glanced at Abby. "Sorry. They…" She really didn't know what to say or how to explain.

Abby leaned a hip against the side of the booth. "No apology necessary. I'd be insulted if kids didn't squabble over my Super Dupers." She bent close to Connor's ear. "I can make another one," she told him, in a stage whisper.

"All right!" Connor set to serious work on the project in front of them.

"So, how are you settling in?" Abby straightened up again. "Is New Skye different from the places you've lived before?"

"Different from New York, certainly." Valerie sucked the ice cream off her spoon. "Ohio is less urban, more like here. But, still, New Skye is the smallest town I've ever lived in."

"Do you think you'll like it?"

"Oh, I already do. What you call rush-hour traffic here is like the middle of Sunday night in Manhattan. And I'm looking forward to less snow this winter."

"Kids adjusting to the new school?" Abby looked at Grace, who flushed, ducked her head and nodded. Connor just kept plowing through the banana split.

"I think so," Valerie added. "I'm sure we'll get to know the girls in the GO! troop really well in no time."

Abby leaned against the side of the booth. "Now, tell me about this GO! program. What is it you do?"

By the time Valerie had gone into detail about the

goals and activities of GO!, Abby was sitting in the booth beside Connor, sharing part of their ice cream.

"Sounds like a good time. Were you in GO! when you were in school?"

Valerie shook her head. "Not until college—the GO! program isn't as old as the Scouts. A recruiter came to my Women in Business class, looking for volunteers to work with troops in the New York area." She pulled a napkin out of the holder and wiped chocolate off Connor's face. "Outdoor experience can be hard to come by in the concrete jungle."

Abby laughed. "I imagine so."

"I did a couple of outdoor adventures in high school and spent summers in college working at a camp in upstate New York. I loved the idea of helping girls develop the kind of independence and self-reliance you can discover in yourself when you know how to perform outside your normal environment. So…" Taking one last spoonful of ice cream, she shrugged. "I've been working with GO! for about ten years now. I was really excited when Grace got old enough to join my troop."

"Lucky you," Abby told Grace. Her smile was rueful. "I wanted to be in Scouts when I was little, but Dad was always working and needed me here. I bet I could've cleaned up on the cooking badges, though."

"We have cooking awards," Grace said shyly. "I want to earn those."

"Her handicap being me," Valerie admitted. "My kitchen skills are really baseline. I do better over a campfire, but I think that's because everybody's so hungry after a day outside that anything would taste good."

"I could help you with your cooking awards," Abby said. "You spend a couple of days with me here, and we'll have a ball. If your whole troop wanted to work with me, I imagine we could arrange that, too."

"Fantastic." Valerie rubbed her hands together. "I'd love to do exactly that—give them a taste not just of cooking, but of running a business for yourself. The best part of being a troop leader is involving the whole community in educating and training these girls for the future."

"You mean, like Rob Warren?" Abby sighed dreamily. "I can see why you'd want to get him involved. He's got to be one of the sweetest, most lovable guys in town."

"H-He volunteered," Valerie stuttered. "I didn't ask him."

"Oh, I know. But you definitely didn't think about turning him down, now did you?"

"Well…" Not for very long, anyway. "I didn't get any other volunteers."

"Really? None of the mothers signed on to help?" When Valerie shook her head, Abby's brows drew together. "Seems strange to me. There are usually lots of volunteers to help out with the kids. Anyway, I'm glad Ginny will be in your troop. She needs the chance to play and to…to expand her horizons."

With the banana split finished, Connor had gone back to practicing his magic on the salt shakers and sugar canister on the next table. Grace had pulled out her latest book and buried her nose in the pages.

Valerie seized the chance to be nosy herself. "I understand Ginny's mother passed away?"

Abby nodded. "Leah was a real sweetheart, like you'd expect if Rob married her. Pretty, petite, wanted nothing more than to be a wife and mother. She was so thrilled to be pregnant, finally. They'd been married five years. But she was toxemic and her labor started early. She had a stroke during delivery and died the next day."

Horror struck Valerie silent.

"Rob has been a wonderful dad, of course, without a single complaint. He's always patient, always careful, always cheerful." She sighed. "Sometimes I wish he'd lose his temper so we'd be sure he's still alive in there. Hasn't happened yet."

Valerie couldn't imagine Rob losing his temper. He seemed happy, despite the tragedy he'd endured. "Does he have help with Ginny?"

"Oh, sure. His mother and sister have cared for Ginny since Day One. And his friends take turns sometimes, just to give him a break. Jacquie Archer keeps hoping he'll take an hour for himself while she gives Ginny horseback riding lessons, though that hasn't happened yet, either. We keep thinking maybe he'll wake up and get a life of his own, find a woman to take care of him."

A sudden sinking sensation developed in the pit of Valerie's stomach. "Do you…would you want…" She blushed again at her own inquisitiveness.

Abby gazed in her direction, but her focus seemed somewhere else. "Me and Rob? No." She shook her head. "We're close friends—I see him almost every day. But…no. He's not for me."

As Valerie swallowed her sigh of relief, Abby got to

her feet. "We did a terrific job on that split, didn't we? Not a drop left." She picked up the dish and deftly managed to corral their drink glasses at the same time. "I guess I'd better get these back to the kitchen and get cleaned up. It's almost closing time."

Valerie got to her feet. "Thanks so much for everything."

"You're more than welcome. Come back any old time. And I'm serious—when you're ready to do those cooking awards, call me. I'll be glad to help out."

"Count on it," Valerie said, as she took her bill to the cash register at the counter. Charlie made change and gave her a smile. "I'll be glad for you to get Abby doing something else besides slinging hash and wiping tables for a change. She spends all her time in this place—not the right life for a young woman like her."

Dishes clattered in the kitchen behind him. "That's enough, Dad," Abby called. "Stay out of my business."

"I don't know what you're talking about," he yelled back. Then he winked at Valerie. "Y'all take care tonight, okay?"

"Sure." She herded the kids to the car and drove out of the diner parking lot smiling. Thanks to Rob, she'd met some really nice people this week. New Skye felt a little bit more like home every day. She didn't even have to think hard anymore about which turns to take to get them to their own little piece of the South.

The peaceful mood shattered as she reached the left turn onto her street. A yellow sports car came screaming down the pavement from the direction of her house. With a screech of brakes, the driver took the corner at high speed and careened into the opposite lane on Valerie's right. She gasped and clutched the steering wheel, throwing her right hand back between the seats as if somehow she could protect Grace and Connor from the coming collision.

But with the luck of fools, the yellow sports car managed to avoid Valerie's car and oncoming traffic. Veering back to the right side of the street, the driver gunned the engine and rocketed away, leaving a cloud of dust and the smell of gasoline hanging in the air.

Shaking her head, breathing fast, Valerie turned carefully and approached her house. Still thinking about the sports car, she pulled into the driveway automatically, shut off the engine and opened the door.

"Look, Mommy. Look!"

She followed the line of Connor's pointing finger with her gaze. They'd left most of the lights on to make the house appear occupied. Against the glow, she had no difficulty seeing what he meant—every window on the front of the house was broken, including the high, small panes on the front door. There wasn't much glass sparkling on the porch, so she guessed that something had been thrown into the windows from outside, a rock or a brick big enough to wipe out each pane.

Valerie let her head drop back against the seat and said a few very ungenteel words under her breath. The windows were broken. Her house, her children and herself were vulnerable to anyone who chose to accost them.

From the darkness of the back seat, Grace's question gave voice to Valerie's only rational thought. "Mommy?

Mommy, that man could come back, or some of his friends. They could get into the house really easy." She gave an audible gulp. "What are we going to do now?"

For a moment, Valerie had no answer. All she knew was the overwhelming urge to hide from the situation, from the decisions. Let someone else take responsibility this time. *Call Rob...*

"No." She said it aloud, sat up straight in the car seat. "No, I can do this." Glancing back at Grace and Connor, she pulled up a sickly grin. "We can do this. Together. First, we call the police."

SHE MADE THE KIDS stay in the car while she went through the house with the officers. Nothing appeared to be missing or damaged, except the windows.

"I wouldn't stay here, if I were you," Patrolman Reilly said earnestly. "Go to a friend's house."

"Or a motel," his partner added. "But stay away from the ones on the highway—we got some troublesome types who hang out at the bars and in the parking lots."

"The Highlander, downtown, is nice. Expensive," Reilly qualified. "I went to a wedding there once."

"Thanks." Valerie walked them to the door. "We'll be fine." She turned back into the living room as the patrol car left, looking at the glass showered over every surface. If she'd been alone, she would have tucked the gun into her jeans and stayed at the house, cleaning up and daring anybody to try a third attack.

But her children were huddled in the car, frightened and miserable. For their sakes, she had to find a safe place to spend the night. Locking up as best she could, she went back to the car.

Grace sat wide-eyed and stiff in the back seat. "Where are we going, Mommy?" Connor had fallen asleep.

Decision time. She'd stayed in The Highlander Hotel when she came to interview for her job—nice enough rooms, though, as Reilly had mentioned, expensive. Valerie visualized walking in at almost midnight to register, bringing no luggage and two incoherent children. The only parking was street level, uncovered and dark, with no attendant or valet. Impersonal hotel hallways and an unfamiliar, empty room would offer them nothing in the way of comfort.

"We're doing what the policeman said," she told Grace. "We're going to a friend's house."

ROB USUALLY RESERVED Saturday night for paying bills and keeping up with his checkbook and his medical insurance statements. The last thing he expected at eleven o'clock was a knock on the door.

Valerie and her kids stood on his front porch, huddled together like refugees from a monsoon. "I'm sorry," she began. "Your address was on the forms—"

He opened the door and motioned them inside. "What's wrong? Did something happen at your house again?"

Valerie drew a deep breath. "They broke all the windows."

"Aw, damn." He propped his hands on his hips and shook his head. "I'm sorry, Valerie. You don't deserve this." He looked at Grace and Connor. "Neither do the two of you. Come on in and sit down."

In the living room, the children hunched close together on the sofa. Valerie walked to the fireplace and turned to face him. "The police came—again—and said they'd keep a watch on the house. But we can't stay there anymore."

"No, you can't."

She made a helpless gesture with her hands. "I hate to impose—we could have gone to a hotel. But…" Even in the low light, he could see her cheeks flush. Her embarrassed gaze shied away from his. "I thought Connor and Grace would feel better in a real home. If you wouldn't mind letting us camp on your couch—"

"I think we can do a little better than that." Rob turned to the kids. "Did you bring clothes and stuff?"

They shook their heads. "Mommy wouldn't let us out of the car," Grace said shakily.

"Good thinking on your mom's part. Follow me." He led them down the hall, past Ginny's room and then his own, to the guest room, where he flipped on the light. "This couch turns into a bed real easily." He pulled off the cushions to demonstrate. "And it's already made up, in case somebody drops by." He took pillows and blankets out of the closet. "There's a TV in this cabinet." He opened the doors to reveal the screen. "And some good videos in this drawer."

In another minute, he scavenged up nightclothes. "A clean nightgown," he told Grace, giving her one of Ginny's, "and a football jersey I wore a few years back." He offered the latter to Connor. "The bathroom's right next door. Change your clothes and I'll bring you a snack to relax with while you get sleepy."

The two children hadn't stopped staring at him with their mouths open, as if they'd never been taken care of before. Rob knew that wasn't true—Valerie was a great mom. "Go on now. Hurry into bed."

Back in the living room, he grinned at the lady herself. "Your turn."

"Just get me a blanket," she told him briskly. "I can sleep on the couch. Or I can sleep with the kids. There's plenty of room for all of us in one bed."

"You'll be almost that close," he said, motioning her to follow him down the hall, past Ginny's door to his own. "You're on one side of the bathroom and they're on the other. Won't you sleep better with the bed to yourself?" He turned on the light in his room as he asked the question, ignoring the traitor in his mind who whispered *"Or with me?"*

"I'm not taking your bed." Valerie stood in the doorway, arms crossed as she glared at him. "That's inconvenient and ridiculous."

He pulled an extra blanket from the top of his closet. "The sheets are clean—I changed the bed just this morning. And I will be more inconvenienced if I feel I have to move all my papers from the dining room into here, so when I keep working the light won't shine in your face. If I take the couch, I can do my paperwork and go to sleep when I'm finished without feeling guilty."

She lifted her eyebrows in suspicion. "You're making that up."

"No, I'm not." He came to stand in front of her, the blanket and his sweats folded over one arm. "Get Connor and Grace settled while I pour them some milk. Then you'll be ready for bed, too."

She stared up at him. Along with defiance, and a shame he didn't understand, he caught the awareness in her eyes, the recognition of where they stood and the possibilities in the room behind him.

As her cheeks flushed, Valerie turned away. "You're too good to be true. Did you know that?"

Rob snorted as he followed her out of the room. "Don't delude yourself, Ms. Manion. I'm just your average good ol' boy, like all the rest."

"Talk about delusions," she muttered.

When he brought a plate of animal crackers and two cups of milk into the guest room, Connor and Grace were tucked into the sofa bed with a classic Disney video playing and the lamp turned low. After a handful of crackers each and a few gulps of milk, the two kids sank back against their pillows, eyelids drooping. By the time Rob returned from putting the plate in the kitchen, both of them were asleep.

"I'll just let the video play, if that's okay." Valerie stood leaning against the doorframe, watching her children. "If they wake up, it'll help them remember where they are."

"No problem." Opening the door to the closet, he took a robe and gown off a hanger pushed to the very back, then, with a deep breath, extended the night clothes to Valerie. "These have never been worn. I'd be glad for you to use them tonight."

She sighed, but didn't automatically refuse, which was a victory in itself. "They belonged...to your wife?"

Shaking his head, Rob left the room for the shadows of the hallway. "My sister, actually. I bought them as a Christmas present, but then discovered that she'd rather sleep in pajamas. I just never got a chance to return them."

It was a weak lie, but he knew she wouldn't wear the gown if she thought he'd bought it for Leah. And for a reason he couldn't begin to define, he suddenly wanted a woman—this woman—to wear the pretty, feminine outfit.

"I'll pay you for them," Valerie said, standing at his bedroom door.

He gave her a level look. "You think so?"

Her chin lifted. "Yes, I do."

"We'll see about that." He took a deep breath. "'Night, Valerie."

"Thank you, Rob, for...for everything."

He managed a half smile. "Glad to help."

Though he went back to the dining room and sat down in front of his papers, any chance of doing more work was shot. He couldn't concentrate on the checkbook, and the insurance reports were worse. After little more than half an hour, he turned off the lights, put on his sweats and laid on the couch, facing the wall.

Sleep wouldn't come, either. He was terribly aware of the woman in his bed, though he couldn't see or hear or even smell her. He could imagine her, though, curled on her side, with her cheek pillowed in her palm.

And he could imagine himself lying with her, his

arm draped over her waist, his fingers relaxed on the soft fabric of the gown. One of the best parts of being married had been waking up with a sweet, sleeping woman within his reach. Leah had always welcomed him when he stirred in the night, especially once they started trying for a baby. Often, she'd been the one to wake him. In the months before she finally became pregnant, he'd begun to feel a little like a vending machine—insert the right change and get a new serving of sperm. Rob flinched from the thought and turned over on the couch to face the room.

"I'm sorry," Valerie whispered. "I didn't mean to disturb you."

In the dark, he could see the white gown and robe in the doorway to the hall. "You didn't. I hadn't gone to sleep yet. Something wrong?"

"No. No, I just…thought a glass of water would help me sleep."

"You're having trouble sleeping?"

"Well…there's a lot to think about. What I'm going to do about the house, where we'll stay. I can't get my mind to stop running."

He sat up and pushed the blanket back. "I know the feeling. And I have a better remedy than water. Come with me." In the kitchen, he opened the refrigerator, pulled a wine bottle from the back and poured two small glasses.

"Harvest wine," he said, handing a glass to Valerie. "Sweet and spicy." With a tilt of his head, he indicated the back door. "The rest of the treatment is out this way."

Wondering and a little wary, Valerie followed him onto the back porch, down the steps, and across the cool grass. Unlike her yard, Rob's was open to the star-sprinkled sky. After the air-conditioned house, the night air felt like a cashmere stole around her shoulders.

"Have a seat." He led her to a grouping of fifties-style metal lawn furniture set near the picket fence. "Harvest wine and Southern nights—the most relaxing combination I know of."

She sat in one of the springy chairs and took a sip of her wine. Cold, sugary syrup carried the flavors of grapes and apples down her throat. "Mmm. I see what you mean." After another taste, she looked at the tables and chairs around them. "Is this all original furniture?"

"Sure is. Fifty years old, some of it. The glider is a little younger, the tables a little older."

"Where did it come from?"

"Lots of folks out in the country still have this kind of stuff in their yards or in their barns. I'll see a piece, every once in a while, and most people are glad to get rid of it. I sand the rust off and repaint."

Her chair bounced gently. "You're right about this, too. Between the breeze and the wine and the stars—you've created an excellent recipe for relaxing."

He toasted her with his glass. "Glad you're enjoying it."

They sat for a long time, not saying much at all. Rob identified for her some of the different sounds in the dark—the whir of cicadas, the burp of bullfrogs, the whistle of a whip-poor-will. Valerie caught the scent of jessamine and pines.

She sighed with pleasure. "Not the kind of nights we're used to in the city."

"I guess not." He set his empty glass next to hers on the table between them. "This is as close to urban as I ever plan to get."

His comment reinforced what she'd already decided—this man wasn't going anywhere else. Kind of like her ex-husband, who hadn't thought his kids or his wife worth leaving New York for. But that was okay—Valerie knew she and Grace and Connor made a great family all on their own. They didn't need a man to complete their picture.

The breeze picked up and turned chilly, just as she figured she could probably go to bed and fall asleep. "A lot of middle-management types I know would kill for a sure method of decreasing stress," she told Rob as they walked back to the house. "Write a book, sell each copy with a bottle of wine—you could make millions."

His chuckle was warm in the night air. "No merchandising for me. I'll sell you the secret and let you franchise it."

Laughing, she turned on the bottom step as he came up behind her. "I'm game. What's your asking price?"

Their faces were at the same level, only inches apart. She could see the fine lines at the corners of his eyes, the glint of gold strands in his hair. A stray beam of light showed her his mouth, carved and elegant in his shadowed face.

"A kiss?" he said softly.

"Rob…"

"We could get it out of the way, find out there's no big deal and go on. Small price, don't you think, for franchising my secret recipe?"

"Sure," Valerie decided, in complete opposition to her thoughts only minutes before. "Cheap."

He nodded. His fingers cupped her chin, tilted her head slightly. And then his lips touched hers.

"Nothing to it," he murmured, in that Ashley Wilkes accent, and drew away…only to return at a slightly different angle. "Simple." This touch was longer, warmer, as their mouths moved against each other.

"Ordinary," Valerie agreed.

With the word, the storm broke over them, a fury of need and want she hadn't seen coming. Rob's arms clenched around her. His weight pressed her back against the porch post and his kisses demanded every ounce of response she could offer. She clutched at his shirt, then at his shoulders, easing herself more fully into his hold while she made demands of her own. It had been such a long, long time since she'd savored the glorious feel of a man who wanted her, whose body, hard and urgent, pressed up against her. A man who would take without leaving her empty…

The warmth of a woman in his arms—Rob had forgotten how it felt, how her swells and dips, her breath and bones, could fill him up. Valerie's curls twined in his fingers, her tongue slid against his and her hips melted into him until his blood pounded against his skin. The white gown and robe were no barrier between them, and he could feel her breasts pressed against him, the tips puckered stiff. He gripped her tightly, too tightly, maybe, but he couldn't seem to get enough....

"Oh, dear God." With a groan, he wrenched his head—mouth—away from hers. His forehead scraped across the rough surface of the porch post; he welcomed the sting. Panting, aching, he loosened his clutch and, finally, stepped back from the woman he'd assaulted. Her hands dragged across his chest as he retreated. Even that meaningless contact turned him on.

He scrubbed his hands over his face, then pressed the heels of his palms into his eyes. "I'm...sorry," he said. "So sorry."

Valerie didn't say anything, though he could hear the fast, ragged whoosh of her breath.

"I had no intention..." He cleared his throat, still without looking up. "I didn't think..."

"No, I know. It's okay." Her voice was a whisper.

"It's not okay. But I promise it won't happen again." He dropped his hands in time to see her nod.

"Sure." She swallowed. "Good night."

He stayed where he was while she went into the house. Valerie should have no doubt that he would leave her alone. He imagined her locking his bedroom door...and then imagined her locking it with the two of them inside.

Rob dropped onto the porch step and propped his head in his hands. Were there words harsh enough to describe his behavior?

Sure. Shameful, to have taken advantage of a woman to whom he'd offered protection. Stupid, to think he could manage a casual kiss or two after nine years of celibacy. Shocking, to discover his own lack of control.

Terrifying, to realize how much he wanted to finish what he'd started.

CHAPTER SIX

GRACE WOKE UP to find *that* girl staring down at her.

"What are you doing here?" she said in a loud voice. "Who said you could wear my nightgown?"

Before Grace could answer, someone else came into the room. "Grace and Connor and their mom slept over, Ginny." Mr. Warren stood at the end of their bed. "There was some trouble at their house again last night and I invited them to stay with us."

"That's my gown." The girl's expression was definitely a scowl—one of the words on last week's spelling list.

"I was sure you would be glad to share." Mr. Warren lifted an eyebrow in that way parents had when they expected you to behave and not make trouble. He had a cut on his forehead, like he'd run into a door or something.

The girl pointed to the TV. "That's my movie."

"Maybe we should turn on a different one y'all can watch while I make breakfast."

She twisted her mouth to the side. "I'm going back to my room."

"Okay," her dad said as she limped past him to the

door. "I'll put in…let me see…" He changed the DVD and the music for the first Harry Potter movie started.

"I want to watch that," the girl said. "I'll take it into the living room."

"No, you can watch in here." Mr. Warren pulled a chair in the corner around so it faced the TV. "Now you've got a front row seat."

With her face still twisted, the girl sat down in the chair. "Give me the remote," she said.

Her dad looked at her for a second, almost frowning but not quite. "I think I'll put it right here, on top of the cabinet." He set it down and then slid it to the very back, next to the wall. "And I don't expect to hear any fighting over the controls. Breakfast will be ready before the troll appears."

When Mr. Warren left, Grace pushed her pillow back and sat up to watch the movie. The girl looked kind of like a troll, sitting there all grumpy in her chair.

Grace knew her mother would expect her to be nice. "Have you read the books?"

"Of course." She rolled her eyes as if it was a stupid question.

"Do you have a favorite? I like the second one best."

"Will you be quiet?" She hissed, like a snake. "I'm trying to watch the movie."

"You should be in the movie," Grace muttered. "Who needs an evil wizard when you're around?"

AS THE SUN CAME UP, Valerie sat cross-legged on Rob Warren's bed, hugging his pillow to her chest while she tried to decide how to approach him this morning. Her cheeks burned with embarrassment when she thought about last night. Worse, her whole body warmed, softened. Wanted more.

With a growl, she threw the pillow at the head of the bed and surged to her feet, pulling the lovely nightgown over her head with the same movement. In seconds, she was dressed in her clothes and shoes from last night, her hair finger-combed, the mascara smudges under her eyes wiped away. She would make up Rob's bed—though he would probably want to wash the sheets—and face him as if nothing had happened. As if she'd never come out last night and…and…

There on the bed, though, lay that pretty nightgown. She picked it up, turned it right side out and held it up in front of her. Made of a soft white fabric, what might have been called "fine lawn" in olden days, the sleeveless gown and its robe were sewn with pin tucks at the shoulders and narrow lace edging the hems and the robe's sleeves. Valerie shook out the wrinkles and looked closely at the structure of those tucks, smoothing her fingers over the fullness they created. Then she froze.

Rob had lied to her. This was a gown for a nursing mother, with hidden slits designed to bring breast to baby. He'd bought it for his wife, Ginny's mother. And he had the sense to realize she wouldn't have worn it last night if she'd known.

After gently folding the gown and robe, she placed them on the straight-backed chair in the corner and then made up the bed. She wouldn't say anything about her discovery. Maybe he didn't mind anymore that the

gown had been for his wife, didn't value it for that reason. If so, why would he have kept it? Why not give it
to his sister, or his mother, or a clothes closet for needy
women?

And if Rob still valued the gown, what did that say
about his feelings for *her?*

Her thoughts flinched at the question. She had no
time, no room, in her life for a man. Or for the feelings men created—the confusion, the irritation, the
pain. Even after barely a week's acquaintance, she'd
been frustrated by Rob's insistence on taking over
when she was perfectly capable of handling a job or
a situation by herself. A Southern cavalier had been
her dream when she was young. But she wasn't
twelve years old anymore. She had to be able to stand
on her own.

Beside her own independence—not to mention the
example she wanted to set for her daughter and the
other girls she might come to know—a thoughtful, gra-
cious, considerate man and his intoxicating kisses simply couldn't be allowed to matter.

When she opened the bedroom door, she heard the
Harry Potter theme playing in the room where the kids
had slept. From the hallway she saw Ginny slouched in
an armchair and Grace propped up against the pillows.
Connor appeared to be asleep still, with his head under
the pillow and his rear end stuck up in his favorite position.

"'Morning, sleepyheads," she said, just as Rob came
to the door of the kitchen.

"Breakfast is ready," he called. "Come and get it."

His face softened as he looked at Valerie—or was that just her imagination? "Good morning to you, too."

She managed a smile back, just as Connor rushed through the bedroom door, followed by Grace. "I guess they're hungry," she said, embarrassed all over again.

"Good thing. I like hungry kids. Ginny, are you coming?"

Valerie glanced into the guest room and saw Ginny, her arms crossed, making no effort to leave the chair. "I'll give her a hand."

She sat on the bed, close to Ginny's chair. "How are you this morning?"

The girl stuck out her lower lip but didn't say anything.

"Kinda weird, waking up and finding us here, I bet."

Ginny eyed her through narrowed lids. "What happened?"

"Somebody threw rocks at all our windows and broke them."

"What did you do that they're being so mean?"

"Good question." Valerie laughed. "I don't think I did anything. The people in the house before us sold illegal drugs, and I guess they forgot to notify all their friends of their new address."

"Why'd you come *here?*"

"Believe it or not, you and your dad are just about our only friends in town so far. I was so worried about making sure Grace and Connor were safe, I couldn't think of anywhere else to go."

She hoped her own weakness hadn't played too big a role in the decision.

"Did you—" Ginny snapped her mouth shut.

"Did I what?"

"Nothing." She turned her face away, pretending to watch the movie.

"You can ask anything you want to, Ginny."

But the girl refused to answer.

"Hey, you two, the pancakes are hot," Rob called from the kitchen.

"Guess we'd better go eat." Valerie stood and extended a hand. "Need some help getting up?"

"I can do it."

"Okay." Valerie turned off the DVD. She made a production of putting the disk in its case and closing the door of the cabinet. But Ginny fought to her feet, settled herself on the crutches and got out the door without help. Slowly, true. But under her own steam.

WITH THE KIDS PRESENT, breakfast passed easily enough. Rob allowed Grace and Connor to help him and Ginny with cleanup while Valerie finished her coffee. He didn't realize she'd left the room until she came back into the kitchen with an armful of sheets.

"Where's the laundry? I'll put these in for you."

He fought off a sudden awareness of how domestic the situation seemed. "Uh…it's the door right next to the back door. Just put them on the washer—"

"I'll get them started… Oh." She stood at the door to the laundry room, surveying the mountain of clothes. "You're a little behind on your wash, aren't you?"

"A little. I'll get to it."

"Now's as good a time as any." She waded in and the door swung closed behind her.

Rob followed her and opened the door again. "Valerie, you don't have to do our wash."

"I won't do all of it." She had started picking through for the obvious girl clothes.

"Don't do any of it." He stared at her, hands on his hips. "I mean it."

"What? Are you the only person allowed to do favors for somebody else? You're the only one who can help out?"

"No. But—"

"You don't want to owe me anything, is that it?"

"Well…"

"But it's okay for me to owe you?"

Rob surrendered with his hands in the air. "Okay, okay. I give in. Knock yourself out doing my wash." He backed out of the laundry room, refusing to think about Valerie Manion washing his underwear. Maybe she wouldn't go that far. She had been a married woman, anyway. She'd seen a guy's boxers before, surely.

As he turned around, a knock at the back door announced Jenny's arrival. "Hey, bro. How's it going?" She saw Grace and Connor drying the last two plates. "Hey, guys. Is this a slumber party? Can I come?"

Ginny got herself across the room to stand between Valerie's kids and Jenny. "They're going home," she announced. "Somebody keeps tearing up their house, but they don't live here." She put her head against Jenny's ribs. "Don't worry about them."

With a smile at Rob, his sister draped an arm around Ginny's thin shoulders. "How about I at least find out their names? I'm Rob's sister," she told Grace and Connor. "Jenny Warren."

"This is Grace and Connor Manion," Rob said. Valerie came out of the laundry room at that moment. "And this is their mom, Valerie. She's the leader of Ginny's GO! troop. Valerie, my sister, Jenny."

For a few seconds, he worried that Valerie would say something about the nightgown that supposedly belonged to Jenny. But the two women chatted about Rob's miserable control of the laundry situation without referring to the gown.

"Mom would be glad to do his laundry," Jenny said, "but Rob refuses to cooperate."

"Some guys won't ask for help." Valerie shook her head. "They think they can handle everything by themselves."

"And there are no women like that, now are there?" Rob glared at the two of them. "Nobody here, besides me, thinks that she can manage a tire plant, take care of two kids, run a GO! troop and a house without asking for a hand now and then."

Valerie put on an innocent look. "Of course not."

"Or," he continued, "somehow keep up with the work at Dad's office and her shift as an EMT and help me out and take care of her own house and dog. Right?"

Jenny crossed her arms and lifted her stubborn chin. "I don't see the problem."

The three kids were staring up at the three of them as if they'd started speaking Martian. Rob shook his head. "I give up. I think we should all go see what we can do about the Manions' windows."

Valerie started to protest, but his glance halted the words on her lips. "Sure," she said meekly. "Let's go."

They found nothing to encourage optimism at Valerie's house. The police might have kept an eye on the street overnight, but somehow they hadn't managed to catch the creeps who threw eggs at the front porch and toilet paper rolls into the trees.

"What a mess." Valerie sagged against the bumper of her car. Somehow, the shattered windows looked even worse in daylight. "I'm in the wrong neighborhood, for sure."

Rob's sister stood with her hands in the rear pockets of her jeans, staring at the wreck. "I'm going to say something to the guys at the station. This shouldn't have happened."

Over Valerie's objections, Rob had taken the house key and gone inside to check things out. "No one's been in that I can tell," he said from the front porch, broom in hand. "There's glass all over the floor, but no other major damage."

"You don't have to do that," Valerie said, her hand held out to take the broom. "You've got other things—"

He gave her a glance that dared her to finish her protest and then continued to gather up the glass that had fallen on the porch.

With a frustrated huff, Valerie turned back to the car. At least her children would follow orders. "Grace, Connor, you two play with Ginny in the backyard until we can get this cleaned up. But stay off the deck."

Broken glass littered the floor of every room, the

kids' included, and covered most of the kitchen counter. Armed with brooms and a vacuum cleaner, Jenny took the kitchen, Valerie, the bedrooms and Rob, the front of the house. For a while, the only sound was the brittle brush of glass over bare wood floors. When Valerie finally returned to the living room, Rob was pouring the last of the shards into a trash bag.

"I hate to say it, but you can't stay here," he said. "You've got to find another place to live."

She dropped down onto the sofa and combed her fingers through her hair. "That's what I get for jumping on a bargain. I didn't ask the Realtor why the price was so low."

"Well, shame on the Realtor for trying to sell you a house that was obviously unsafe." Jenny sat down and put an arm around Valerie's shoulders. "There might even be some kind of legal measure you can take about that. I wouldn't be surprised if we couldn't get some of your money back."

"Kate Bell's dad is a lawyer," Rob said. "We could ask him to look into that. Meanwhile, Jenny has made a suggestion, and it's a good one."

Valerie looked at him suspiciously. "What suggestion?"

"I think," Jenny said, "you should move in with me."

VALERIE ARGUED HARD and long, so long that Jenny finally took the kids off to pick up hamburgers and fries for lunch. For every reason Rob offered in favor of the plan, she produced an excellent objection…every reason but one.

"When it comes down to it, you'd be doing me a

favor if you moved in with Jen." He sat down on the opposite end of the sofa from where she'd thrown herself in frustration.

Valerie glared at him. "I don't believe you."

Elbows propped on his knees, he stared at his linked fingers. "I wouldn't lie to you. See, Jen was supposed to get married last summer. Her fiancé was a police officer. That house she lives in was where they planned to be together."

"He broke up with her?"

"I wish. He was killed in a shooting incident, by a drunk teenager. A week before the wedding."

"Rob. How awful."

He nodded. "Jen's done okay—got the presents returned, put the dress away, started her new job and stays in that house with just their dog, Buttercup, for company. But I know she's lonely." Looking up, he pinned her with a solemn blue stare. "I can't help thinking that having a family like yours around would really brighten her days. And nights."

After that appeal, she accepted the offer with what grace she could muster. "I pay rent," she insisted, when Jenny and the kids returned with the food. "Or I find somewhere else to live."

"Rent sounds reasonable," Jenny agreed. "We'll work it out tonight. Meanwhile, y'all get the things you need packed up. Rob will take me home to get my truck and I'll be back in a few minutes to help you move."

Grace whined about leaving her pale pink room and Connor played with his toys instead of gathering up the ones he wanted to take with him, but by late afternoon most of their clothes and valuables had been stowed in the back of Jenny's truck for transport across town. Valerie did a final check of her own closet and came across one important item she'd neglected to pack.

When she came into the living room, Jenny stared at the gun case and the separate box of shells Valerie carried. "A weapon? Bullets?"

"A .357 Magnum." She hefted the case in one hand. "Don't worry—I'm an expert marksman."

"That's good." Pale and wide-eyed, Jenny didn't look in the least reassured. "What about Connor and Grace?"

"They know this box is strictly off-limits. I keep the case and the gun inside locked unless I have it in my hand to fire, and the shells are in a different place. The ammunition chest also locks." She showed Jenny the catch and its keyed padlock. "I've never had a single bit of trouble."

"Still…" Jenny took a deep breath. "Valerie, I'm sorry, but I'm gonna be really uncomfortable with a gun in my house."

"I can't blame you." She offered a smile. "It's okay—we'll go back to the hotel plan. No problem."

Rob stood up from the couch. "What if I keep the gun?"

Valerie stared at him. "What? Why?"

"Jen will be comfortable, you'll know where it is and you'll have a decent place to stay. I don't have a gun in my house, but I don't have a problem with keeping one for a while. How's that sound?"

Though she didn't like becoming even more indebted to Rob and Jenny, Valerie decided that leaving the gun with Rob would work. Before dark, she and the kids were settled in Jenny's spare bedrooms, and Grace and Connor were arguing over which of them got to sleep with Jenny's golden retriever puppy.

"This will be fun," Jenny assured her that night, as they sat at the kitchen table with their coffee. Rob and Ginny had shared their spaghetti supper and then gone back to their own house across the yard. "I feel like I'm rattling around in this place when I'm here by myself." She gazed into her mug. "It wasn't supposed to be just me and the dog."

Surprising herself, Valerie put her hand over Jenny's. "I know. I'm so terribly sorry."

Jenny blinked hard. "Thanks. Anyway, Buttercup will love having kids to play with."

"Does Ginny like dogs?"

"Sure, but Rob doesn't let her play... I mean, she *can't* play as rough as your kids can. He's always felt she was pretty fragile, which is why he never got himself one. And they only have Mat the Cat because he strayed into the yard and refused to leave again." She hesitated for a moment, her lips pressed together. "I was a little surprised, in fact, that Rob signed Ginny up for GO! It's a pretty active program, isn't it?"

"It can be, depending on the interests of the girls and the leader. As a first-year troop, we're not going rappelling or white-water rafting, of course."

"Glad to hear it." Jenny returned her smile. "Even hiking over uneven terrain is going to be a challenge for Ginny."

"That's why we're starting with a neighborhood hike at next week's meeting. She'll get a chance to warm up to a long walk on good surfaces before we go out into the wild. I think she'll do okay. And Rob will be along, in case she needs extra help."

"Right. Rob will be there." Strangely, his sister didn't seem at all reassured by that idea.

AT THE MEETING on Wednesday, the girls were excited when Valerie announced the hike. "First, though, Mr. Warren brought ingredients for us to make our own snack."

"Candy bars?" Kendra asked.

"Cupcakes?"

"Brownies?"

"Chocolate chip cookies?"

Valerie held up her hand for quiet. "GORP."

The girls stared at her in confusion. "What," Ginny said loudly, "is GORP?"

"It's a hiker's tradition. The word stands for good old raisins and peanuts. But our version has some extra ingredients. Let's go see."

Rob waited at one of the lunch tables with a huge plastic bowl in front of him and a long line of small paper bags on either side. "We're going to slide this along the table," he said, "and each of you will dump what's in your bag into the bowl. Then everybody will get a chance to stir as the bowl comes back to me. Don't peek at your bag until you dump it."

This activity had been his idea, and Valerie had to admit that the girls got a lot of fun out of the surprise ingredients they added to the mix—breakfast cereal, popcorn, fruit candies and chocolate, dried apples and bananas and cranberries, plus the standard raisins and different kinds of nuts. Everyone took a stir at the bowl and then filled their own plastic bag with the snack before lining up two by two at the outside door.

"Stay with your buddy," she told the girls as they headed outside. "And stay behind me. No running ahead, no lagging behind. Let's go!"

Rob brought up the end of the line, with Ginny as his buddy. He'd suggested she find one of the other girls to pair up with, but she clung tightly to his hand. He thought that was probably to be expected on this first expedition. She would warm up soon enough and venture out on her own.

The August afternoon was mild, under a sky where the sun played hide and seek with low clouds. Dressed in their uniforms, the girls skipped along the sidewalk, chattering like little blue and tan birds. Valerie had made up a scavenger-hunt list of things to look out for on the hike—everything from squirrels and bird feeders to safety signs and fire hydrants. Each buddy pair that found at least half the items would get a surprise when they returned to the school.

"So," Rob said, holding up the list, "we're looking for a bunch of things. Seen any Stop signs?"

Ginny had her eyes on the sidewalk as she hopped along on her crutches. She shook her head.

"You have to look around to see stuff, Gin. And I've gotta keep my eyes on all these other girls. Give me some help, here."

His daughter didn't reply and didn't lift her head. Rob bit back his irritation. "This is supposed to be fun, honey. Can't you try a little?"

Valerie had mapped out a fairly level course, so Ginny wasn't working too hard to keep moving. She simply didn't want to cooperate.

Ahead of them, Grace had been paired with Connor so she could keep an eye on her brother. Just as Rob glanced their way, Connor took off at an angle to the sidewalk and headed for a small dog yapping at them from behind a fence.

Grace stopped. "Connor! Come back here." When her brother ignored her, she resorted to the age-old threat. "I'm gonna tell Mom."

Rob shook his head. "Your mom's got her hands full. Why don't you and Ginny walk together and I'll get Connor back in line?" He didn't wait for the girls' agreement, but jogged over to the fence, where Connor was doing his best to get his fingers snapped off.

"Let's go, buddy." Rob put a hand on Connor's shoulder. "Mrs. Burton's dog isn't safe, like Buttercup. She'll take a hunk out of you before you know what happened."

"Why?"

"Mrs. Burton always trains her dogs that way. She had a poodle when I was your age, and I swear that dog would've eaten me alive if I hadn't climbed a tree to get away." He turned the boy around and pointed to the old oak in the corner of the yard. "That tree, right there. I had to sit there one day until Mrs. Burton came home from work at six and took the poodle inside. Got all my homework done sitting on a branch in that tree."

Connor eyed him with suspicion. "You're kidding, right?"

"Nope. Ask Jenny tonight. She'll tell you I got yelled at for being late."

They caught up with the line of girls, and Rob saw that neither Grace nor Ginny were cooperating in the scavenger hunt. They walked side-by-side, avoiding each other's gazes. Whatever the problem between them might be, nobody was making an effort to solve it.

The hike ended back at the school with five minutes to spare before the meeting ended. Valerie handed out sheets of stickers to all the girls who presented a scavenger hunt sheet. When she looked at Ginny and Grace with her eyebrows lifted, Rob, standing behind them, shook his head.

Not until all the other girls had gone home did they get a chance to discuss the problem. "Neither of them participated?" Valerie shook her head. "That doesn't sound good."

"I think pairing Grace with her brother might be part of the problem," Rob told her. "Seems to me she doesn't really get to be part of the troop, you know? She's either watching Connor or helping you."

"Grace has plenty of opportunities to participate." Valerie's cheeks took on a bright pink flush. She planted her hands on her hips. "She likes helping me."

"I know she does. But it sets her apart from the

group. She's not just one of the girls. She's the leader's kid."

"Since you're so great at analyzing, what do you think Ginny's problem is?" Valerie sure was cute when she got mad.

But he didn't like making people mad. He held up his hands in surrender. "I'm not trying to make trouble, here. I just thought I'd tell you what I see."

"And do you see why Ginny doesn't participate?"

He gazed over at his daughter, sitting alone at one of the long cafeteria tables. "I guess Ginny's still uncomfortable with the group. She's not used to fending for herself in the midst of so many girls."

"She fends for herself all day at school."

Rob felt his own anger stir. "Troop activities are different. I think she'll come around."

"I hope you're right. Even one girl who doesn't co-operate can dampen everyone else's experience."

Now his hands were on his hips, too. "Are you saying Ginny spoiled the hike for the other girls?"

"She certainly spoiled it for herself and Grace."

"Grace wasn't any more cooperative than Ginny."

They faced off, staring at each other, breathing hard. Finally, Valerie looked away and backed down. "We shouldn't argue about this. They both had a bad day. Next week will be better."

"You're right." Rob rubbed a hand over his face. "I'm sorry I got so riled up. But…" He looked at her from underneath his brows. "Maybe it would help if Connor didn't have to come to the meetings. Then

Grace wouldn't have to be responsible for him and you wouldn't have to worry about him."

"That sounds good, but where would he go? He has to have some kind of supervision."

Rob snapped his fingers as the answer came to him. "You know, my mom really does a good job with little boys."

CHAPTER SEVEN

THE WARREN FAMILY Labor Day picnic started at three in the afternoon. Long before then, Valerie was a nervous wreck.

"I don't want you running and yelling," she told Connor as she ironed the T-shirt and shorts he would wear. "Say *please* and *thank you* and *yes, ma'am* and *no, ma'am.*" Rob had asked his mother if she would keep Connor during the GO! meetings and she'd agreed, though they hadn't tried out the arrangement yet. If he didn't behave today...

Making appropriate rocket engine sounds with his throat and lips, Connor zoomed his space cruiser around the guest room, then ran across the bed, hopped to the floor and headed out into the hallway. Valerie winced at the noise. At least they had the house to themselves—Jenny was at work. So the picnic would be, as Rob described it, "no big deal—just the boys and the old folks." His parents, in other words. *His parents.*

"Connor, did you hear me?" she called.

Grace came to the door of the bedroom. "Is this okay to wear?"

Valerie considered the outfit—a black tank top that

showed off Grace's pretty shoulders paired with a camouflage print skirt and flip-flops. "I don't think the skirt works. Do you have something a little less…aggressive? I'm not sure Mrs. Warren will appreciate the military fashion statement."

Rolling her eyes, Grace went back to the room she shared with Connor. The situation wasn't ideal—each of the kids should have their own space. On the other hand, she didn't have to worry so much about vandalism and outright assault while they stayed at Jenny's. And she'd made sure she paid a generous rent.

What she did have to worry about, of course, was too much of a good thing. That would be too much of Rob Warren dropping by his sister's house to share a cup of coffee or a glass of iced tea. Too many opportunities to step through the trees and into his backyard, where it seemed her children spent most of their time when they weren't in school. She wasn't sure which was a bigger enticement for Grace and Connor—Buttercup, the retriever or Rob, the father figure.

The same closeness had not developed in her relationship with Ginny. More often than not, Rob's daughter sat removed from the general fun, with Mat the Cat on her lap and a distant expression on her thin face. Their games weren't always beyond her skill, but she steadfastly refused to participate. Valerie wondered if this afternoon at her grandparents' house would play out the same way.

Grace came back with a white skirt. "How's this?"

"Do you think you can keep it clean? Something darker might be better."

They went through three more options before they agreed on a pair of denim shorts and a yellow tank top with sneakers.

"That's good," Valerie decided. "Bring me your brush and I'll braid your hair."

"Mom! I don't want braids."

"But it's so neat, and it keeps your hair out of your face."

"I'm too old for braids."

"You're too young to wear your hair down all the time. You'll be a mess before we've been there twenty minutes." And Mrs. Warren would think her a terrible parent who couldn't keep her children presentable.

The ensuing half-hour argument—conducted while Valerie supervised Connor's bath and got him dressed—left Grace with tears in her eyes and a single braid down her back. Valerie conceded far enough to give her a zigzag part on top of her head.

"Cute." She smiled at Grace through the mirror, but her daughter was too angry to reciprocate. "As soon as I change, we'll be ready to go. Right on time, too—Rob will be here in fifteen minutes."

When Rob knocked on Jenny's back door, however, Valerie was still in her bedroom, trying to figure out what to put on over her underwear. Sundress? Shorts and a casual top? Slacks and a blouse? Sandals? Sneakers? Perfume?

"Like this is a date?" she asked herself in the mirror. "Like he isn't the last man in town you should get excited about?"

"Like I can help it?" her reflection demanded in return.

Grace knocked on the door. "Mom, Mr. Warren's ready to go. He's bringing the van around to the front of the house."

"I'll be right out," Valerie said through gritted teeth. She'd narrowed her options down to which shirt and shoes to wear with olive capri pants. She liked the gold sandals, but they didn't work with the red shirt...

Five minutes later. "Mom, Mr. Warren's parked outside."

Swearing under her breath, Valerie defaulted to a white sleeveless shirt and the gold sandals, added earrings and a clatter of tortoiseshell bracelets, then ran a comb over her head. Thank goodness her hair, at least, required no choices. The Southern humidity guaranteed an abundance of curls.

"Coming!" she finally said, with truth.

Rob smiled at her as she climbed into the passenger seat. "Good afternoon, lovely lady. Ready for some fun?"

Valerie didn't have an answer that wasn't an apology or a defense. She'd expected impatience or, at best, resignation. Weren't men always irritated when a woman kept them waiting? "Um...sure."

"How about you folks in the back seat? Got your swim suits?"

"No," Connor and Grace said at the same time.

"Better go get 'em."

That errand entailed Valerie unlocking the house again and searching for towels while the kids fetched their suits. Back in the car, she glanced nervously at Rob. "I hope these aren't Jenny's good towels. They were the only ones I could find."

"Don't worry about it," he said, gazing into the rear-view mirror as he backed out of the driveway. "Mom's got plenty of towels for everybody. We can just leave those in the van."

Valerie dropped back against her seat, feeling like a deflated balloon. How could he be so...so relaxed? Didn't he realize what an intense, nerve-racking occasion this was? Was the man immune to pressure?

The absurdity of her questions struck her right away. This was Rob's family. Why should he be nervous?

Though they lived outside the New Skye town limits on a couple of acres of land, Rob's parents' home was not the grand plantation house she'd expected. The lawn was large and green, but the building itself was a single-story brick ranch. Black rocking chairs and wrought-iron tables occupied the long front porch, with clay pots of red geraniums added for a splash of color. Graceful, but not intimidating.

"Come in," Rob said as he opened the front door for Ginny. The hall inside was big enough for Connor and Grace to ease in beside her, with Valerie following. Instead of the formality she'd expected, the house was decorated in a "country" style—checks and plaids in blue and red, rag rugs on hardwood floors, furniture that looked comfortable, not elegant. Her breathing relaxed just a little.

As she followed Rob through the house, she saw that photographs of children filled one wall of the family room. Valerie was immediately drawn to a picture of three boys and a little girl, ranging from probably twelve years old down to four or five. Each smile featured at least one missing tooth. Two of the boys had dark hair and eyes, but the middle boy and the little girl were both towheaded.

She felt Rob standing behind her. "I knocked one tooth out in baseball and the other when I smacked my chin on the diving board. Lucky they were just baby teeth."

"You were a good-looking bunch."

"We've got great gene donors. Come and meet them."

Out on the deck beyond the sliding glass doors, a man who could only be Rob's father sat at a round glass table with a dark-haired, smiling woman.

Ron leaned into the shade of the large umbrella to give the woman a hug. "Mom, Dad, this is Valerie. Valerie, Mike and Carolyn Warren."

Mr. Warren got to his feet, setting his cigarette in a nearby ashtray as he did so. "Pleased to meet you." He shook her hand, and his voice was friendly enough, but she immediately missed Rob's grin in such a familiar face.

"Welcome, Valerie," Mrs. Warren said. Her relationship to Rob was there in their shared smile—wide, graceful, relaxed. "Have a seat and Rob will get you something to drink."

Ginny came to stand by her grandmother and was immediately pulled into Mrs. Warren's lap. "Hello, there, Ginny love. How are you today? Enjoying your time off from school?"

Grace and Connor were hanging back shyly, but before she took her seat, Valerie moved them forward.

"Mr. and Mrs. Warren, these are my children, Grace and Connor."

Mr. Warren only nodded, but his wife held out her hand. "I'm glad to meet you both. Ginny, why don't you show them where the bathroom is so they can change into their swimsuits? And then you can all get into the pool."

Ginny frowned, but at a raised eyebrow from her dad she turned and went into the house. Valerie nodded at Grace's questioning glance, and her children followed.

Then, finally, she felt free to sit down. Rob propped his hands on the back of her chair and leaned forward to look into her face. "What would you like? Lemonade, soda, beer…?"

Looking up at him over her shoulder felt…well, intimate. "Lemonade sounds great." She turned quickly to face his mother again. "Your home is beautiful, Mrs. Warren. And this backyard is a child's paradise."

"Thank you. And call me Carolyn, please." She waited while Rob set down a tall, frosted glass beside Valerie's hand on the table. He had brought out a beer for himself. "Mike built the swings and climbing gear for the kids when they were young, and we just left it, figuring we'd have grandchildren one day. So far, only Ginny uses it."

"Don't give up, Mom. We're all still able to reproduce." Rob sprawled comfortably in his chair, as if he didn't have a care in the world. He wore a dark blue T-shirt and white cargo shorts which revealed the long, tan length of his legs. Valerie took a deep breath, trying to keep her gaze away from those really great legs, dusted with fine golden hair, like his arms. Underneath the perennial baseball cap, his hair shone gold, and hung a little long, as usual.

And, as usual, he took her breath away—a luxury she could not afford. "Mr. Warren, I understand Rob works with you in the family business. I guess you must be really busy all year round."

He nodded somberly. "There's no season on locksmithing. Somebody's always building somewhere, needing locks. Folks shut their keys in the car every day of the year."

"Maybe a little more often during the Christmas rush," Rob said. "They're too busy, with too much on their minds, and they forget to take the keys out of the ignition before they lock all those presents in the trunk."

"Nah." His dad shook his head. "There's no real difference between one time of year and another."

Valerie bit down on her irritation with the uncongenial Mike Warren and turned to his wife. "Do you work outside the home, Carolyn?"

She shook her head. "I stayed home with my children too long to have any really marketable skills. But I volunteer at the cancer clinic three mornings a week. A couple of days serving dinner in the shelter downtown, a morning tutoring elementary school children in reading... I keep busy."

"That sounds like full-time employment to me." She hesitated, then decided to be direct. "If you're too busy to mind Connor during the GO! meetings, I'll certainly understand."

"Not at all." Carolyn patted Valerie's hand on the

table. "It'll be fun to have a little boy around the house again. I was something of a tomboy, myself, and I've missed those rowdy days. I'm looking forward to playing with Connor. Now, it sounds to me like you're the busy one, working full-time with two children. Rob says you're employed at the tire plant?"

"Yes, ma'am, I'm the vice president in charge of production. It's my job to keep those steel-belted radials rolling off the line."

"My goodness..." The older woman stared at her with wide eyes and raised brows. "You must be very talented, to be in such a top-level position. And so young!"

"I've gotten some good breaks in my career," Valerie admitted. "And I've taken advantage of my opportunities."

Grace and Connor came through the sliding glass door just then, and she suddenly realized how faded their bathing suits had become over a summer of use. Connor's suit trailed a couple of threads from the hemline, and Grace had actually almost outgrown hers. In Ohio, they'd gone to the pool almost every day after she got home from work, for lessons and play. She should have remembered and should have bought new suits before this weekend. What would Rob's mother think?

But Rob's mother glanced past her kids to Ginny. "Oh, that new suit I got you fits perfectly, doesn't it? I thought we'd love that red—it brings out the red in your hair."

Ginny had come out onto the deck using her crutches, but without her braces. "It's okay," she said. "Can we swim now?"

Rob got to his feet. "Sure." To his mother, he said, "Thanks for the new suit, Mom. The old one was starting to wear through pretty bad." He looked at Valerie and gave a wry shrug. "I just haven't had time to do much clothes shopping. Thank heaven for mothers. Are you coming in with us?"

"Oh, no." She hadn't thought the swimming invitation applied to her. "I didn't bring my suit."

"Are you so used to giving orders, you don't listen when you're told what to do?" Shaking his head, he clucked his tongue. "How did you get to be such a stubborn woman?"

Before she could answer, he pulled off his shirt and, with an unconscious ease, tugged down his shorts to reveal basic black swim trunks. No designer label, no special fabric—Valerie was beginning to think he shopped for his own clothes in one of those superstores that carried everything from food to diamonds and computers to automobile parts.

But Rob Warren did not need the enhancement of a well-designed, expensive swim suit. As he ambled over to the pool with Ginny, the hot sun glinted off his smooth back, toasted a terrific nut-brown by hours outside. His bare shoulders looked broader, more buffed, than she would have imagined. She made a deliberate effort not to stare at his butt, but one glance confirmed her impression. The man had an awesome body.

And he used it well. On the rim of the pool's deep end, he stood poised for just a second, then knifed into the water like an Olympic swimmer going for the gold. In seconds he came up at the near shallow end, his hair slicked back and his long lashes sparkling with water droplets.

"Come on in, kids, the water feels great."

With a cry of joy, Connor leapt into the sparkling water with his knees clasped in his hands—the classic cannonball. He sent up a big enough splash to wet Rob again.

"Good one, Con, my man." Rob clapped his hands. "Do it again. Your turn, Grace."

One place Grace felt at home was in the water. With a couple of skipping steps, she, too, cannonballed Rob. Not as big a splash, but successful, all the same.

Rob moved to the ramp which sloped into the pool and held out a hand. "Come on, Gin. I'm here."

She stood at the side, where Connor had gone in. "I want to jump."

Her father shook his head. "Just walk in like you always do."

"I want to jump."

"Ginny, you know that's not safe."

"I can do it. I can!" She glanced at Grace and Connor, paddling around in the deep end of the pool. "And I want to swim down there."

"First you have to get in." By his tone, Valerie could tell Rob's patience had frayed. "Walk in and then I'll take you down to the other end."

"I want to jump. And I want to swim by myself."

"That's not—"

"Let the girl do what she wants." Fists clenched, face red, Mike Warren exploded out of his seat, kicking his chair backward in the process. "She's not going to drown with you standing right there. You're making a big deal out of nothing." He stalked into the house, leaving a long moment of silence behind.

Valerie kept her eyes on Rob's face, hoping her own didn't betray embarrassment at his dad's explosion. When their eyes met, she nodded in encouragement. Ginny deserved a chance to be just another kid, as far as she was able. A little freedom might improve her attitude in other situations.

With a small nod in Valerie's direction, Rob turned back to his daughter. "Okay, your granddad thinks you should jump. So…" He held out his arms, backed away from the side. "Jump."

The crutches clattered onto the deck. Ginny stood unsteadily on her own thin legs for what seemed to be an eternity, stopping Valerie's heart with fear. Beside her, Carolyn drew an unsteady breath.

Then Ginny fell face-first into the pool. After an endless second, she came to the surface, sputtering and paddling, keeping herself afloat.

Valerie laughed and clapped her hands. "Way to go, Ginny!"

Rob reached out to hold the girl under her arms. "That was terrific, Gin." He glanced over at Valerie and shared her smile of approval. "Want to do it again?"

Over the next hour or so, he even relaxed enough to let Ginny swim in the deep end by herself—arm strokes, mostly, with occasional kicks to keep her afloat. Valerie sat on the side of the pool while Rob treaded water a few feet away, both of them watching like hawks as the three kids laughed and splashed and played together.

By the time they all came back to the table, Rob's brothers had arrived. Once another round of introductions had been made, the kids went into the house to change.

"Where do you find all these beautiful women?" With the air of a man embarking on a serious hunting trip, Smith Warren sat in the chair Rob had used and pulled it even closer to Valerie. Trent, the eldest, went into the house for more drinks.

"'All these beautiful women?'" Rob pulled his shirt over his head and came out with his jaw clenched. "What are you talking about?"

"Well, there was Leah, and now Valerie… You're batting a thousand, far as I can see."

"We can all see that you're a jerk, Smith." Rob cuffed him on the ear as he went to sit on the far side of the table. "Engage your brain before you open your mouth, why don't you?"

But Smith wasn't about to be stopped. "I just think you have good luck with the ladies. What's wrong with that?"

Trent brought three beers and a glass of lemonade to the table in his big hands. "Let's see…could be it's a little rude to mention a man's dead wife in the context of 'women' in general. Not to mention making assumptions out loud about a couple's relationship without having enough information. Just for starters." He set Valerie's lemonade in front of her. "I apologize for the overall stupidity of my little brother."

"I didn't mean any offense," Smith complained.

"None taken," Valerie said. Across the table, Rob had

tensed like a panther ready to pounce. She didn't know what to make of his attitude, couldn't contemplate the implications. "Let's change the subject."

"Okay," Smith said. "What are you doing next Friday night?"

She looked at him in amusement. "Laundry," she said lightly.

He took the rebuff with a laugh, and the conversation moved on to safer subjects. The Warren brothers were certainly a trio of attractive men. Trent and Smith possessed their mother's dark hair and eyes but the same lean height as Rob and their father. Smith seemed a little young for his age, and a lot spoiled. She got the feeling he hadn't heard the word *no* very often, and almost never from women. Trent, on the other hand, rarely smiled, and when he did, his eyes remained wary. Valerie only needed a few minutes to decide that Rob was definitely her preference among the three.

Not that she would have to—or want to—make the choice, of course.

Mr. Warren—she couldn't think of him by his first name—came back outside to start the gas grill, then lit a cigarette and sat down with them at the table. "Busy today?" he asked Smith.

The younger man shook his head. "Nah. Nobody's worried about locks on Labor Day. I turned on the answering machine and left the pager at the shop. Whatever they want will wait till tomorrow."

"You left the pager?" Mr. Warren sat up straight. "What kind of fool move was that? You know how much business you could lose me, not answering the emergency calls?"

"Relax, Dad. I told you—I didn't get a call all day. If they haven't figured out they need a locksmith by five in the afternoon, don't you think they can hang in there another twelve hours?"

"What I think is that you've got no more sense than a grasshopper." He puffed hard on his cigarette and then ground it to dust in the ashtray. "Somebody's gotta be responsible for running the business right."

"Then I'd say you're lucky you've got the three of us." Smith offered his opinion with a cheeky grin, but his father wasn't impressed with the argument.

"Bullshit," he said distinctly.

"Come on, Dad," Rob protested. "Watch your language."

"You watch yours, boy. Since when do you get off correcting me?"

"Since I brought guests to the house, including children." Rob glanced at the climbing gym out on the lawn and Valerie followed his gaze. Connor and Grace were exploring the equipment. Ginny sat alone in a chair swing, moving slowly back and forth.

"I'll say what I please, how I please." Mr. Warren took another cigarette from the pack. "And you'll shut up about it."

The harsh words fell into an uncomfortable silence. Valerie knew she was flushed with embarrassment at witnessing—causing?—this family argument, while Rob looked both furious and mortified.

"I think I'll see if Carolyn needs any help with the food," she said, and made her escape.

Rob watched Valerie retreat to the house and waited to be sure the door was shut before turning to his dad. "What is the matter with you? I've never seen you act this rude in front of company."

Mike's expression turned mulish. "I won't be criticized by my own flesh and blood."

"You're being a jackass, Dad," was Trent's assessment. "This is a holiday, for God's sake. Lighten up."

"I might be able to lighten up occasionally, if I had the least hope that any of the three of you would take the responsibility for maintaining what I've managed to build all these years. As it is—"

"As it is…" Trent pushed back from the table and got to his feet. "As it is, the three of us work our butts off for you six to seven days a week and it's still not enough. I, for one, didn't come over here to be beat up on. I'll see you at work tomorrow." Without looking over his shoulder, he went into the house. In another minute—time enough to kiss their mom goodbye—the front door slammed and the roar of Trent's Harley flared and then diminished with distance.

"Okay," Smith said with a cautious expression. "I think I'll get another beer."

Rob didn't announce his own departure, but left the table and crossed the grass to join the kids at the gym set.

"Want me to push you?" He went around behind Ginny in her swing. "Fasten your seat belt."

With a little frown, she did as he asked. Pretty soon,

though, she was laughing as he sent her swinging into the air. "I'm flying," she called, stretching her arms out to the sides, straightening her legs. "Higher, Daddy, higher!"

Rob was happy to oblige. The momentum of the day changed at that point, restoring his balance and his peace of mind. His mom brought hamburgers out for Mike to put on the grill, and Valerie came out to the swing set. Soon, he was alternating between pushing Ginny and pushing Valerie, both of them giggling with delight.

He'd forgotten that a grown woman could giggle, or maybe Leah never did. He couldn't remember her as well these days as he once had.

Grace sat in the third swing and pushed herself as high as the other two, while Connor experimented with different ways to go down a sliding board. This, Rob knew, was the way a family holiday should feel.

Not that Valerie and her kids were his family. Even though the moment seemed so right…

With his mother outside, Rob was relieved to see that his dad behaved better during the meal. He wasn't the jovial, patient man they'd all grown up idolizing, but at least he wasn't downright rude.

The kids finished their burgers and took slices of cold, sweet watermelon out onto the climbing gym to enjoy. Even Ginny participated in the seed-spitting contest. On the deck, the adults ate their watermelon with forks and then sat with coffee and cookies as the sun started to set.

"Valerie was telling me about her vandalism problems," Rob's mother said. "I can't believe her Realtor didn't warn her about the house's history, not to mention the neighborhood." She retold the story for the benefit of Mike and Smith, with specifics added by Rob.

"That sucks." Smith put his hand on the back of Valerie's chair, behind her shoulder, with a proprietary attitude which tempted Rob to kill him, right then and there. "The police should do something."

"They try." Valerie shrugged and shifted in her seat, sitting sideways and slightly out of Smith's reach. "But they've got a whole town to monitor. They can't spend all day every day watching my house."

Smith sat forward, leaning his elbows on the table. "See, Dad—there's a bona fide example of the people we could help if we invested in the alarm business." He winked at Rob. "Seems to me I've heard some talk like that around the shop now and again. Maybe it's time you listened."

Mike's fist slammed down onto the glass table. Valerie jumped in surprise. Rob's mother squeaked. "Michael Warren!"

He ignored her. "I am not about to waste time and money on such a-a-a foolhardy idea. The security business calls for more expertise and training than all three of you boys put together can claim, yet you expect me to just throw away forty years of my sweat and blood so you can sit all day in front of some damn computer monitoring alarm signals. Well, I won't do it."

He stood up, grabbed up his pack of smokes and headed for the steps. "I'm going for a walk," he said over his shoulder and, without another word, stalked toward the woods which lined the backyard.

"Good night to you, too," Rob muttered. Under his breath, he added, "you arrogant son of a bitch."

WHEN THEY FINALLY left the Warrens' house, the children were exhausted from swimming and playing outdoors all afternoon. Valerie was exhausted, as well, but for purely emotional reasons. The conflict between Mr. Warren and his son had been more bitter than she would have believed possible, given Rob's easygoing personality.

"I'm sorry about my dad," he said, turning the car onto Jenny's street. He hadn't said another word on the drive into town. "He's always been stubborn, always set in his ways. Lately, though, I feel like he's getting downright mean."

"This is a hard time to be a small business owner, with the economy struggling and the world situation so uncertain." She hesitated, then ventured a little further. "If he's anything like my dad, I imagine he's worried about seeing everything he's worked for vanish due to forces he can't control. So he controls what he can."

Rob gave her a sidelong glance as he pulled the van into Jenny's driveway. "You're perceptive. And generous."

"I'm not the one he was yelling at. And I'm not his son." The comment won her a small smile. "I also know that patience isn't easy. You said, didn't you, that you've talked with him in the past about expanding into security systems?"

"And you saw his reaction."

"That's too bad, because I think you're right. You could tap into a good market right here in New Skye. I'd be your first contract."

"The first of quite a few. I've got a lot of friends who would like the comfort of an alarm system in their house." He rolled his shoulders and then blew out a deep breath. "But that's not a problem we can solve tonight. Let me help you get Grace and Connor inside. Ginny will be all right out here for a few minutes."

Grace was awake enough to walk on her own, but Rob picked Connor up out of the van and carried him toward the house. Valerie tried to block the images that crowded her brain—dad and mom and kids returning from a day of fun…the family dog wagging her tail behind the gate across the kitchen door…children tucked into bed and kissed good-night…husband and wife alone together, at last, with nothing and no one to consider but each other—

"He can sleep in his clothes," she told Rob, as he set Connor down on the bed. "Just slip off his shoes and socks."

Now they stood together in the dimly lit upstairs hallway. Except for the sleeping children and Buttercup, they were alone in the house. And Rob was as aware of the fact as she was. The air around them practically shivered with that knowledge.

He cleared his throat. "Guess I'd better head toward my side of the neighborhood and get Ginny into bed. Tomorrow is a work day."

"Right." She nodded too vigorously, turned away

too quickly toward the stairs. "I need to let Buttercup out."

"It's lucky for Jen that you're here right now to take care of the puppy." Rob followed her down the steps. "And it's good for Buttercup to have so much company."

"It's the least we can do. I seem to be taking more and more advantage of your family." They'd left the front door open, and she stood well back, giving him plenty of room to leave without an unexpected encounter. A nearby lamp provided just enough light to see the glint in his eyes—Rob recognized exactly what she was doing. And he didn't like it.

Surely, as an intelligent man, he understood that they couldn't become physically involved. If his male pride suffered a dent or two over it, he'd recover soon enough. Far sooner than if they actually gave in to this…this *lust* between them.

For a moment, though, she thought he was going to challenge the barrier she'd erected. She tensed her body to fight not only any move he might make, but her own treacherous attraction.

"Don't worry about it," he advised. "We aren't." Then he pivoted on his heel and walked out the door. His "Good-night," floated back to her on the breeze. Without watching him leave the driveway, she shut the door, turned the dead bolt…and suddenly remembered the dog, now whining in the kitchen.

"Sorry, baby," she crooned, stepping over the pet gate. "You've been a good girl, haven't you? No messes anywhere. I bet you're really ready to go outside."

Jenny had erected a nice picket fence around her backyard, so Buttercup could be sent out without supervision. But the cool night felt so wonderful that Valerie stepped outside, as well. The most important part of Rob's relaxation recipe was the solace of a Southern summer night, right?

Such was the power of the process that when the trees beyond the fence started to move, she didn't even wonder if she should be afraid. Or maybe she was reassured by Buttercup, whose tail wagged in recognition of the man standing at the back gate.

"I heard her tags jingle," Rob explained. "And thought I'd...come say hello."

"Sure." Sitting on the steps of Jenny's back porch, Valerie made no effort to get up, to move closer. "It's a beautiful evening."

"Yeah." He stood on the other side of the fence, only his face and hands visible in the dark, and she willed with all her heart for him to stay there. If he came near, she wouldn't be able to resist. Her throat closed, waiting for him to make a move.

She stared through the night until her eyes crossed with the effort to see. Finally, she squeezed her lids together, then blinked and opened them again.

Rob had vanished. She heard the quiet clatter of his back door as he entered his house. This time, she knew he wouldn't come back.

"Let's go, Buttercup." She whistled for the dog. "Come on, girl. Inside."

While Buttercup curled into her bed, Valerie set the automatic coffeemaker to produce the magic elixir of work in time for her own departure and Jenny's return home. With nothing left to do, she made her way to the bedroom upstairs, checking on the kids as she went by. They were her life, the reason for everything she did. The time had come to remember that fact and to put these foolish hopes for more...for true and lasting love...where they belonged.

In the realm of make-believe.

CHAPTER EIGHT

THE TUESDAY NIGHT after Labor Day was the first meeting of the Parent-Teacher-Student Association. Rob always attended to learn what issues were being addressed and whether he and Ginny had a stake in them.

Tonight, Jen had volunteered to watch the kids so he and Valerie could drive together—conservation of fossil fuels, and all that. The different fund-raising projects for the year were displayed on tables around the cafeteria, with chairs set up in the center for the actual meeting. Roaming past the exhibits, Rob and Valerie traded irreverent comments in their quietest voices. They agreed they'd rather just write a check than try to sell wrapping paper or roasted nuts.

"Rob Warren, how are you?" Kellie Tate, wife of the former mayor, caught his arm and kissed his cheek. "I haven't seen you all summer. But you look like you spent some time at the beach."

"No, just mowing the yard." He disengaged from Kellie and stepped back to include Valerie in the conversation. "Have you met Valerie Manion? Valerie, this is Kellie Tate, wife of our former mayor."

Valerie offered a handshake, which Kellie returned with a limp wrist. "Oh, yes—I heard we had somebody new at the school this year. You came from New York, is that right?"

"We lived in Ohio last but, yes, we're originally from New York."

"Must have been fascinating." She turned a shoulder to Valerie and spoke to Rob. "How's your little girl? I always feel so sad when I see her."

"Ginny's great. Valerie has started a Girls Outdoors! troop for the school and I'm the assistant leader. Don't you have a daughter between eight and ten? She'd probably love what we're doing."

Kellie took a step back, putting up her hands to ward off contamination. "Oh, no. No, thanks. Marcia is a real girl's girl—she loves dance and modeling." She wiggled her fingers in a goodbye wave. "See you later, Rob."

He unclenched his teeth and turned to Valerie. "Don't worry—she's a witch to everybody. That's one reason her husband lost the election."

But over the next few minutes, they encountered several other parents, and the reactions were all similar.

"You're from up north?" Rita Jones asked. "That's so…interesting. You must feel really out of place down here."

"Hey, Rob." Lee Franklin shook his hand. "Good to see you. I hear you're a troop leader these days—for the little ladies. You teaching them the latest hairstyles…or are they teaching you?"

Valerie's hand on his arm kept Rob from shoving that comment right back down ol' Lee's throat.

Then there was the meeting itself. Welcome, Reading of the Minutes, Treasurer's Report, Old Business… Rob thought the reports would never end. When the president asked for items of new business, several people in the audience raised their hands, Valerie among them. Some of the issues involved considerable debate, and the meeting dragged past its allotted time by half an hour, then forty-five minutes.

Finally, when all other speakers except Valerie had been acknowledged, the president banged her gavel. "I'm afraid that's all we have time for tonight," she said. "Please come back next month when we'll report on these issues and address any new concerns that arise."

"All I wanted," Valerie mused, as the crowd began to disperse around them, "was to propose a school-wide directory. How much easier would it be for new families—not to mention the ones already here—if there was a book listing teachers, subjects, students and their parents? I would even volunteer to produce the whole project." She shrugged. "I just wanted to help."

Rob choked on a thick dose of shame—for his town and the people he'd grown up with. "I can only apologize," he told her. "I can't imagine what's got into these people. I'd suggest you hightail it back up north where the 'rude' people live."

"But that's what they want," Valerie told him. "I'd rather stay right where I am, like a stick in their craw.

I'll be as visible as I can manage. And I'll make them miserable."

"Go for it." He allowed himself the pleasure of a quick, one-armed hug. "I'm with you all the way."

ON WEDNESDAY, Valerie began preparing the GO! girls for their first cookout. "We'll drive to a nearby park on a Saturday morning," Valerie told them. "We'll hike, do some nature studies for our Outside Adventure award, and then we'll make potluck soup on the camp fire."

"What's potluck soup?" Keisha wanted to know.

"That's the fun part." Valerie gathered the attention of every girl as she looked around the circle. "When you come to the cookout, each of you is going to bring one can of food. Could be vegetables, like green beans or corn or peas. Could be soup—tomato, chicken noodle, vegetable beef. Or hot dogs and beans, chili or tuna fish. Bring whatever you have on your shelf at home or buy at the grocery store. As we did when we made the GORP, we're going to dump everybody's can into the pot, stir it all together and that's our potluck soup."

"Eww," Ginny said, and she wasn't the only one. "That sounds disgusting. What if somebody brings canned liver?"

"Or snails," another girl added, giggling.

"Or worms."

"Or ants."

"Or poison!"

Valerie held up a hand. "My suggestion would be to bring only something that you would want to eat. I've done this with many different groups, and I can honestly say I've never had a potluck soup that wasn't delicious."

They went on to discuss dishes—unbreakable, in a net bag such as oranges came in—then clothes, equipment and all the innumerable questions little girls could devise concerning their first big outing. Rob watched and marveled at Valerie's patience. He remembered being told what to do as a Cub Scout, no questions allowed. At least for little girls, Valerie's way was better.

And little boys were better off somewhere else during the process. After the Labor Day picnic, Connor had felt comfortable enough to leave school with Rob's mother this afternoon and to be dropped off at Jenny's house before dinnertime.

They did more work with the compasses, and then Valerie passed out information sheets for parents. "You must bring back the signed permission slip or you can't go with us. The blue sheet explains to your parents what we're doing, what our schedule will be and what you need to bring. The pink sheet is a list of our meetings for the rest of the year so they don't get confused about holidays and stuff like that."

Rob shook his head. Not only organized, not only typed, but color-coded. The woman was an efficiency fiend.

He was still trying to catch up on the laundry she'd discovered at his house three weeks ago.

"One thing I still don't get," he said, once the girls had gone home, "is the net bag. Why not just recycle one of the plastic grocery sacks?"

"Because we're going to wash the dishes while we're

there. And then we hang them up in our drip bags, so they're clean and dry when we go home."

He thought for a minute about the process of third graders washing dishes. "Clean?"

Valerie's mischievous look showed off her dimple. "Relatively. But since you brought it up…" She delved into her file box, which he'd begun to consider a bottomless pit of paperwork. "You're going to have to take a training course before you're qualified to act as assistant leader on these outdoor expeditions. I've got first aid training, so we don't need to look for anyone else, but the first aid adult can't be the same person as the camping-trained adult. So we have to get you certified."

"Is this some kind of initiation rite? Black candles and robes? Human sacrifices?" He risked a joke. "Or maybe an orgy?"

"Only the orgy part."

"Sounds good to me." He rubbed his hands together. "Where do I sign up?"

"Right here." She handed him yet another form to fill out. "This training session is a weekend experience, Friday night until Sunday afternoon up in the mountains."

"A long way to go."

"We'll drive up, spend the weekend in tents, you'll get your camp training card and we'll be good to go."

"We?"

"I need a refresher course." She didn't meet his eyes. "So I thought we could both go at the same time. And I checked with Jenny. She's free that weekend, so Grace and Connor could stay with her. Ginny, too, she said."

For a wild and crazy minute, he'd completely forgotten about Ginny. What kind of father was he? "Is there another way to do this? Like weekly sessions? I don't go out of town without Ginny."

"But I told you—Jenny will keep her. And your mother—"

Rob shook his head. "Doesn't matter. I'm her dad, and she needs me in town, where I can be reached easily if there's trouble." The idea of being four hours away when Ginny needed him cramped his gut.

"But you wanted her to be part of GO!, and having a troop requires somebody to get this training."

"One of the other parents'll volunteer, if you ask."

"What makes you think I haven't asked?" She flung her hands out from her sides in desperation. "Every single parent in the troop said they had other commitments. *Every single parent*—which is two adults for each girl except mine and yours."

"That's absurd."

"Maybe. But true. So either you go—or the girls don't."

Valerie left Rob alone to think about it while she packed up her supplies. For once, he didn't even attempt to carry the boxes or load the van. He sat at one of the tables they'd used, staring at the registration form, while she did all the work. A strange victory, but she'd take it.

He came out into the parking lot as she shut the back door of her van. "Okay," he said slowly. "I'll have to talk to Ginny about it, but assuming she doesn't mind too much, I'll take the training. Here's the form."

"Excellent." She smiled up at him. "It's not Yosemite, but you might have a really good time, spending the weekend outdoors with a bunch of women."

His grin was strained but gallant. "You may just be right. What were you saying about an orgy?"

GINNY'S PROTEST didn't take the form Rob expected. When he broached the subject, she didn't really care that he was going. But she didn't want to stay at Jenny's.

"I want her to come here." They were doing her evening exercises, prescribed to preserve and, maybe, increase the range of motion and muscle strength in her legs and hands. "They get to live with her all the time. I want Aunt Jen to stay with me."

"But, Ginny, that means Grace and Connor have to come, too." He switched from her right leg to her left, providing resistance against which she had to exert force. "It would be easier to move one person instead of three. And there's Buttercup. She doesn't live here. Mat the Cat wouldn't put up with having her as a guest."

"I want to be in my own house." She kicked at his hand and rolled over, effectively ending the session. "I won't go over there."

Rob consulted Jenny. "Would you mind coming to my place with Grace and Connor?"

His sister closed one eye and squinted at him through the other. "You're the dad, right? You make the rules."

"I'm talking about leaving her for the first time in her entire life, Jennifer. I think she deserves a little extra consideration."

She pretended to tremble and cower. "Oh, boy, you're mad. You're using my whole name."

"Don't be smart. Can you do this for me or not?"

"I suppose. But someday you're going to have to take a stand with Ginny and stick to it whether she likes it or not."

He gave her a dirty look. "Like you, she's already had enough unchangeable, unpleasant truths to deal with in her life."

Jen punched him hard on the shoulder. "Jerk." There were tears in her voice.

Ignoring the comment, he slammed Jenny's screened door behind him as he walked out. "And I really don't think it's my job to provide more."

ON THE OTHER HAND, telling his dad that he needed three days off work provoked exactly the reaction Rob expected.

"You're crazy." Mike threw the screwdriver he'd been using into a drawer and then slammed the drawer shut. "I can't possibly spare you for that long."

"It's only two days of actual work at the shop. Trent says he doesn't mind taking calls on Friday and Sunday."

"Yeah, that's right, abuse your brother."

"I think he'll survive, Dad. Sunday call isn't usually too tough."

"And if something happens and he needs backup?"

"Smith will be here. You'll be here."

"So we all get to pay for your little R&R?"

"I'm not going on some damn vacation. I need this

training weekend to work with Ginny's troop. I wouldn't go otherwise. Doesn't that make a difference? *It's for Ginny.*"

He thought his dad hesitated. But then he said, "She'd be better off if you'd let her go on these trips without you."

Rob slapped his hand on the workbench. "I'm there to make sure she's safe. It's my responsibility, my obligation in her life. Why the hell do you keep pushing me to let go?"

"You think you're some kind of god? You think bad things aren't going to happen just because you're right there?" Hunching his shoulders, Mike turned away from him and leaned an elbow on the bench. "The more fool you."

"Do I get the days off, or not?"

"Whatever. I can't stop you, can I?"

All you'd have to do is ask. But Rob wasn't going to admit that weakness. Not right now. "You know, Pete Mitchell asked me again last Saturday about putting an alarm system in his house. I've looked on the Internet, and I can get most of the training up in Raleigh. We could hire one experienced guy—"

Mike turned on him, red-faced and snarling. "More salary. More overhead. More inventory. You think I'm made of money? What do you expect your mother to use for food and medicine in her old age? How are we supposed to take care of ourselves if we spend everything I've made on your reckless ideas?"

He stalked forward, backing Rob up against the wall with a finger jabbing his chest. "I've got a plan for you, boy. You don't like it here, don't like the way I work, the way I think, the way I run things...well, get out. Go open your own business. Run it your own way. I won't stop you. And when you fail, when you can't pay your bills and your shop goes belly-up... I'll take you back. Same pay, same work. No hard feelings. You just make the choice. Let me know what you decide." With a final jab, he went into the office and slammed the door between them.

Rob looked at the clock over the work bench. Two o'clock. The shop would be open for three more hours. There was always extra work to finish up after closing.

For about a minute, he considered the pros and cons of leaving. Then he picked up his jacket and lunchbox, took his keys out of his pocket, and walked out the door. A sunny September afternoon greeted him.

What did a guy do on a great day like this?

And who did he do it with?

HUNCHED OVER HER DESK, Valerie was frowning at an excruciatingly dull production report when her secretary buzzed the intercom.

"Call for you, Ms. Manion. A Mr. Warren."

Ridiculous, how just the prospect of talking to him brightened her day. "Hi, Rob. Something wrong?"

"Nothing unusual. I just wondered—what view do you see out of your office windows?"

"I beg your pardon?" He repeated the question. "I don't know if I've ever looked out my windows." She went to the blinds and twirled the rod to get maximum visibility. "Um…I'm looking at the nursing home across the highway, then the trees around our parking lot and the lot itself."

"See anything else?"

Valerie looked left and right, up and down. "No, I…" She stopped on a gasp. "Is that you? Are you out there in the middle of a Thursday afternoon in that terrific car? With the top down?"

"Wanna go for a ride?" His grin came through loud and clear.

She wrestled with her conscience. Working lunches at her desk for six weeks—surely that entitled her to an hour off. She'd stay late tomorrow. She'd come in on a Sunday. She just had to get a ride in that car.

When she reached the sidewalk, Rob had shifted to the passenger seat. "Thought you might like to drive," he said casually.

"You are a prince among men," she told him. "Can I put my jacket and purse in the trunk?"

"Be my guest."

"Where shall we go?"

"North, south, east, west…you pick."

So Valerie pointed the Thunderbird south and started driving. They were out in the country soon enough, flying along under a brilliant blue sky with the wind in their faces. No need for conversation, no reason to talk. Pure, perfect escape.

After thirty minutes, Valerie slowed down. "I probably ought to head back. I can't be gone too long."

"I know." Rob sighed. "Take this next right up here, and we'll find a place to turn around."

She realized that he knew exactly where they were and what they would find on the narrow country road—a tiny brick church nestled under big oak trees. Nearby, a cemetery bounded by low brick walls sat on a rise above the bank of a clear, free-running stream.

Valerie gave him an innocent glance. "Is this where you want me to turn around?"

His eyes glinted in the way she'd come to love. "Since the road dead-ends at the creek, looks like you'll have to."

Without consultation, they got out of the car in the small parking lot and went to lean on the wall. Under the trees, the breeze picked up, turning the day cool and ruffling Valerie's hair. She could have stayed all afternoon.

She turned to sit on the wall, the better to see Rob's face. "What in the world brought this on, in the middle of the work day?"

"I asked my dad for time off to go to the camp training."

"Ah." No need to ask how that went over.

"And since our talk was going so well, I decided to propose the security business idea again."

"Timing is everything."

"He told me…" Rob looked away. "He told me to go open my own business. See if I could make it on my own. And if I didn't, he said he'd take me back. No hard feelings." He shook his head, still staring at the horizon. "I never quite expected to get kicked out by my dad. Not when I was thirty-four years old, anyway." His tone of voice conveyed all the hurt he wouldn't express.

"I have to admit," Valerie said carefully, "that the thought has crossed my mind."

Finally, he looked at her. "What do you mean?"

"Why not start your own security business?"

He held up a hand, ticking off the reasons. "One, lack of money. Two, losing my insurance for Ginny. Three, lack of money. Four, lack—"

Laughing, she held up her hand. "I get the picture. Why are you so sure you don't have the money?"

"Last time I looked at my checkbook, there were only six digits in the balance, and two of them were to the right of the decimal."

"Rob, nobody starts a business with their own money."

He drew his eyebrows together. "Explain."

"You need investors. A business loan. You can start your business with capital somebody else provides. Then you split the profits—without having shouldered the initial costs."

"Okay, but I'm supposed to just walk into a bank and ask for a business loan?"

"Doesn't your dad do business with one of the institutions here in town?"

"Sure."

"Well, then, you've got a contact. But you could also investigate other sources of funds. Got any rich friends?"

"As a matter of fact, I do." Dixon made big bucks writing songs and playing the stock market. Adam came from a wealthy family to begin with and had done very well with his construction company.

"Would they have an interest in staking your business?"

"Maybe. Maybe they would."

"So talk to them. Make a proposal. I can help you write up a business plan—a formal expression of what you intend to do and how, what kind of results you expect and when. Present it to the bank, to your friends…what could it hurt?"

He took the two strides that closed the distance between them. "Absolutely brilliant, is what you are. Where have you been all my life?"

She felt herself flushing. "New York, Ohio…the usual places."

He cupped his hand along her cheek and brushed his thumb over her lips. A thrill went through her, and her heart started to pound in anticipation of the kiss to come.

But, for once, her head was on straight. As his gaze dropped to her mouth, she found the strength to put her hand on his chest and push lightly.

"No, Rob."

His hand lingered against her skin just a second longer, then dropped to his side. A deep breath lifted his chest. "You're right. Sorry."

He turned away from her, toward the stream. Pulling off the baseball cap, he ran a hand through his hair, then tugged the cap on and faced her again. "So…ready to head back?"

"Sure." And she was…because being with him and keeping control was harder, now, than being alone. "You drive."

Rob showed up at Saturday's 7:00 a.m. basketball game with enough energy to take on the other five guys by himself. Anger, frustration, nerves…his tank overflowed with adrenaline.

Himself, DeVries and Bell teamed up against Pete Mitchell, Tommy Crawford and Dixon's stepson, Trace. Rob surged up at the tip-off, batted the ball directly to Adam, racing to be in place beneath the basket when the mayor dribbled down the court. His layup missed and he barreled after the ball. When Tommy got in the way, they both ended up on the ground.

"Basketball is not," Crawford panted, "a blood sport. Watch where you're headed, Rob."

He couldn't feel guilty, even though Tommy stood nine inches shorter than his own six-four. As soon as Pete threw the ball inbounds, Rob was running, pushing, grappling for control. The next time he and Tommy tangled, the shorter man came up with his fists clenched.

"What is your problem?" He pushed the heel of his hand into Rob's ribs. "I'm not invisible, man, and I'm not running away. Settle down."

Trying to be careful, Rob played cautiously for a while. But he missed several shots, and DeVries yelled out, "Come on, Rob. Focus."

The next thing he knew, he was sprawled on the ground with both Dixon and young Trace crashed on top of him.

"That's it." Dixon staggered to his feet, grabbed Rob's wrist and pulled him up. "We've all got Jacquie's wedding to go to this afternoon. My wife's not going to like it if I show up with broken bones or a concussion. So let's get some breakfast…" He pushed Rob in the direction of the diner. "…and figure out just what the hell your problem is, anyway."

A short time later, with half a plate of Abby's pancakes sweetening his disposition, Rob managed an apology. "I'm seeing red everywhere I look these days. Sorry, guys."

"Seeing red about what?" Tommy sat as far away from him as possible and hadn't recovered his good humor.

"My dad practically fired me," Rob admitted. "Told me I could leave the business any time I wanted."

"Don't know if that would be such a bad thing," Dixon commented over his coffee cup.

Rob shrugged. "Maybe not. But then I'm committed to go out of town in a few days, to a training session up in the mountains. Without Ginny."

Pete stared at him. "What kind of training?"

"Camping," he muttered through a mouthful of grits.

Trace gave a laugh and quickly choked. The other guys stared at Rob like he'd grown another head.

"Camping?" Adam tilted his head. "Why?"

"The GO! troop," Pete answered. "You have to get training to camp with little girls?"

"Laugh," Rob ordered, his teeth gritted. "It's the rules."

"So you spend a weekend in the mountains." Tommy shrugged. "Big deal."

"With a bunch of women," Rob explained.

"Women campers?"

"And…" He dragged in a breath. "Valerie."

They all dropped their gazes to their plates for a silent minute. "Now I understand." Tommy picked up his coffee mug. "You've got problems with a woman."

"No. I mean, it's not like that. We work together, is all." The pitying looks coming his way demanded a defense. "Seriously. I'm not…"

Pete nodded. "Involved?"

"Dating?" Dixon asked.

"Serious?" Adam shook his head. "Yeah, right."

"Lost?" Tommy added. "After being on the receiving end of your tackles this morning, all I've got to say is…" Hand on his heart, he stood up and looked around the table, catching each man's eyes. "It's time for a salute, boys."

Rob's friends—the guys he'd counted on for most of his life, the comrades who'd helped him keep his sanity all these years—got to their feet, imitated Tommy's gesture and, with grins on their faces, intoned the final verdict.

"Another one bites the dust."

CHAPTER NINE

GRACE DIDN'T UNDERSTAND whose wedding they were going to, or why. All she knew was that, for the first time in her life, she would get to see a real bride and groom. She had a brand-new dress to wear, new shoes and a necklace she had picked out all by herself. And a purse to carry. The new clothes were nearly as exciting as the wedding itself.

The ceremony started at four, her mom said, and so she had to wait all through the long Saturday morning and eat lunch before she could start getting ready. She claimed the bathroom first, and made sure every inch of her was perfectly clean. Mom had to force Connor to do the same—through the open windows, Grace heard him complaining all the way across the backyard, up the stairs and down the hallway. Con really didn't like baths.

Grace knew Ginny was going to the wedding, too— they were all riding together in Mr. Warren's van—and wondered what kind of dress the other girl would wear. Would she be mean and moody, as usual? Sometimes Grace had the strongest urge to reach over and slap the frown off Ginny's face. Didn't she see how hard her dad and her aunt tried to make her happy? And how hurt her dad was by all her grouchiness?

The knock on her door was her mom. "Ready to get dressed, Gracie?"

Grace opened the door and gasped. "Oh, Mommy. You look so beautiful!"

"Thanks. I really do like this dress. You've got great taste in clothes, Miss Manion."

Grace had been the one to spot the dress in the store. She'd had to drag her mother to the rack and then force her to try it on. The midnight blue fabric had a shine to it, like stars twinkling in the night sky. The sleeves of the jacket ended a little way below her mom's elbows, and the dress underneath was smooth and straight, but not shapeless. Her mom wore silky gray high-heeled shoes and stockings, silver earrings and a long silver chain with a big, dark blue stone hanging down.

"You look like a princess," she sighed.

"So will you, when you're ready." Her mom picked her dress up off the bed. "Here we go."

Her own dress was in her favorite dark purple, but there were also streaks of gold and red and green, in a sheer material that floated when she twirled around. The sleeves fluttered over her arms, and if there hadn't been a dark purple lining, people could have seen right through the rest of the dress. Her shoes and purse were shiny black and her necklace was a circle of purple stones. Her mom had taken her to Arlene's Beautyrama and they'd cut about three inches off her hair, so she could wear it loose today…as long as she promised not to run around at the wedding.

Really, though, she was old enough to know better than that.

The biggest surprise of all, though, was when Mr. Warren knocked on Jenny's front door. For a second, Grace didn't recognize him, he looked so completely different than usual.

"Well, well," Jenny said. "You do clean up nice."

"You're not bad yourself. For a tomboy." He opened the screened door. "I see Mr. Connor Manion has managed to get himself all slicked up. Good to see you, my man." He and Con exchanged some kind of complicated handshake before Con ran across the porch to the van. Grace wanted to yell at him to walk, but she was afraid to interrupt what Mr. Warren would say next. Did he think she looked…okay?

"Somebody's gonna have to introduce me to the princess," he said, looking around the room. "I'm not sure I recognize this beautiful young lady." Then he took her hand. When he smiled, Grace felt comfortable again. "Such a pretty dress, Grace. Can I have a dance at the reception?"

She could feel her cheeks getting red. "Y-yes. Thank you." Was she supposed to say thank you?

He held her hand as she walked down the porch steps and helped her into the van as if she really were a princess.

"All the guys will be jealous of me this evening, that's for sure."

Grace watched him go back for her mother and Jenny, watched him walk toward the van with a lady on each arm. He was such a gentleman. She wondered if she would ever meet a boy even half as…what was the word?…*gallant* when she grew up.

When everybody was inside and the van started moving, she looked over at Ginny. Her dress was pretty, too—a soft golden-orange color with long sleeves and a ruffle around the hem. She wore beige tights and nice brown ballet-slipper shoes.

"I like your dress," Grace said. "Did you pick it out?"

The other girl shook her head. "I don't get to go shopping much. They think I get too tired. My grandmother bought it."

"At least she didn't choose, like, red plaid or something. My grandmother would have bought a sweater and a white shirt and a pleated plaid skirt. With penny loafers and white socks."

Ginny wrinkled up her face. "Gross."

Grace rolled her eyes. "Tell me about it."

"I—I think your dress is pretty." Ginny's pale cheeks turned pink, and she looked out the window without waiting for Grace to answer.

"Thanks," Grace said, loud enough to be pretty sure the other girl could hear. Then she looked at Mr. Warren again, noticing that he'd gone to the Beautyrama, too—his hair now curled just over the collar of his crisp white shirt. His dark gray suit had tiny blue lines running through it, and he wore a silver tie. He couldn't have matched her mom's dress any better if he'd tried. They would look awesome dancing together.

As the wedding ceremony unfolded, and then the reception, Grace let herself pretend this was her mom's wedding…her mom and Mr. Warren. He would be such fun to live with. He listened, he laughed, he played and spent time with kids when he probably had a million more important things to do.

More importantly, he made her mom laugh. Nobody had done that since Grace could remember. With Mr. Warren around, *she* didn't worry so much about her mom, because there was somebody else to help out. She wasn't sure her mom realized it yet, but Mr. Warren would make the perfect husband. The perfect dad for her and for Con.

Even if they had to put up with Ginny the Grouch as part of the deal.

VALERIE MET ROB'S friend Jacquie for the first time in the receiving line at the wedding reception.

"I'm so glad you came," the bride said, giving Valerie a kiss on the cheek. "Rob's told me all about the GO! troop and how much fun Ginny's having. I think you're just terrific for organizing something so important to the girls." Her wedding dress was a slim, sleeveless sheath of ivory silk. A sheer, gold-flecked stole covered her shoulders and, instead of a veil, she wore a simple circle of braided satin ribbon, its long streamers mingling with the shining flow of her strawberry blonde hair.

"It's my pleasure. I've never seen such a lovely wedding. And this old stone house is gorgeous. Rob says you'll be living here full-time?"

"We just signed the contract to make Fairfield Farms our own." Jacquie put a hand on her new husband's arm.

"This is Valerie Manion," she told him, "a friend of Rob's."

Rhys Lewellyn took Valerie's fingers in his. "I'm glad you're here to help us celebrate." He was an amazingly handsome man, with black hair, ice-blue eyes and an intensity she'd often seen in high-achieving executives. "Please make yourself at home."

"You have the most impressive friends," she told Rob a few minutes later, as he lifted two glasses of champagne from a nearby tray. "Olympic riding champions and hit songwriters among them. How can such a small town be home to all these different kinds of people?"

"We're not quite as simple down here as you might have been led to believe." He toasted her with his wine. "Speaking of impressive, I haven't had a chance to mention how beautiful you look today. Here's to you…all the things you are, all the things you do." Gazing into her eyes, he took a sip.

"Rob…" Blinking hard, she looked away from him and across the wide reception room of the grand house. "You're making this impossible."

"Sorry, I don't— Hey, there, Dixon. How's it going?" She turned back and saw him shaking hands with Dixon Bell. "Valerie, you remember Dixon. And this is his wife, Kate."

There were hugs and kisses all around, but before any real conversation could begin, they were joined by Pete Mitchell, whom Valerie had met a couple of times at Rob's house, and his wife Mary Rose, who carried her son Joey on one hip. Adam and Phoebe DeVries arrived, and the group became a kind of minireunion. The relationships weren't quite clear to Valerie, but she couldn't miss the affection flowing between them all. Jacquie and Rhys stopped by as they worked their way through the crowd, adding to the good spirits.

To her amazement, there were no veiled insults about her northern origins, no snubs or pointed comments—just friendship, extended without reservation. For the first time in years, she began to feel comfortable. *Settled.* Friends like these could tempt her to stay put for a long time, promotion or no promotion.

"Should we worry about the kids?" she asked Rob during a lull in the conversation. "I haven't seen them since they headed out to the stable."

"Ginny knows her way around," he assured her. "She rides here several times a month. I don't think even Con can get into serious trouble. Besides, Rhys's son and Jacquie's daughter were going out with them. So…relax." He took her glass away, made it vanish. "Dance with me."

It would be impolite to refuse, imprudent to accept…but she moved with him to the dance floor on the other side of the entry hall. At the instantaneous feelings of comfort, strength, support and acceptance she found in his arms, she could only sigh.

"Tired?" He pulled her closer into his body. "Would you rather sit down?"

"No. Oh, no."

Rob heard the longing in her voice and almost lost the last of his good intentions. Dancing with Valerie wasn't smart, wouldn't offer any defense in his constant battle against wanting her. But at least he'd have something to remember, a few moments with her body close to his, her hair under his chin, her palm tight against his own. He could build a lifetime of memories during this one evening, couldn't he?

Between the slow dances they talked with his friends and his brothers, who'd surprised him by showing up.

"I always wanted a look inside this house," Trent said. "We used to drive by and park on the shoulder of the road, planning to build a house like this some day." He shrugged and popped a tiny ham biscuit into his mouth. "Luck follows the lucky, I guess."

Valerie gazed after him as he walked away, then looked back at Rob. "We?"

He nodded, impatient for the music to begin again. "He and his girlfriend. Trent went up to N.C. State University on an athletic scholarship—football. The sportswriters were already hyping his professional career, even before his senior year. Over that summer, he got engaged to his high school sweetheart. He was being courted by several pro teams, and his biggest challenge was deciding whether to sign for five million or six."

He took a deep breath, reliving that one November afternoon. "The last regular season game of his college career, he took a bad hit. Ripped his knee to pieces, did some damage to his spine. His career ended in less than a minute."

"That's terrible."

"It got worse. The money went away, of course. And so did his fiancée. She visited him once in the hospital to give him the ring back. I like to imagine she ended up a stripper in Las Vegas—that seems a fair enough retribution."

"So now Trent works for your dad."

"Right. He earned his degree in history, but hasn't used it for anything. He goes to work, he goes home, he shows up sometimes where you least expect him. I keep hoping he'll snap out of it, but after all these years, I'm beginning to wonder."

"Your family has gone through its share of hardship."

"Every family has. If you're lucky, the folks around you help you through."

The music began again and they eased onto the floor. Valerie nodded against his shoulder. "I think you have a wonderful support system. Friends and family who care deeply about how you are and what you're doing." He felt, more than heard, another sigh. She didn't say anything more.

You could be part of this, he wanted to tell her. *We'd all be glad to draw you in.* But he kept quiet, and the moment passed, as they always did.

Eventually, Rhys and Jacquie climbed the winding front staircase so she could throw the bouquet. As soon as she tossed her flowers into the air, they fell into much smaller sprigs which rained down on everyone. Ginny caught one, as did Grace. Beside Rob, Valerie stared at the flowers nestled between her palms as if she didn't know what to do with them.

He took the nosegay—baby's breath and white roses—and tucked it into Valerie's dark curls, anchored behind her ear. In a different life, he would have followed up the gesture with a kiss.

But this wasn't a different life, so he simply smiled and turned to applaud as Rhys and Jacquie disappeared upstairs. They reappeared shortly, dressed for travel. The honeymoon, he'd heard, was a horse-buying trip in Europe. Jacquie kissed her daughter and stepson, hugged her parents, and then the married couple disappeared into a waiting limousine. Within a few minutes, the crowd began to disperse.

His particular group of passengers was quiet on the drive home. Somehow, Jenny had ended up in the front seat instead of Valerie, who sat in the back with Connor falling asleep on her lap.

Jenny sat up straighter as he turned onto her street. "Did you notice that Mom and Dad didn't make the wedding?"

He thought back, frowning. "Not at the time. Were they planning to come?"

"I thought so."

"Maybe they changed their minds. The way Dad's been lately, I wouldn't go anywhere with him I didn't have to." He'd told Jenny about the Labor Day arguments, but not about his more recent confrontation and the ultimatum he'd received.

"I don't think he's feeling too good," Jenny countered. "He seems stiff, and tired a lot of the time."

"I'd tell him to take some time off, but I'm dead sure he wouldn't listen."

"No. He wouldn't listen."

In the driveway of Jenny's house, Rob helped Valerie get out of the van with Connor sound asleep in her arms. Grace walked unsteadily beside Jenny to the porch.

"Thanks for coming," he said quietly. "I enjoyed being with you."

She laid her cheek against Connor's bright hair, avoiding Rob's eyes. "Thanks for asking. We all had a marvelous time."

He could smell the rose in her hair, the perfume she wore, and the need inside of him expanded unbearably. "You're welcome. Sure you don't want me to carry him?"

Valerie shook her head and walked toward the house. Rob followed, in case she needed steadying on the steps. As he opened the screened door, Jenny came barreling down the hallway. "Rob? Are you still here?"

When she saw him, she came to a sliding stop beside the stairs. "Oh, thank God. Get Ginny out of the van right away. Valerie, can you stay with the kids?"

"Of course."

"What's wrong?" Rob didn't really need to ask. "Dad?"

Eyes wide, Jenny nodded. "There's a message on my machine, and yours, too. Mom took him to the hospital about eight o'clock.

"She said it was his heart."

UNABLE TO SIT in the waiting room, Rob paced the long corridors of the cardiac unit at New Skye Medical Center, where shadows of the past mingled with the present threat. He'd spent many long hours in the children's unit during these last eight years, waiting for Ginny to come out of corrective surgeries on her back and legs. She'd had a few reactions to medications and a couple of bad bouts of pneumonia. He'd survived the waiting then, and he knew he would now.

The blackest memories came from further back…the two nights Leah had spent on the obstetric floor, trying to survive the delivery of their baby. The first night hadn't been so bad—childbirth was supposed to be a time of joy, though Leah's blood pressure had tinged the happiness with worry. But the twenty-four hours after Ginny's arrival, with his wife lingering in a no-man's-land between life and death…

Rob rubbed his hands over his face, dragged them through his hair. He'd avoided the black hole of those memories for the last eight years. He wouldn't fall into them now.

"Rob?"

He looked behind him and turned around to face the white-coated doctor striding down the hall in his direction. "Hey, Tim. How are you?"

Tim DeVries, Adam's brother and a classmate of Trent's at New Skye High School, was the cardiologist on call tonight. "Pretty good. Is your family inside the waiting room? Let's go have a talk." He ushered Rob through the door and pulled up a chair so he could sit knee to knee with their mom, holding her hands.

"Okay, Mrs. Warren, you did a good job tonight, getting your husband to the ER so fast."

Trent interrupted. "Did he have a heart attack?"

Tim smiled. "No, thank goodness. But I've talked to Mr. Warren for quite a long time this evening, and it turns out he's been having this chest pain for a number of months now."

Rob closed his eyes. He should have known.

"Lately, Mr. Warren says, the pain has been getting more frequent and more intense, as it was tonight. Tomorrow, we're going to perform some tests, including cardiac catheterization, to see just what is happening with his heart."

Rob's mom took a deep breath. "Is he going to be all right?"

Tim explained how the tests would help determine the best treatment. "We'll get him on his feet and home in just a few days, and he'll be back to normal in no time. Ideally, though, he's got to make some major changes in his life. The smoking must stop. He should follow a healthier diet and drop some weight. At his age, a decrease in stress would help his overall health. I think all of you could help him alter his lifestyle and ensure that he'll be around for a long time to come."

Smiling, he got to his feet. "So the news isn't too bad tonight, after all. Do y'all have any questions?"

"Can I see him?" Rob's mother asked, and Tim walked with her down the hall to their dad's room.

Rob slumped in his chair and closed his eyes.

"So he's going to be okay, right?" Smith stood at the window, gazing out into the hospital parking lot. "This is no big deal?"

"Heart problems are always a big deal." Trent sat beside Rob, elbows on his thighs and head buried in his hands. "If your heart stops working, you're kinda screwed, you know?"

"But that's not going to happen to Dad." Smith tapped his knuckles on the glass in front of his face.

"They're gonna fix his arteries and he'll be back to normal."

"Unless he doesn't quit smoking," Jenny said. "That's the number one risk factor in coronary artery disease. And he needs to lose weight. When's the last time you saw Dad pass up a second helping?"

"I bet he'll straighten out, after this."

Hearing the desperate note in Smith's voice, Rob sat up straight. "You're pretty determined to be optimistic, little brother. What's going on?"

"It's just…well, I had made some plans…"

"Haven't we all?" Trent got to his feet. "What kind of plans?"

"Me and a few buddies were thinking about a trip."

"Now's not the time for a vacation, Smith." Jenny stood up. "Give it a couple of months."

"Not a vacation." Hands in the pockets of his slacks, Smith finally turned to face them. "I'm leaving for California. In ten days."

BETWEEN THE UPROAR over Smith's desertion and their dad's hospital stay, Rob doubted that he would be able to fulfill his commitment to the GO! training next weekend. While Valerie was nothing but sympathetic, he couldn't help feeling he would let her down, along with all the girls in the troop.

But then his dad went home on Tuesday and seemed to be pretty much his old self…grouchy and hard to get along with, as usual. Smith agreed to delay his plans for a month, just to be safe. Suddenly, as of Wednesday night, the camping trip looked feasible after all.

He met Valerie at her house Friday morning to help load her camping gear into her car. They stood side-by-side in the overgrown front yard, staring at the house.

"Doesn't look like there's been any trouble here for a while," Rob decided. A couple of Adam's workers had boarded up the broken windows and Kate's dad had agreed to take on the task of nullifying the sale. "Do you see any new damage?"

Valerie shook her head. "I don't think so." Then she sighed. "It's just so sad. I really liked this house."

He quelled the impulse to put his arm around her shoulders and give her a hug. "There are lots of nice houses in New Skye. We'll find you another one." The picture of her in *his* house—his bed—flashed through his mind. "So...let's get this stuff you say we need."

Two small tents, a camp stove, pots and pans, a fire grate, buckets, tubs and water jugs... "Man, you really are prepared." Rob added a water cooler and an ice chest to the collection. "Are you sure we need all of this? Isn't anybody else bringing stuff?"

Valerie carried a box of cooking utensils out of the garage. "I volunteered a lot of the equipment we all would use, because I've collected most of it over the years. Do you have a sleeping bag?" Rob nodded, but she thought he looked a little uncertain. "Are you sure? I've got two really warm ones and I'd be glad to share."

For a long moment, he stared at her across the width of the driveway, with an expression in his eyes that left her in no doubt of what was going through his mind. "I appreciate the offer," he said finally, with a smile. "But I'll be fine."

"Great." She wasn't about to touch that subject again, not with a twenty-foot pole. And she left the extra sleeping bag in the garage.

Back at his house, they ate lunch with Jenny and then loaded their personal gear into her car.

"This is a list of phone numbers," Rob told his sister, handing her a sheet of paper filled with his small handwriting. "Doctors, dentist, pharmacist, therapist—"

Jenny looked at the page. "Do you think I don't remember my own parents' phone number? Or your cell phone? Or 911?"

"Just being careful." He offered another sheet. "These are menus, and a list of the food that's in the house. You don't have to stick with this—they're just suggestions."

"Rob, you're being stupid. I know what to cook for my niece."

Yet another page. "Medicines, schedule, therapy moves."

"Like I haven't done all of that for years now."

He delivered the final sheet. "GO! training information. The numbers for the camp—there's an office phone and the ranger's private number, Valerie's cell number and mine, again. A map with our location marked in red, Valerie's license plate number, the nearest hospital and its emergency numbers." He blew out a deep breath. "I'm hoping that'll cover the possibilities."

"For a nuclear assault?" Jenny stacked the papers together on the counter underneath the kitchen phone. "We'll be just fine, Rob. Ginny will be safe for two days and two nights. Connor and Grace and I will make sure nothing happens to her but happy thoughts and sweet dreams." She reached for her brother's face and squeezed his cheeks between her hands. "Go away now! Valerie, please get him out of here."

Laughing, Valerie took his wrist and pulled him from the kitchen, through the dining and living rooms, to the front door. He hesitated there, but she dragged him over the threshold and onto the porch. "Everything will be okay. I promise." She put him on the passenger side of the car and waited until he had buckled his seat belt to close the door. "Stay put. Don't move."

Before he could remember anything else he'd meant to do, she hurried around the hood and into the driver's seat. Jenny came out onto the front porch with Mat the Cat in her arms and waved goodbye.

Valerie started the engine. Rob sat up straight in his seat. "Wait a minute, I meant to tell Jenny—"

"Too late," she told him, backing out as fast as she dared. "Just sit back and close your eyes. Take a nap. Listen to the music." She turned up the oldies station on the radio. "You're in my power now. The power of GO!"

He looked over with that same sexy glint in his eyes. "You mean that?"

She took hold of her courage. "I mean it."

Rob pulled his cap down over his eyes and slid down in his seat, smiling like the cat who got the cream. "All right, then. I can hardly wait."

CHAPTER TEN

AT FOUR O'CLOCK Friday afternoon, Rob and Valerie sat on the ground, along with twenty other women, to receive their introduction to the next forty-eight hours.

"What we're aiming for is to reproduce your basic camping experience the way the GO! girls should experience it." The trainer was a very tall, very thin woman with short gray hair whose nametag read "Call Me Fluffy." "At the end of the weekend, you'll know what you're shooting for when you go back to your troops."

Rob had received his own tag to wear, and just barely resisted the urge to write "Call Me Outa Here." He hadn't given serious thought to the fact that he would be surrounded by females this weekend, and the reality nearly overwhelmed him.

He was required to set up his *male* tent a fair distance away from all the *female* tents, to use and clean his own bathroom, and to pay due respect to the supremacy of estrogen in the natural hierarchy. He liked all women very much, and one woman in particular more than he knew how to deal with, but…what was so wrong with being a guy?

Dinner Friday night consisted of hamburger, potatoes, onions and carrots wrapped up in aluminum foil, then burned to a crisp while lying on the too-hot coals of the fire. The beverage of choice was fruit punch. Dessert, at least, was a success, with the traditional roasted marshmallows, chocolate bars and graham crackers combined to create s'mores. Then the singing started, and the skits.

He grinned as he watched Valerie portray a grizzly bear chasing hapless little girls through the woods, only to be turned into a loving pet by magic "GO! Power." For his turn, he acted in pantomime to a rousing rendition of "Oh, Susannah" by the ladies and then gladly took his place again in the dark beside Valerie.

"You didn't mention anything about torture," he whispered in her ear. Her shoulders shook on a silent chuckle.

The campfire broke up at eleven with threats from Fluffy about an early morning. Leaving the women to their nightly routines, Rob strolled to the edge of their campsite, on a rise above a bend in the French Broad River. Footsteps in the underbrush behind him announced Valerie's approach.

"Your first night as a GO! inductee. Do you think you'll survive?"

"I'm reserving judgment and hoping breakfast turns out better than dinner."

"You do have to be careful with those foil packs. We should've let the coals die a little longer."

"Or gone into the nearest town for a steak dinner."

She punched him lightly on the arm, but he could see

her smile in the dark. "Get with the program, Mr. Warren."

"Yes, ma'am." They both stood quiet for a few minutes, appreciating the sound of water flowing over stone, the deep peace of a mountain night.

Valerie leaned back against a convenient tree trunk. "Are you doing okay without Ginny?"

"I called," he admitted sheepishly. "The machine said, 'Rob, we've gone to the movies. Find something else to do with your time.'"

"She knows you so well. It must be such fun to grow up in a big family."

"You don't have brothers and sisters?"

"It was just me."

"There must be advantages to being the only child."

"Depends on your parents, I suppose. My dad expected me to stay in my place as a female, so he really didn't have much time for me."

Rob tried to read her face in the dark. "Your place?"

"Homemaker and childbearer, seldom seen and even more seldom heard."

"That was your mom?" He shook his head at the very idea.

"And my grandmothers, kept completely dependent on their husbands. Until the husbands die and they're suddenly supposed to manage the bills, figure out insurance and taxes and mortgage payments…and they never even learned to drive a car." Valerie took a deep breath. "I swore my life would be different. My daughter's life will be different."

Before he could commend her intention, Fluffy's

voice rang out through the woods. "Lights out! All campers to their own tents. Immediately!"

"That's clear enough." Rob turned with Valerie as she headed back to camp. "Do we have to be this regimented with our girls?"

"Don't worry." She patted him on the shoulder as they parted ways. "By nightfall on our first day, you'll be grateful for every single, solitary rule you can lay your hands on."

BECAUSE THEY WORKED with the same troop, Rob and Valerie were paired with other leaders for the weekend's activities. While Valerie's patrol cleaned the bathrooms on Saturday morning, Rob entertained the women cooking breakfast with his old-fashioned courtesy and charm. The cooks were allowed to eat first, so by the time Valerie got through the line, there was nowhere to sit at Rob's table. Even the women on his crew had to squeeze in to get everyone on the benches beside him. Fluffy stood at his shoulder as she ate.

In default, Valerie found a seat with two leaders from the Raleigh area. "You're the lucky one," Anita said. "You get to work with him every week."

"I'd be holding planning sessions over romantic candlelight dinners." Lucy gave a dreamy sigh. "And my husband could baby-sit the kids while I did it."

Valerie managed to be polite, though she was far from amused. "Rob is a terrific leader. A great dad."

"And single," Lucy added. "What's wrong with the women down your way? Are they blind?"

Anita chuckled. "Maybe he's a Dr. Jekyll/Mr. Hyde

type. Turns into a monster when he gets home from work."

"No." Valerie did smile at that one. "He has a daughter with cerebral palsy who takes up all his time. I don't think he feels there's room in his life for another relationship." A fact she was trying to keep in mind, with limited success.

"The man's a saint." Lucy threw her hands up in the air, then crossed them over her heart. "Talk about your most eligible bachelor!"

Valerie agreed wholeheartedly...and that was the problem.

Summoned by Fluffy to finish washing their dishes, Valerie demonstrated the proper technique for Rob and supervised as he duplicated the process. "Soapy water, hot rinse, bleach rinse, drip bag. See, it's easy—even for a guy," she said with a wink.

"We're spending a lot of time cooking, cleaning up and eating," he protested. Hands in the pockets of his jeans, he surveyed the campsite and all the women scurrying around like a hive of bees. "When do we get to the good stuff, like fishing and taking a nap?"

Fishing and napping weren't on the agenda, but they had plenty to do—lashing sticks together to build a table and making individual ovens to cook their midday pizzas while they talked about troop dynamics, plus projects that involved whittling, ax and saw work, and leaf identification. Rob turned out to be more skilled than the instructors where tools were involved. Instead of working on his patrol's project, he floated from group to group, offering advice.

"How's it going?" He came up to Valerie's team as they worked on their table.

"We're doing well," Sybil announced with a bright smile. She had elected herself the group's leader. "Our table's almost done."

Rob pushed on the rickety structure with his finger. "I…uh…believe your knots need to be tighter. Feels a little loose, don't you think?"

"Oh, no," Sybil insisted. "We'll brace the legs with rocks, and it'll stand up just fine."

"But—" Rob looked at Valerie. "Maybe a few more sticks in those bare spots would add stability."

"Sybil thinks the open spaces are decorative," she told him in a neutral voice.

"Right." He backed away, smiling. "Good luck, y'all."

And, of course, when they tested their table against all the others, theirs was the first to collapse. Sybil sat down with a *harrumph*. "You didn't tie the knots tight enough, Valerie."

"I didn't tie the knots at all, Sybil. You and Margaret did."

"We needed more sticks."

"I believe I mentioned that, even before Rob came over."

Sybil *harrumphed* again. "He probably helped the other teams more than he did us. Why do we have a man here, anyway?"

Late in the afternoon, they were given a free hour before dinner preparations would start. Most of the campers trailed off to their tents with comments about naps and aching feet or backs. Valerie didn't want to spend any part of the gorgeous afternoon inside and opted for a walk to the nearby river instead.

"Want some company?" Rob caught up with her at the edge of their clearing. "Or would you rather be by yourself?"

She was torn—being alone with him was a risky choice. But how much trouble could she get into in a camp full of women? "We're supposed to always have a buddy when we leave camp," she reminded him. "You can be my buddy."

He snorted at the idea, but fell in step beside her down the hillside. "GO! is pretty rigid about rules and regulations, aren't they?"

"For the girls' safety." Valerie stepped around a sprig of poison ivy encroaching on the path. "And probably for legal reasons. Unless you establish specific guidelines that the parents understand and then guarantee they were followed to the letter, when something bad happens, you're very vulnerable to criticism."

"Not to mention lawsuits."

"Exactly."

"But usually nothing bad happens, right?"

"At this age, that's true, because we don't take many risks. But as they get older, some of the activities will be inherently dangerous. And girls have gotten hurt."

He was silent for a minute, falling in behind her as the path narrowed. "I don't know if Ginny will ever be up to much danger."

"She may have other interests by then. Ginny said she loves riding horses. That's not a completely safe activity."

"I trust Jacquie and Rhys to keep her safe. And I'm always there."

"Of course. And Ginny will find her own place." *If you allow her to,* was on her tongue, but she left the words unsaid as they stepped out of the tree cover onto the bank of the river.

"Wow," Rob said, stepping to the edge of the water. "This is terrific."

With a sigh of satisfaction, Valerie settled on a conveniently placed rock. "All the fog in my brain clears up in places like this. It's as if I can finally hear myself think."

Rob took the boulder next to hers. "The city—even a little place like New Skye—can produce a lot of mental noise."

"I'm supposed to be a city girl, but if I don't get away pretty often to somewhere like this, I start feeling tired all the time. Beaten."

"Well, you have had a pretty hard time so far this fall, with the move, the new job and then the trouble with your house. Anybody would be stressed."

"Says the man who bears nonstop responsibility for a daughter with special needs." She pivoted on her rock to look at him. Now they were sitting knee-to-knee. "Plus working a full-time job and taking care of the house by himself. You should be feeling stressed all the time."

He looked at her with a half smile on his lips. "I'm not feeling stressed right now."

She should have looked away, but couldn't. "I told you, this is a great place."

"I'm thinking it's less the place than the company."

Trying to keep things light, or just to keep her head, she said, "You enjoy being romanced by all these women, don't you?"

His fingers twined with hers. "Just one of them."

"At a time?"

"Ever." His gaze dropped to her mouth. "I know this isn't the right time or place, but I have to kiss you."

"Or what?"

"Or I will turn into Mr. Hyde." His wink acknowledged that he'd heard what was said at her table during breakfast. "You wouldn't wish that on all these ladies, would you?"

She couldn't breathe, couldn't think straight. "I guess I'll have to sacrifice myself to save them."

"Good idea," he murmured against her lips.

In just moments they were going wild together. Rob eased her to stand between his knees, then locked his arms around her hips and drew her body against his. She didn't have to bend far to keep their mouths fused, to keep their hearts in touch.

No one intruded on their privacy. He could have taken her down to the sand and satisfied them both. While the idea played in his mind, Valerie broke away and hid her face on his shoulder.

"We have to stop," she said breathlessly. "They could come down here any second."

Rob's deep breath was as unsteady as her voice. "I know." He loosened his hold, then couldn't help stroking his hand along her curves, from shoulder blade to sweet, rounded hip. "I know."

"That doesn't help." She pulled away without looking at him and walked to the edge of the water. Rob watched her for a moment, then propped his elbows on his knees and buried his face in his hands. The sun was just as warm on his back, the day just as beautiful. But now he did feel tired. Stressed. Why did everything have to be such a struggle?

He would have taken a dip in the cold river, but couldn't think of an explanation to give the rest of the group that wouldn't embarrass Valerie with its patent untruth. So he sat where he was, listening to the water slip by his rock, thinking about spending another night in a too-short sleeping bag on the hard ground—a prospect which should dampen his enthusiasm for anything but getting home to his own house, his own bed.

Unless he imagined sharing that sleeping bag with the woman he'd just held in his arms.

Voices coming down the path put that idea completely out of his mind. When he looked up, Valerie had wandered even farther away, around a curve and across some boulders. And here he sat, relaxed on a rock. The least suspicious picture they could have presented.

But he hadn't taken Sybil into account. Followed by several of the other campers, she stumbled into the clearing, puffing from her trek down the hill. "We wondered where the two of you had ducked off to." Her smile had an edge of meanness. "This is a nice secluded spot to spend an afternoon."

"Yes, it is." Rob stood up and deliberately stretched his arms high over his head. He had nothing to hide.

"We were talking about our girls and kinda just wandered down here. But I think I'm scheduled to show up for latrine duty about now. I'll see y'all at dinner. Later, Valerie," he called, and got a careless wave in return. She would have to fend for herself against Sybil and her minions. He didn't doubt she would win, hands down.

Crouched on the stones in the shallow water at the river's edge, Valerie heard Rob's efficient strides as he made his way up the path behind her and Sybil's heavy breathing as she approached.

"Looking for diamonds?" she asked brightly.

Valerie straightened up. "My son Connor likes to collect rocks. I thought I'd gather a few for him while I was here."

"Rob is a really nice guy. That smile of his is sweet enough to eat." She pretended to consider the treetops around them. "He makes me think of Ashley in *Gone With The Wind*."

Valerie hated sharing her fantasy with Sybil, of all people. "I thought that, too. But Rob's got more backbone than Ashley ever had."

"Sort of Rhett and Ashley combined?" Sybil followed as Valerie started back across the loose rocks to the beach at the bottom of the path.

"Sure." She'd agree to anything, if the woman would just be quiet.

"I always—" The words broke off in a scream. Valerie whirled around to see Sybil stagger and then crash into the shallow water. "Oh, God. Help me! My ankle…" she moaned.

From where she stood, Valerie could see that Sybil's

foot had slipped down between two rocks and was stuck there, twisted. No wonder she was in pain.

"Relax." Valerie crouched over the foot, putting her hand on a chubby leg. "We're gonna get you out in just a second, but you have to calm down."

Sybil's cries dissolved into gulping sobs and then to wet sniffs. The other women started to approach, but Valerie waved them back. "The stones shift easily. Let me see if I can get her foot out first. Somebody get the first aider."

Neither rock would roll easily, and she couldn't lift them on her own. "I'll be right back," she told Sybil, and took a straight-line path to the nearest trees.

"Where are you going? What are you doing?" Hysteria edged the shrill voice.

As she reached the undergrowth, Rob jogged back down the path. "What happened?"

Valerie nodded toward Sybil. "She's got a foot stuck under two rocks I can't lift. I'm looking for a lever."

"I'll see what I can do." He made his way toward the fallen woman. Valerie knew she didn't have to tell him to be careful.

When she came back with a stout stick, Rob shook his head. "I can't lift them, either. Let me lever the rock, and you get her foot out."

Without a word, Valerie handed him the stick and went to kneel by Sybil's legs. "We'll have you out in a minute," she promised, hoping it was true. Sybil moaned.

After a second's survey, Rob fitted the stick in exactly the place Valerie would have chosen, and wedged it in as tightly as possible. "Ready?" He grinned at Sybil. "Take a deep breath and we'll be done."

And it was that simple. He bore down on the stick, the rock shifted up and away…and Valerie drew the imprisoned foot free. Sybil, of course, screamed at having the foot moved at all. But at least she was no longer caught.

"Okay." Rob threw the stick back into the trees. "Now we're gonna get you on better ground." He put an arm around Sybil's shoulder. "Valerie's gonna hold on to the other side and we'll take you to that nice rock over there where you can sit. Ready?"

At Sybil's tearful nod, they lifted her upright and carried her over the remaining rocks without either foot touching the ground. By the time they got her seated, their first aid specialist, a nurse, had arrived.

"Not broken," she announced after an examination. "Scraped and bruised and sprained slightly."

"Slightly?" Sybil put her head back against the friend standing behind her. "It hurts like hell!"

Sandy, the nurse, patted Sybil's knee. "I know it does. I'm gonna clean the scrapes and wrap you up tight, then we'll get you up to camp. I've got pain meds. You'll feel better in no time."

Sandy's prediction proved true, mostly because—in Valerie's opinion—Sybil allowed Rob to carry her all the way up to camp. Once seated in the only chair, with her foot propped up and iced, she was quite happy to be the center of attention. Rob, of course, got due accolades as hero.

Valerie just wanted to go home. Not because she

didn't get a share of the credit, because she did. Not because Rob's group burnt the bottom of the Dutch-oven lasagna for dinner, or because the weather changed some time during the night into a fine, chilly rain which fell all Sunday morning and afternoon as they cooked and cleaned and packed up for the return trip.

She wanted to go home because she had to get away from that man. Had to stop watching his good-natured teasing with each woman in the group, completely unflirtatious and yet somehow special. Jealousy had rarely taken hold of her emotions—by the time she discovered her ex-husband was seeing another woman, their marriage had already ended.

Now, she seemed to see everything through a green haze. Her jaw clenched when she heard Sybil's giggle as Rob brought her a cup of coffee and then rolled up her sleeping bag and took down her tent. Valerie took down her own tent with ease and needed no assistance with her sleeping bag. She didn't want help with her gear. She prided herself on her independence, her competence, her self-sufficiency.

She just wanted Rob Warren with an ache that threatened to consume her. No amount of rationalizing—and she'd spent most of the night on all the logical arguments—could dissolve the sheer need she felt, the immense longing just to lose herself in his arms, in his eyes, in the pleasure of his hands. It wasn't even about sex, so much, as a craving to get as close as possible to this special man, sharing the warmth and acceptance which seemed so much a part of him.

The fact that an intimate relationship with Rob Warren would create a huge disaster on almost every level of her life seemed to matter less every day.

In the meantime, the campout ended with congratulations all around as each leader received a card certifying their participation in GO! outdoor training.

"You're all qualified to take a GO! troop camping," the director told them. "Remember the safety rules, don't forget to complete all the paperwork, and…oh, yes…have fun!"

Rob stowed the last of his gear in the back of the car and shut the door. "Do you want to drive or should I?"

Valerie avoided his eyes. "I'll drive, thanks."

With a sigh of relief, he buckled himself into the passenger seat beside her and adjusted the heater to deliver warm air at a high speed. "That's better. Amazing how chilled you get, working in wet clothes, even if the temperature isn't all that cold. I'm glad to be out of the rain."

Valerie nodded but didn't say anything. Rob introduced several subjects—the weekend just past, the events they'd planned for the troop, the music on the radio—but the most she could manage was a nod or, occasionally, a smile.

Finally, he turned in his seat to face her. "Something wrong?"

She pretended to be surprised. "No. Not at all."

"You're pretty quiet."

"I'm not usually a chatterbox."

"No, but you are full of ideas, plans and suggestions. I'm not hearing any of that this afternoon."

"Tired, I guess." She shrugged. "And, like you said, a little chilled."

"We could change into dry clothes at the rest station coming up. Or we could check into a motel."

She jerked her head around to stare at him. "What did you say?"

"For a warm shower," he clarified, with an innocent look. "Before the dry clothes."

Because she wanted him so much, she couldn't smile at the joke. "I don't think so," she said in a severe voice and added more weight to the gas pedal.

"I can't apologize for yesterday," he told her when a few miles had passed beneath the wheels. "Because I'm not sorry."

"I didn't ask for an apology," she said quickly. Several heartbeats later, she added, "I'm not sorry, either."

After that confession, they drove from the mountains, through the Piedmont, to the southeastern part of North Carolina called the Sandhills without saying much at all. The silence didn't mean they weren't communicating...they were, but on a different level altogether.

Just after ten, Valerie eased the car into Jen's driveway and turned off the engine and the lights. The rain in the mountains hadn't reached New Skye, and the October night surrounded them, cool but clear.

She pulled in a deep breath against the tension in her chest, and other places she didn't want to think about. "Now, I guess, it's time to go back to the real world. Kids, jobs, bills, traffic..."

Rob rolled his head against the back of the seat to look at her. "I wouldn't mind a cup of coffee, first."

Everything inside of her went completely still. His

blue eyes seemed dark tonight, his voice rough and very deep. No lights shone in the house beside them— the kids and Jenny would still be on the other side of the backyard and the trees. If they went in together, they would be alone. Very alone. "I—"

He didn't touch her, didn't make the decision easy. "I'm not promising anything," he said. "Except to start the coffee pot."

When he came around and opened her door, she gave him her hand, let him pull her to her feet. He kept his fingers around hers as she locked up the car and then turned toward Jenny's front porch.

Just like that, her decision was made.

Inside, he turned on the light above the sink but left the overhead lighting off. Shadows huddled in the corners of the kitchen and outside the doors. The house was very quiet.

"Buttercup must have gone to my house for a visit." Rob plugged in the coffeemaker. "I wonder how Mat the Cat likes her company."

Valerie couldn't think of an answer, couldn't force words through her closed throat.

With the coffeemaker set, he glanced at her where she still stood just inside the door. "Go sit down in the living room. I'll bring your coffee as soon as it's ready."

He followed and knelt to set a match to the firewood already piled in the grate. Valerie switched on one of the smaller lamps, but most of the light in the room came from the flames now leaping in the fireplace.

"I love that snap and crackle," he said, standing up again. "And the whisper of fire—do you hear it? Like a very small wind." He smiled. "I'll have as much fun at the campfire as the girls will."

She recovered her poise enough to answer. "I don't doubt it. You can always tell when a man has built a fire—there's a huge amount of wood, probably some incendiary liquids involved, and a tower of flames shooting up into the sky. In GO!, we build just enough fire for the purpose."

"Where's the fun in that?" His grin teased her. "Have a seat, and I'll bring in the coffee. Black, right?"

"Right." She looked around the room after he left, trying to make the fateful decision of where to sit. There was a love seat, two armchairs and the couch. The armchairs would convey that she was turning him down, the sofa would be an invitation. What did the love seat say?

She was pretty sure she didn't want to know.

Music entered the room as she debated—Frank Sinatra, an album of his classics. When Rob came back with two mugs of coffee, she lifted an eyebrow. "You're a Sinatra fan, too?"

He handed her one mug. "Jen got the habit from me." His glance took in the empty chairs. "Hard choice, isn't it?"

She frowned at his insight.

With his free hand, he drew her to the couch. "You can take one end and I'll take the other, if you want."

Defiantly, Valerie sat in the middle, holding her mug in both hands with her elbows on her knees. "This is great."

Rob sat down beside her, just outside of touching range. The fire snapped loudly in the silence, and Valerie took a gulp of her coffee.

What next? She should drink down and tell him to go, she decided. The tension was only getting worse—her expectations, or his, had thickened the air to the point where she could barely breathe.

In the second before her fingers started to loosen on the cup, Rob took hold of the mug's handle, lifted it out of her hand and set it on the table.

"Relax," he said, his voice soft, husky. "Nothing will happen here that you don't want." With a hand on her shoulder, he pressed her back against the couch. She found that he'd slipped his arm behind her shoulders without her being aware of the move.

"The question," she managed to say, "is not what I want, but what's best."

"There is no best," he countered, turning his head to set his chin on her hair. The small move melted her insides into something sweet and rich. "Only better or worse. Is this better than being alone?"

Valerie squeezed her eyes shut. "Oh, yes."

"Worse than playing it safe?"

She sighed, and nodded. "Probably."

"Well," he said as his fingers touched her cheek, "if you keep having second thoughts, just stop me. Meanwhile…" His mouth slipped from her temple, along her jawline to her lips and settled there, warm and gentle.

She gave a small gasp, and her mouth opened slightly. Rob didn't take advantage, didn't force the moment. He wooed her sweetly; instead, his hands tender, his mouth persuasive. They slid from comfortable to aching to desperate, through subtle stages of delight, until Rob's hands were in her hair, his fingers stretched long and wide over her skull. She couldn't escape if she'd wanted to.

But Valerie had no desire to escape, only a desire for more. With his shirt gone, she kissed his bare shoulder, tasting the strong, sleek muscles, feeling the graceful curve of a collarbone against her cheek. He dragged her sweater over her head, and his mouth claimed hers again as they pressed belly to belly, chest to chest, only her bra between them. A quick twist of his clever locksmith's fingers vanquished even that barrier. They sighed together, in pleasure and relief, then plunged back into the heat.

Rob shaped Valerie's curves with his palms, grateful and panicked at the same time. He wanted *now,* wanted to lose himself inside of her, wanted the sheer physical release her body promised.

But he wanted to pleasure *her,* as well. Wanted to bring her something new, something she'd never found with another man. All he could do was try to convey, with every touch, every kiss, every thrust of his hips, how much he'd come to value her in his life. How wise and funny and talented and brave he thought she was. How much he needed her.

He grabbed a condom from the pocket of his jeans as she slid them off his hips, and—glory be—she helped him put it on. She took him inside her and tightened her legs around his waist until he saw black in front of his eyes from the sheer beauty of the moment. He shook his head to clear his vision and stared down at her, at a loss for words but doing his best to tell her, in the strongest, deepest, longest way possible, how much he loved her at this moment.

She cried out, and he knew she understood. Letting go at last, Rob took hold of the comfort Valerie offered. They held each other tightly, while the fire he'd started consumed them both.

CHAPTER ELEVEN

ROB HAD ONLY SLEPT with one other woman, so he'd never had to worry about what to say "afterward." He'd never realized until tonight how being married simplified sex.

Not that he was sorry…if he wasn't in his sister's house, with a child for whom he was responsible next door, he'd probably wake Valerie up this minute and start all over again. So far, they'd covered just the basics. He could think of several variations he wouldn't mind exploring.

"Rob?" Her whisper was sweet in the firelight, and he couldn't suppress a sigh of pleasure as she rubbed her cheek against his shoulder. "What time is it?"

"About midnight."

"Jenny will wonder where we are."

"Blame the rain."

"Good idea." She lay so still, so soft against him, that he thought she'd gone back to sleep.

But then she stirred, stiffened and sat up. Grabbing the corner of the afghan folded on the back of the sofa, she wrapped up into a cocoon of green crochet stitches. And started to walk away.

"Hey." He hooked his finger into an empty space in the pattern. "Where are you going?"

"Clothes," she said, indistinctly. "Pajamas. Sanity."

"Was this insane?"

She looked at him over her shoulder. "I think so."

He felt disadvantaged by the fact that he was still naked. He pulled on his jeans without bothering with his shorts. "I don't." The jeans were stiff and still damp and felt miserable against his heated skin. "I've wanted you since the first time I saw you."

"So we scratched the itch and—"

"Bullshit." He didn't swear too often. "I haven't had sex in nine years and was prepared to go ninety. This was not any stupid itch."

Valerie looked down at her feet. "Okay. I'm sorry. But…" She met his gaze again. "I don't want… I can't do this again."

"I was that rusty, huh? That clumsy?"

The joke fell flat. "You know what a bad idea this was. We can't have an affair. Not in a town this small, not with children to think of. Not when we work together with the girls."

"We could have an engagement. A marriage." He couldn't believe he'd said that. He couldn't believe the thought had been in his mind so long, without his recognizing it.

"No."

Rob took a step back. "That might just be the fastest refusal on record."

"I don't want to marry you. I don't want to marry anybody."

"Why not?"

"I've lived all my life with some man's expectations dictating my behavior. My father, my husband, more bosses and managers than I want to remember. I'm not doing that anymore."

"You're putting me in the same…class…as your grandfathers? Men who dominate women instead of partner them?" He clenched his fists against a surge of anger. "I'm nothing like that."

"You want control, Rob. I've seen it with Ginny."

"I take care of her for her own good. It's not the same thing."

"I've heard that before. I think marriage would make us both miserable." She smiled sadly. "I care about you too much to hurt you that way."

Rob didn't protest when she left this time. He put all his clothes back on, except for the shorts he stuffed into the pocket of his jacket. Pushing the burning coals to the rear of the fireplace, he turned off the coffeepot and then let himself out the kitchen door for the walk to his house.

Back to real life, indeed.

DESPITE HIS NEW training certification, Valerie gave Rob the next Wednesday off, mostly just to give both of them a break from the agony of being together. In his place, she enlisted a couple of parents to provide transportation and together they took the girls to Charlie's Carolina Diner for a cooking lesson with Ms. Abby Brannon.

She waited for them in front of the counter, wearing

a big white apron and a floppy chef's hat. The girls giggled as they settled in at the long table she'd set up, complete with a miniature picnic basket at each chair.

"Don't laugh," Abby warned, smiling herself. "This is a chef's toque—a respected sign that you're dealing with an experienced professional. An artist." Then she pulled the toque off and tossed it onto the counter. "But most of us are just people who like to eat and need to know how to cook. Even here at the diner, where I cook all day long for other people, I don't wear a toque. Just a ponytail, to keep my hair out of the food. So, everybody who has long hair, there's a ponytail holder in your basket to pull your hair back."

The girls delved into their baskets and some of them pulled out the paper toques Abby had put there. "Sure," she said, in answer to their question. "If you want to wear your toque this afternoon, you're more than welcome. There are some aprons, too, to keep your uniforms clean. So let's get dressed, and get cooking."

Abby had organized her presentation so well that Valerie had almost nothing to do except offer an occasional helping hand and serve as official taster for the recipes. The troop divided into groups of four or five, each group assigned part of a meal to prepare. From finding and using recipes to measuring ingredients and calibrating ovens, Abby's lesson gave the girls a real sense of the business and the pleasures of cooking.

Grace's group was assigned dessert and given a recipe for strawberry shortcake. "Where are the little cakes?" Manda asked. "And the can of whipped cream?"

"You have to bake the cake," Valerie told her, studying the recipe. "And whip the cream."

Manda's jaw dropped. "Huh? So where's the cake mix?"

Valerie pointed to the bag of flour on the counter. "Right there."

The girl shook her head. "I still don't get it."

Grace calmly took the recipe from her mother's hand. "I know what to do. First, we have to cut up the berries."

"Don't they come frozen in a little bag?"

Across the room, Ginny's crew had started on the main course under Abby's supervision. While Abby explained the recipe for lasagna, Ginny wandered across the kitchen to the dishwasher. "Abby, what's this?"

"That's how the dishes get clean. Come back, Gin-Gin, or you're going to miss figuring out what you need to do."

The girl shrugged. "I don't have to cook. My dad does all that."

"You expect to eat this afternoon?" When Ginny answered with another shrug, Abby clicked her tongue. "Well, unless you want to watch while all the other girls enjoy this meal, you'd better help us out."

Determined to win the power struggle, Ginny wandered farther away. Valerie followed her to the rear door of the kitchen.

"Ginny, come back to your group. The other girls need your help."

"No, they don't. They don't need four people to make lasagna."

"Why don't you want to participate?" Valerie propped a hip on a nearby stool, hoping to get some insight regarding this uncooperative attitude. "And don't just shrug. What are you trying to say?"

Ginny rolled her eyes. "Nothing. I just don't want to cook. I don't like to cook."

"Why?"

"It's messy. You get food everywhere and then you have to clean it all up again."

Granted, from what Valerie had observed, Rob was not the neatest kitchen worker in New Skye. "There are ways to cook without wrecking the kitchen."

"Not when you have to use crutches."

Ah. "I imagine your crutches do complicate cooking." She pretended to consider. "I bet it's pretty exhausting to have to push yourself back and forth when you have to get ingredients from the refrigerator and the pantry."

"It's hard to carry stuff at all," Ginny confessed. "I must've dropped hundreds of eggs before—"

Before, Valerie guessed, she'd given up in self-defense. "Does your dad get mad about cleaning up?"

"N-No." She sighed. "He almost never gets mad. Doesn't matter what I do, he's really patient. Takes care of everything. Puts up with anything."

Valerie kept her voice quiet. "Is that a problem?"

But Ginny had finished with making confessions. "No. That's the way I like it. Can I go sit down out front? I'm tired."

"Sure. She's tired of standing," Valerie said, in answer to Abby's questioning glance. "I bet she'll come back in a little while."

Ginny did return in time to layer the lasagna. The salad group managed to cut up carrots, cucumbers, tomatoes and celery without slicing any fingers, and no one burned a hand on the ovens. When they finally sat down to their meal, Valerie felt a real sense of accomplishment.

And on top of it all, the girls thought their dinner tasted "awesome."

They weren't so enthusiastic about cleaning up, but the automatic dishwasher proved fascinating enough to forestall most complaints. Even Ginny's.

"This was fantastic," Valerie told Abby, as parents began arriving to take their children home. "You're a natural teacher."

With a relieved sigh, Abby leaned back against the counter. "I had a great time. This was such a change from the usual daily grind— I'm thinking I should offer cooking classes every afternoon."

Charlie snorted as he passed by with a tray of drinks. "And leave me with the dinner rush? You'll put me out of business, girl!"

Abby sent a mock frown after him. "I'm trapped in diner hell. Forever." Taking a deep breath, she straightened up. "But he's right. I've got a responsibility here. And I do love it, most days." She put an arm around Valerie's shoulder and gave her a hug. "I had a great time today. Thanks."

Valerie reciprocated with an even bigger hug. "Thank *you*. You're a friend in a million."

And that was *true,* she realized with surprise. Abby was a friend in a million—*Valerie's* friend. Jenny, too.

How long had it been since she'd really taken the time to form relationships outside the workplace?

How hard would leaving be if she had to abandon friends like Abby and Jenny?

And a man like Rob?

ROB SPENT MOST OF his free afternoon at the shop, working on files, cleaning, repairing and straightening the storeroom. When closing time arrived, he still had an hour left before he was supposed to pick up Ginny at the diner. Just enough time, he decided, to drive out and check on his dad, but not enough time for a major argument. He preferred to err on the side of optimism.

This time, his perception paid off. When he reached the house, he saw his mother on the front porch, trimming and watering the geraniums. "What a nice surprise," she told him, after a welcome kiss. "You're just the person I wanted to talk to. Sit down and I'll bring you out a drink."

He did as he was told, and sipped his iced tea while she puttered with the flowers. "Where's Dad? And my man Connor?"

"I checked on them while I was inside. Your dad's napping in front of the baseball game. I thought he needed the rest, so I didn't wake him up to tell him you're here. Connor is spending his daily hour with the video monsters."

"Sounds good. I just thought I'd drop by, see how the old man's getting along."

"Very well. We went back to see Dr. DeVries yesterday, and he's really pleased with your dad's progress. Well, except for the smoking."

Rob sat up straight in the rocker. "He hasn't quit?"

His mother pressed her lips tightly together and wordlessly shook her head.

"That's insane. Did Tim talk to him?"

"Of course. Your dad walked out of the office and lit up before he got into the car."

"Damnation." For once, she didn't correct his language.

"He's eating better, though. And we've taken a walk every night this week."

"That's something, I guess."

She worked with her flowers for a while longer, while Rob took the chance just to relax. He still had a few aches and pains from sleeping on the ground for two nights. Not to mention the emotional bruises he'd picked up fighting with Valerie.

"Robbie, I want to talk to you." His mother came to sit in the rocker next to his. "I hope you won't mind too much what I'm going to say."

His mind immediately leaped to an unwelcome conclusion. Did his mom know…sense…how he felt about Valerie? "I don't expect I'll mind. What's going on?"

"Your dad told me about the argument you two had, back before he got sick."

Rob relaxed a little. Not Valerie. "He shouldn't have bothered you with all that."

"He tells me everything." She smiled proudly, then sobered. "And in spite of what he says, I do understand your point. I even agree that your idea about combining the security business with the shop has real potential."

"Then maybe you could help me convince him—"

She shook her head. "I've never interfered in the business. That's your dad's place, his world."

"Okay." A shiver went down his spine. "Don't worry about it."

"I can't help but worry," she responded. "Part of his problem, Dr. DeVries tells me, is the stress of his work. He's always taken everything that happened at the shop personally. If something goes wrong, your dad can get very disturbed."

"I know, Mom. I grew up here. Remember?"

"And so I know that he's extremely concerned about the difference of opinion between the two of you. He told me he suggested you could go out on your own, if you didn't like the way he runs the business."

"He did say that."

Reaching over, she placed her hand on top of his. "Oh, Robbie, please, please reconsider. It would just about kill your dad to lose you. Especially now, with your brother so determined to take off for the other side of the country." He saw her eyes fill with tears before she looked away from him. "I've already tried to convince Smith to stay. I wanted to give you the room to make your own decision."

She drew a deep breath. "But Robbie, you know Smith has never been really...*engaged* by the business. He's done what your dad asked him to, but reluctantly. Even sullenly. Now, for the first time in his life, he's being stubborn. Your dad argued with him, too. But nothing I've said, nothing Trent or your dad can say, will change his mind. Smith is leaving. I don't really think he'll ever come back to stay."

Though he knew now what was to come, Rob waited for the rest of her argument.

"And Trent's heart has never been with locksmithing. He's reliable because that's the kind of man he is, not because he likes the work. But you—" She patted his hand. "You're our rock. Your dad's foundation. Just the fact that you'd like to expand the business proves how dedicated and concerned you are. Have always been."

You really have them all fooled, Rob thought to himself. *Good job, Warren.*

"And I think it would just simply kill your dad if you walked out on him, especially now, when he's weak. He counts on you, though, of course, he wouldn't ever say so."

Of course.

"So I'm asking, Robbie, if you'll drop this idea of starting your own business. We need you—your dad needs you. I'd like to keep his stress level as low as possible, and that's going to be difficult as long as there's even the slightest chance that you might walk out on him. Please, son." The tears finally spilled over. "I don't know what I'd do if I lost your dad."

The hurt in his chest was so sharp, so big, that he wouldn't have been surprised to look down and find himself bleeding from a knife wound. To think he'd questioned the reality of Valerie's fears, her belief that marriage threatened her independence.

But his mother's needs were equally real. "Sure, Mom." He turned his palm up and clasped her hand with his. "Don't worry about this for another minute.

I'm part of Warren and Sons Locksmiths for as long as I'm needed."

She threw her arms around his neck. "Oh, Robbie, thanks so much. I knew I could count on you." After a moment, she pulled back. "Can you stay for dinner? Why don't you go get Ginny at the meeting and bring her back out? I've got a turkey breast roasting in the oven and a big salad already put together."

Health food, with a vengeance. He felt sorry for his dad. "Thanks, but I'd better get Ginny home early. We've got a cookout this weekend for the troop, and I want her to have plenty of rest beforehand. I'll take Con with me and save everybody a trip."

"Sunday, then?"

Rob stood up, then bent and kissed her cheek. "I'll let you know. Tell Dad I was here."

"Of course."

On the trip back to town, he encouraged Connor to explain the fine points of his new video game, keeping his own mind blank except for the thought involved in safe driving. They arrived at the diner to find that Ginny was the last of the girls to be picked up.

"Sorry," he told Valerie. "And I'm usually the one complaining about the parents who show up late."

"It wasn't a problem." She studied his face, her forehead wrinkled with worry. "What's wrong? Is your dad doing okay?"

"Sure." Rob looked away from that probing gaze. "He's great. The doctor says he can come back to work at least part-time next week."

"Then why—"

"Come on, Daddy, let's go home." Ginny came up beside him and pulled on the sleeve of his shirt. "I'm tired."

He allowed himself a glance at Valerie's soft, seductive mouth, remembered the taste and feel of those lips against his own. *Me, too.* "Coming, coming, *coming,* Miss Impatience. And you've already had dinner, haven't you? Man, I wish I'd been here. Lasagna and salad sounds too good to be true."

"I layered the lasagna," Ginny told him proudly.

"Very impressive."

"Rob?"

Reluctantly turning back, he found Valerie offering him a carryout container. "We thought you'd like to sample what we cooked. The girls made up a meal for you, too."

His heart melted. "That's terrific. And heavy," he added, feeling the heft of the box. "I'm glad I'm feeling starved." He couldn't suppress his grin. "You're the best." And grinned even more widely when he saw her blush.

Unfortunately, he realized as he drove home, he was a man who would from now on always have to settle for less than the very best.

FOR THEIR FIRST COOKOUT, Valerie took the troop to a community park near the school. Parents dropped their girls off at 10:00 a.m. on Saturday, and would return at three.

Rob had helped her unload all the equipment and arrange it under the picnic shelter for the girls to use. She was forcibly reminded of the camp training weekend, and the distance that had existed between them since. He'd been much less visible at Jenny's house this last week than at any time since she'd moved in. As the afternoons grew shorter, the kids tended to stay inside when she brought them home, unless they romped with Buttercup in the backyard. Excursions into Rob's domain simply didn't happen.

Which was for the best, she'd told herself frequently. Her life did not—could not—depend on any man's attention.

"Okay," she told the girls, once they'd all arrived. "We're going to start cooking about eleven o'clock. Before that, we'll have a snack, and between now and snack time…we hike!"

Most of the troop cheered the announcement, but Valerie heard Ginny's groan under the celebration. And she saw, by his worried gaze, that Rob had heard, as well. In their planning, he had volunteered to conduct this activity, but if Ginny didn't go, he would be torn between his daughter and the troop. Déjà vu all over again.

As the girls got in line for the hike, Valerie caught him by the arm. "Ginny can stay here in the shelter, if she'd rather. She certainly doesn't have to hike. Keisha's mom is going to stay here with her baby and watch the food and gear."

He nodded. "Considering how warm it is today, that sounds like a good idea. I'll talk to Ginny."

In only minutes, Rob took his place at the head of the line and headed out into the wooded area of the park. Valerie brought up the rear, with Grace as her partner. Connor stayed with Carolyn Warren for every GO! event these days and, as Rob had predicted, the change had improved the troop dynamics and her relationship with her son. She saw Rob cast one final, concerned glance back at the picnic area, but then he put his mind on the job. For the next hour, the girls were fascinated and busy as they put their compasses to practical use. His concluding exercise—a team race back to the picnic shelter using directional navigation—challenged and entertained the troop as well as any she'd ever seen.

Once everyone had a chance to get water and visit the bathroom, the clamor for food became overwhelming. Since she and Rob had set up the site ahead of time, the different patrols were able to start on their tasks right away. From where she stood outside the shelter, supervising the fire-building process, Valerie soon heard Ginny's shrill voice.

"Me, first. I want to put my food in the pot first." *At least,* Valerie consoled herself, *she's enthusiastic.*

For a first cookout, events proceeded smoothly, and soon their big pot of soup sat on the fire. Leaving Rob to watch the cooks, Valerie gathered the other girls nearby and, with Grace's reluctant help, taught them some traditional campfire songs. The cooking time passed quickly and painlessly. Right on schedule, they all sat down in a circle on the grass to eat.

"Oh, yuck!" Beside Valerie, Laura Taylor threw her bowl into the center of the ring, rolled violently onto her hands and knees and spit out a mouthful of soup. "That's so gross."

Several of the girls sat staring at Laura, their spoons held halfway between bowl and mouth. Others had already taken a taste.

"Eeuuww." Keisha swallowed, but screwed her face into a wrinkled mask. "Mommy, that's awful." More protests—more revulsion—followed. Across the circle from Valerie, Zoe Miller turned around just in time to lose her breakfast, as well as that one taste of soup.

Rob jumped to his feet. "Drink, girls. Get the taste out of your mouths." He grabbed up the bottle of clear soda they'd brought and started refilling cups. "Swish it all around your teeth and spit it out. Who knows how to gargle? Who can gargle the longest?"

Valerie's admiration for his quick thinking warred with panic and confusion. What was wrong with the soup? Had someone tampered with the food while they were gone? But wouldn't Ginny and Keisha's mom have noticed?

She took an experimental sip of her own serving. A bittersweet taste coated her tongue, curdled in her throat. Almost certain she could identify the source, she spooned a full dose into her mouth. Yes, there was no mistaking that flavor. Soap.

Taking her bowl with her back to the shelter, she opened the dishwashing box and extracted the liquid soap bottle—the brand new, never-been-opened soap bottle, now with a telltale drip of blue liquid along one side of the cap. Maybe a quarter of a cup of the detergent had been squeezed out. Into their potluck soup, Valerie was certain.

But who…?

Hating her suspicion, she looked for Ginny out in the circle. Rob had brought her special chair along so she could sit on the ground with everyone else. Unlike the girls around her, Ginny had nothing to say about the taste of the soup. She still held her bowl, and stared into it as she made patterns through the goop with her spoon. Valerie would have bet a year's salary that she hadn't tasted so much as a single drop.

Why, oh, why would she be so cruel?

That question would be settled later. In the meantime, crisis management was in order. She stepped back into the center of the troop and held up her hand for quiet. "Is everybody okay? I know it tasted bad, but I think there must have been some soap left in the pot the last time it was washed, and that soap got mixed in with our soup. Soapy soup, you can call it." She gave the girls a chance to exclaim over the idea of eating soap. "Some of you might have a little stomachache this afternoon, but nobody's going to get sick or feel much worse than they do right now. And I just happened to bring along bread, peanut butter and two kinds of jelly, so we don't have to go hungry. Remember—it's always good to have a backup plan in case something goes wrong."

Between PB&J sandwiches, cleanup, and a craft involving peanut butter, pine cones and bird seed, the girls were all back to normal by the time their parents arrived to take them home.

Rob loaded boxes into her car as Valerie stood in the parking lot, explaining the problem to each and every adult. She would have to file a report with GO! headquarters on the incident and probably endure an interview. *Thanks, Ginny. Thanks so much.*

When only the four of them were left under the picnic area, Valerie suggested in a quiet voice that Grace wait for her in the car. Rob's eyes narrowed in question, but Ginny pretended innocence.

"Can I go, too?"

"Um, no, Ginny. I want to talk to you."

Rob had straightened up to his full height. She'd never seen his posture quite so stiff. "What's the problem?"

Valerie didn't answer him directly. "Ginny, how did soap get into the soup?"

"How should I know?"

"You were here while the rest of us were hiking. Did you see someone going through the boxes of equipment?"

"I didn't watch. I put my head down on the table and took a nap. Maybe Keisha's mom saw something."

"She said she stayed busy with the baby, and carried him to her car to change his diaper. What happened, Ginny?"

The little girl shrugged. Rob made a quick movement with one hand, but then stood still again. To his credit, he didn't say a word.

Valerie let the silence stretch between the three of them until Ginny began to fidget. "I don't know why you're looking at me. Why would I put soap in the soup?"

"Good question. I'd like the answer."

After another long pause, Ginny said, "Nobody got hurt, anyway."

"No. But I think it was a very mean trick." Ginny's cheeks flushed a bright red. "And the cookout wasn't nearly as pleasant for the rest of us as it could have been. Whoever did this must have really wanted to ruin the day."

With her white-knuckled fists wrapped around the handles of her crutches, Ginny looked at her father. "Can we go home now?"

"Sure." As he looked at Valerie, Rob's expression conveyed both apology and anger. "I'll talk to you later tonight."

Valerie nodded. She knew a promise when she heard one.

ROB GOT GINNY into bed around nine-thirty, tucked her in, wiped her wet cheeks one more time, and kissed her good-night. "Love you, Ginny-girl."

A damp sniffle was his only answer.

He stumbled through the hall and into the kitchen, where he pulled two beers out of the fridge. Then he and Mat the Cat went outside. The day had been warm, but the night was cool…and moonless, so at first he didn't see the woman sitting out in his furniture on the grass. Rob hesitated, then headed in that direction.

"Hey." Dropping into his usual chair, he held up the bottles. "Want a beer?"

"No, thanks. I don't like beer."

"Oh, good. I do." He twisted the top off with the tail of his flannel shirt and took a long swig. "You were right, of course. Ginny put dish detergent in the pot while we went hiking, then poured her beans in first so nobody would notice."

"Did she say why?"

Another long draw on the beer. "Not directly."

Valerie leaned forward and braced her elbows on her knees. "Indirectly?"

He closed his eyes, heard again the mumbled words, the incoherent accusations. "What good grades Grace brings home…how much fun I have wrestling with Connor…how I danced so long with you at the wedding, didn't dance with her at all."

"But—"

He waved his free hand. "Never mind that she spent the entire reception in the stable." A few more glugs and the first bottle hit the grass. The second popped open. "All I ever wanted to do was give her a normal childhood."

Valerie's hand closed on his knee. "You're doing a great job under amazing conditions. I've met very few men who would have done half so much."

Rob moved out from under her touch. His self-control had reached the breaking point. "I'm just trying to do the right thing. Hoping I can make up for—" He shut his mouth with a snap of teeth. So much for self-control.

"Make up for what?"

"Never mind." On his feet again, he walked to the back fence, hiding in the shadows underneath the oak limbs.

She followed him, of course. "I'll listen, if you want to talk. Or I can go away."

The beer loosened his tongue. Or maybe he needed just to say it, finally, aloud. "I hated her."

"Who?" There was a moment of silent shock. "Your wife?"

He breathed in the scent of drying leaves. "Ginny."

CHAPTER TWELVE

VALERIE HEARD the self-loathing in Rob's voice, and her heart broke for him. "Because Leah died, you mean?"

He nodded, and the leaves brushing the top of his head rustled. "I loved Leah so much…and having the baby killed her. So I hated the baby—this small, defenseless, wrinkled little girl with no idea what she'd done." His voice dropped even further. "A little girl who would miss her mother more than I possibly could."

She put her hand on his shoulder. "What did you do about this…hate?"

"I—" He shook his head. "I couldn't *do* anything. I had a baby to take care of. We didn't know about the CP then. I took her home and buried Leah and went on with life."

"More or less," Valerie said under her breath. "I have to say, Rob—you really had me fooled. I never realized you hate Ginny so much."

He whipped around to stare at her. "I don't hate her! Not now. Not for a long time."

She hid her smile. "But—"

"That first day, when Gin was in the nursery and

Leah was gone, when I was trying to make arrangements and I knew I had to go back to our house without her…yeah, that was bad. I didn't see the baby at all that day. Didn't want to. I—I'd wished she'd never been born."

Valerie waited in silence.

"But my mom brought her to the memorial service and gave her to me to hold. I couldn't refuse, not in front of all those people. I couldn't listen to what they were saying, either, or I wasn't going to make it through. So I sat in the church and watched the baby sleep. She had Leah's eyes, and hair, but I could see a resemblance to my mom, too. She woke up once, and I thought for sure she'd start to make a fuss. But she just looked up at me with those dark eyes, and it was like looking at Leah. Like being with Leah, somehow. I…" He shrugged. "I've loved her with everything in me ever since."

Stepping close, Valerie reached out and gripped him above the elbows. "How many days of love do you suppose will atone for that one bad day? How many days of devoted fatherly care, beyond the limits of emotional and physical strength, will erase your very natural reaction to the worst experience a husband can know?"

"Valerie—"

Anger coursed through her body, and she shook him. Hard. "You continue to punish yourself for the one day out of the—what?—more than three thousand in Ginny's life that you haven't been totally supportive, completely understanding and unfailingly protective. Don't you think you could stop now?"

"I—" Rob felt his jaw hanging loose, and he closed his mouth. The question made him sound ridiculous. "It's not that easy."

"Probably not." She dropped her hands to her sides and stepped back. He immediately missed the warmth of her touch. "We all would prefer to hide behind the shields we build against other people."

"I do not—" He stopped, thought. And couldn't continue.

Valerie nodded. "Right. I wouldn't begin to believe you."

Crossing his arms, he looked at her in the night's shadows. "I'm not the only one."

"No," she agreed, in a small voice. "I know."

He could have pushed her, then, could have touched her, kissed her, maybe even asked her—again, and with better style—to marry him.

"I think," he said instead, gently, "we've been through enough for one day. Let me walk you home."

She didn't protest as he opened the back gate for her and followed her through the trees. Buttercup was in Jenny's backyard and she woofed at the sight of them, then dashed around wildly until they reached the back door and let her into the house. Rob waited at the foot of the steps as Valerie crossed the porch to open the door.

"Good night." A shaft of light coming through the doorway put her face in shadow.

"I'll talk with Ginny some more tomorrow," he promised. "She'll make an apology at the meeting on Wednesday."

But Valerie shook her head. "Let's not do that. Let's leave it an 'accident.' Somebody forgot to rinse the pot well. No one was hurt, and she'll never do anything like that again, I'm sure."

"That's awfully generous. She deserves more punishment."

"Knowing she's disappointed you may well be the only punishment she needs."

"Okay." Rob couldn't help but be grateful. "We'll play it your way. Thanks."

He couldn't see her dimple in the dark, but he thought she smiled. "Sleep well."

After today's crisis, not to mention its resolution, he was more than weary enough to follow her advice.

IN PREPARING FOR the troop's horseback adventure and evening cookout, Rob decided against another lecture to Ginny about how she should behave. Their long discussion after the first incident had surely made enough of an impression. Maybe he had indulged her over the years, but didn't she have a right to be spoiled, considering the bad tricks nature had played on her? She would behave from now on. He trusted his daughter.

For this trip, they met the girls in the school parking lot on Saturday morning. Valerie had assigned each vehicle specific passengers, mixing the girls up so they'd get to know everybody. All drivers had contact lists, safety and health forms, first aid kits and snacks.

"Have you considered working for the U.S. Army?" Rob asked as they waited for everyone to load up. "I think Special Forces could learn a thing or two from you about deployment skills."

Valerie rolled her eyes, but he could tell from her dimple that she appreciated the compliment.

Ginny rode in his car, since her equipment was already stowed there, along with four other girls sitting in the back seat. He listened to them chatter about school, boys, TV, music and clothes, waiting for Ginny to join in.

But his little girl faced forward and watched the road, contributing nothing to the conversation. Rob tried to ignore the bad feeling in the pit of his stomach. Sometimes she got carsick—looking backward was a sure way to trigger that problem. She'd feel better when they reached the camping area.

He frowned a little as he stopped the van in the gravel parking lot of their destination. Ginny had trouble maneuvering her crutches on this kind of loose, round rock surfacing. But the point of his daughter being in GO! was to conquer obstacles, right?

Once out of the gravel, the gentle slope led down to an open-sided shelter with four picnic tables underneath. Beyond, on level ground, a large ring formed by tree trunks surrounded the fire pit. Wood-sided cabins with screened and shuttered windows and doors offered beds for campers at a safe distance from the fire. Tall oaks stood sentry around the edge of the site and along the fence surrounding the pastures, where horses grazed in their naturally scenic way.

"Everybody get your backpack," Valerie called as soon as they had all left the cars. "We'll unload our gear, then walk over to the stables for our tour and ride. Each girl should help carry food and equipment to the picnic area."

Some girls tried to slide out of their responsibilities, of course, but overall the spirit of cooperation remained high. Rob took charge of an ice chest and walked beside Ginny as she inched across the slippery gravel toward the grass. The walk to the shelter wasn't long, but they were both relieved when she sank down onto one of the benches.

"You wait here," he told her. "I'll go back and help with the rest of the stuff."

She nodded, watching the other girls tote boxes of food and firewood toward the tables.

He picked up another ice chest and started back, coming up behind two girls just in time to hear Sabrina say "She always gets to be lazy."

Beside her, Molly nodded. "I think she's just pretending to need those stupid crutches. I've seen her walk without them sometimes at school. She could if she really wanted to."

"If she wasn't such a pill," Sabrina added, "it wouldn't be quite so bad."

"If only," Molly agreed.

Rob stopped in his tracks and let the girls get far enough ahead of him so that they wouldn't think he'd heard. Unfortunately, he couldn't ignore what they'd said. And as much as it hurt, he couldn't deny the part about Ginny's attitude. The other girls didn't like her. If he'd doubted that before, he'd been slapped in the face by the truth today.

As he set the ice chest down in the shelter, he saw Valerie double-checking that they'd brought out all the equipment. She glanced at him, then did a double take, her brows lifted in question. His face must have given something away. Luckily, the girls were clamoring around her, demanding to see the horses, and she didn't have the opportunity to question him. By the time they had a chance to talk, he might have come up with some kind of explanation.

They all trekked—in a double file of buddies, of course—over the gently sloped grounds toward the riding stable. He kept pace with Ginny, who managed more easily here than in the parking lot. Her gaze was fixed on the corral and the horses in the distance, and she moved as fast as she possibly could to get there.

"Slow down," Rob told her, putting a hand on her shoulder. "You don't want to fall."

"I'm not going to fall," she said sharply, and pulled away from his touch. "I want to be able to pick my horse. Come on."

They arrived at the stable along with the rest of the girls and were introduced to Trini, their instructor. "We're going to take a tour of the stables and talk about horses, first," she said. "Then we'll get you all sorted onto the different horses and go for a ride."

"Can't we ride first?" Ginny called. Rob kept his groan to himself.

Trini shook her head. "We need to learn some things about horses before we start handling them. Like…how should you act around a horse you don't know?"

"Careful," Ginny called, though others raised their

hands. "If you talk too loud or act crazy you might spook them. You should talk quietly and move carefully. Watch out for their feet, don't walk too close behind them."

"That's all correct," Trini said, with a startled look. "You must have been doing some riding."

"I've ridden lots of times." Ginny moved forward in the group of girls. "My friend Jacquie is a farrier—that means she puts the shoes on horses. And she lets me ride hers."

"That's great." The instructor led them into the tack room. "So who knows what the two kinds of saddles we have in here are called?"

Again, Ginny had the answer. And so the lesson went, with some girls knowing this or that, and Ginny supplying all the extra information any of them could want.

"She's an encyclopedia," Valerie commented as they moved through the stables, talking about stalls and hay and other fascinating details.

"She's learned a lot from Jacquie. Riding lessons are the one time she's completely focused on what's being said." He shook his head. "She really does love horses."

"So do some of the others," Kara Marsh, one of the mothers who'd driven, commented as she passed them. "It would be nice if they had a chance to participate in the activity."

The snide comment felt like yet another kick in the ribs. He glanced at Valerie and shrugged. "Sorry if she's monopolizing the conversation. Ginny's not usually the best at anything."

Her hand closed around his arm for a second. "Don't worry about it. Molly is one of those girls who wants to be the best at absolutely everything. And Kara encourages her. It won't hurt either of them to realize there are other people with talent and passion."

Outside in the corral, the girls finally met their mounts. Ginny picked out a black-as-pitch mare with a white blaze on her face and four white socks. "I want this one," she told Trini.

The instructor shook her head. "Raven's one of our more spirited lesson horses. You'd be better off with Waldo over here." She pointed to a quiet white horse standing with his eyes closed and one rear hoof resting. "He's a really sweet guy."

"But I ride big, fast horses," Ginny said loudly. "I can canter, too. I want to ride Raven."

Trini looked at Rob. "I've got liability, here," she said in a low voice. "Can you talk to her?"

"She does ride," he said. "I'm her dad. I think you and she will both be okay if she takes Raven. I brought her special saddle."

The instructor shrugged. "If you say so."

Rob smiled and went to help Ginny change saddles and get onto her horse. Heaven only knew what would have happened if he hadn't been here to settle this issue. Ginny might have thrown a tantrum, leaving Valerie, the parents and the other girls subject to the unpleasantness and a messy situation.

He felt really good about having his decision to work with the troop confirmed.

With Ginny settled on Raven, he went to help the

other girls and meet his own horse. Soon enough, Trini brought out a big bay gelding, which she mounted without assistance, and then led the string of riders and their horses out into the fields.

His horse, Bella, fell into line a couple of places behind Ginny and Raven. He kept an eye on all the girls he could see as they rode up and down the low hills, through a grove of pine trees and along the fence—always at a walk. He couldn't hear her voice, but he didn't doubt that Ginny would be chafing at their speed, wishing for a trot, or even a gallop. He hoped…

Even as the thought crossed his mind, he saw Raven break away from the string and strike off across the pasture land on her own. The rest of the horses stopped. All eyes were fixed on his daughter.

"Ginny!" he yelled, and heard Valerie's voice in echo.

Part of him was furious that Ginny had disobeyed his instructions and Trini's directions. But a greater part of him was proud as hell to see his little girl—his *handicapped* little girl—flying across the ground on the black mare as if flying were her natural gait. Still showing off, she turned and headed back to the line of riders at a brisk trot. Raven, understanding the expertise of the rider she carried, did a little showing off of her own. Neck arched, tail swinging, she demonstrated her breeding and training for the crowd to appreciate.

With Ginny and Raven back in line, the procession moved on. In a half an hour or so, they wended their way back to the stable, the horses brightening as they recognized the way home.

Rob and the other adults held the horses and tied them up as the girls dismounted. Trini came over to Rob as he left the last animal.

"That," she told him with anger in her voice, "was scary as hell. She could have been killed." Then a twinkle lightened her gaze. "That's what I thought, at first, anyway. She's good, even with her disability. If she wants to take lessons out here, I'll be glad to teach her. She's an example for anyone who wants to ride."

Savoring the praise, Rob joined the group of girls and mothers. He was aware of the adults' glares, the extent of their displeasure. Valerie came up beside him, her irritation obvious.

Now was not the time to argue the issue. "I'm sorry," he said, reading the signals in her set jaw, her narrowed eyes. "I didn't expect her to do something like that."

"You didn't? I expected exactly what she did." Then the anger faded. "Rob, she really has to be in better control. This behavior affects the whole troop."

"I'll talk to her. I promise."

In short order, it became obvious that Valerie was right—the troop dynamics had changed. Impressed by what they'd seen, girls who had rarely spoken to Ginny in the past now flocked around her, listening to tales of her rides at Jacquie's farm. As one group began preparing dinner under Rob and Valerie's supervision, Ginny and her audience collected their packs and went inside the nearest camp cabin. Their giggles floated through the screened window and made Rob grin. Finally, his plan for Ginny was beginning to pay off. Maybe she hadn't chosen the best way to demonstrate her abilities, but she'd certainly caught their interest.

Valerie called another group of girls, Grace among them, out of the cabin to light the fire for dinner. Keisha came into the fire circle with her hair down around her shoulders. Valerie told her to go get a band to pull her hair back, but Keisha hadn't brought a hairband, so Grace went in to get an extra one out of her backpack. Always prepared, just like her mom.

Rob looked up as Grace stumbled out of the cabin again. He saw the shock on her face, but before he had time to wonder what had happened, she had reached her mother and was tugging on Valerie's sleeve.

Focused on watching the girls set up the fire, Valerie only glanced up. "What is it?"

When Grace didn't say anything, Valerie turned to face her directly. "What do you need? Is there a problem?"

Grace pointed wordlessly at the cabin. Valerie stared for a long moment into the girl's face. "Sit on the logs," she instructed all the campers, in a voice that brooked no argument. "I'll be right back."

She walked quickly to the cabin, opened the door and stepped inside. All the giggles died away, so Rob could hear her next words clearly.

"Where did you get that?" The sharp tone surprised him.

No one answered, which surprised him even more.

"Ginny, where did you get it?" At the tone of that question, Rob stepped out of the shelter and headed toward the cabin. Behind him, around him, and inside the building, there was only silence.

After a long pause, his daughter said, "At home."

"And who does it belong to?"

Rob couldn't hear that answer, even though he now stood right outside. He put his hand on the screen door handle, just as Valerie spoke again.

"Ginny," she said gently. "Ginny, give me the gun."

CHAPTER THIRTEEN

ROB TALKED without stopping almost all the way home. The words poured out of him in a stiff, ragged voice—his disappointment in Ginny's judgment, his embarrassment, his actual fear that she would do something to endanger the other girls. The earlier stunt with the trail ride got a separate condemnation, as did the soapy soup incident, followed by more exasperation, indignation and chagrin. Finally out of words and losing his voice, he allowed the silence take over.

As they approached New Skye, Ginny spoke for the first time. "I'm hungry. Can we eat at the diner?"

A glance at the clock showed him it was, indeed, dinnertime. His stomach felt as if he'd swallowed an anchor. His heart ached at Ginny's apparent callousness.

But she needed regular meals for her health's sake. Maybe a time-out would give him a chance to understand the puzzle that was his daughter.

Charlie's was crowded, but Abby gave them a booth for four rather than a table for two. She bustled back in a few minutes with the coffee he'd ordered and a glass of milk for Ginny.

"What's for dinner?" she asked them, flipping

through her order book. Then she looked up with a frown. "Wait—I thought the cookout was this afternoon. What are y'all doing here when you could be eating beside the campfire?"

Ginny kept her eyes on her napkin as she folded it into one of those guessing game contraptions with different moveable panels that revealed the answers. Rob took a deep breath. "We came back early. Ginny…didn't feel comfortable."

Abby met his gaze for a second. "Sure. So what would you like to eat? The special tonight is country fried steak."

Ginny nodded. "Sounds good," Rob said. "We'll have two orders."

When Abby had left, Rob sipped his coffee, hoarding all the strength he could muster. He had no idea what more to say to his daughter. She'd stepped over the line this time, so far that he was pretty sure what the outcome of this disaster would be.

Suddenly, even without Jenny—and Valerie—to point it out to him, he wondered if that was exactly the reaction Ginny had hoped to provoke. Had she deliberately played the worst prank she could think of, intent on inducing a serious, even permanent, split between him and the Manions? Between him…and Valerie?

He couldn't talk about anything if he didn't address this issue first. "Ginny, look at me."

It took a long moment, but she finally lifted her head and met his gaze.

"You had to know that bringing a gun to the cookout was absolutely the wrong thing to do. We talked about guns when I brought it into the house. Do you remember promising me that you would never try to find it? That you wouldn't touch it if you did?"

She stared at him, unmoving, but he read confession in her eyes.

That, however, was not enough. "Ginny, do you remember?"

"Yes."

"You broke that promise, and I want to know why." He almost said *need,* but he couldn't afford to soften even that much.

Abby appeared with their plates, another glass of milk and a glass of tea for Rob, because she knew he didn't drink coffee with his food. She didn't say anything as she served them, but she set her hand on his shoulder a second before she left again.

Rob picked up his fork, but couldn't quite manage to spear up a bite of one of his favorite meals. "I asked you a question."

Ginny used her fork to push the food around on her plate. "I don't know," she said finally.

"Not good enough." He made himself cut off a bite of steak and put it in his mouth, though he thought he might throw up when he tried to swallow. "What are you thinking about these days? What made you decide to bring the gun with you today?"

"I thought it would be fun." When he didn't say anything, she offered, "I thought the other girls would like it."

"Did you think about me at all? Or about Mrs. Manion and what she would say?"

"I didn't think you would find out."

"And that makes it okay?"

"You say no to everything, anyway. I didn't bring the bullets, so I knew nobody could get hurt."

His attention was drawn to the first statement. "I say no to everything? What does that mean?"

Ginny shrugged and didn't answer.

"How's dinner?" Abby asked in the silence. Her gaze moved from Rob to Ginny and back again. "A rhetorical question. Sorry." She hurried away, leaving them alone.

Rob pushed his plate to the side and leaned forward, hands clasped, forearms braced on the table edge. "I want an answer, Ginny. Because from where I'm sitting, I feel like I do everything I can to be sure that you have a good time. Riding lessons, the GO! troop, school…what do you want that I haven't given you?"

"But you're always there," she burst out. "Right beside me, or behind me, watching, waiting for me to do something wrong."

"Not at all. I just want to be sure you're safe."

"I'm tired of being safe." She looked almost as surprised as he was that she'd said it.

Rob shook his head. "I don't understand."

"People are always watching me anyway. 'Look at the funny girl, see how she walks. She's weird, she doesn't move her fingers much. Bet she's retarded, too.'"

"Ginny…"

"And you do the same thing."

He couldn't find a single word to say in denial.

"You're always watching to see if I mess up. Am I gonna trip? Can I make it up the hill? Will I fall off the horse or trip over a crack in the sidewalk? I have to have somebody in the bathroom while I take a bath so I don't drown—how much of a baby does that make me?"

Rob stared across the table at the face of his daughter—so like her mother's and, at this moment, so furious.

"Go to bed early, eat healthy, do your therapy, take your medicine, watch out, be careful, don't try, don't hurry, don't risk it, don't, don't, don't…" Her voice rose with each repetition.

He'd only thought he hurt before. His brain ached with the effort of trying to understand. All he'd done to help his daughter had only added insult, literally, to injury. His heart broke out of pity for both of them, but especially for the eager spirit he seemed to have crushed. His soul—well, his soul had forsaken hope nine years ago. Any little stirrings due to occurrences in the last few weeks could easily be extinguished. Or so he wished.

Meanwhile, he had Ginny to deal with. "I'm going to have to think about what you've said. I certainly didn't mean to cause problems for you. We'll have to talk more and see what we can do to change your situation, make it more comfortable.

"But…" He steeled himself to look her in the eye. "You deliberately created a disaster today on the cookout. You owe the girls and Mrs. Manion an apology. I think I know what the outcome of today's stunt will be, and you probably do, too. Maybe that's what you wanted to achieve. I'll call Mrs. Manion tomorrow and talk things over with her. I expect you to write a note to the girls in the troop for her to read at the next meeting."

"Now," he said with a deep breath, sitting back against the seat, "let's finish our dinner."

Though they pretended to eat, they had a large box of food to take home when they were ready to leave. Ginny wanted to go to the bathroom before they drove home. As Rob waited, his mind blank, Abby slipped into the booth across the table from him.

"What in the world happened? You both look like the world ended."

"Ginny brought a gun—unloaded—to the cookout." Abby sat back. "Oh, wow."

"It's not the first time she's disrupted an event."

"No…" She looked at him from under her lashes. "She was a handful when they came here to work on their cooking badge."

"Ah. Valerie didn't tell me that." He shrugged. "Ginny says I'm overprotective. I don't…trust her…I guess is what she thinks."

"You're a great father, Rob." Abby put her hand over his. "She's a kid—take what she's saying with a grain of salt. Make that half a pound of salt."

He called up a half smile. "Maybe. But I doubt that'll be a problem now. I expect Valerie will ask me to take Ginny out of the troop."

"That would mean—"

"Yeah." Ginny came out of the restroom and he got to his feet. "We'll see you soon, Abby. Thanks."

She stood, as well, and gave Ginny a hug before they left. "Y'all take care."

As an effort of good faith, Rob let Ginny take her bath alone that night. He sat in his chair in the living room the entire time, butt barely settled on the edge of the seat, head bowed and hands gripped hard together. The cry for help he anticipated didn't come. Ginny left the bathroom a wreck, but she survived her first solo bath.

While he supposed that was a good thing, somehow the outcome only made Rob feel worse.

He still reserved the right to tuck her into bed. "Sleep tight," he told her, as he did every night. "I love you."

She peered up at him in the dim light. "I—I'm sorry."

"I know." He kissed her on the forehead. "It's okay, Ginny. Everybody makes mistakes. The point is to learn to do better the next time."

Back in the living room, he dropped into his chair and closed his eyes. "If only I could figure out what better actually means…"

HE DIDN'T WAIT for Valerie to call him on Sunday. As soon as he finished dinner at his mom's after church, he drove straight home and walked through the backyard to Jenny's house.

Grace and Connor were outside, playing with Buttercup, as usual.

Rob gave them a wave as he passed. "Hey, you two. Throw a couple of Frisbees for me."

The two children stared at him wide-eyed, as if they couldn't believe how brave he was for even showing up. But maybe that was simply his imagination.

Jenny called, "Come in," when he knocked on the back door. She sat with Valerie in the kitchen, both of them drinking iced tea. The table was covered with papers, the papers covered with lists, written in Jenny's scribble and Valerie's precise print.

"What's going on?" He tried to be casual. "Deciding early this year who's been naughty and nice?"

Jenny got to her feet. "We're planning the annual Warren Halloween party, and we volunteered you for the ugly monster. Typecasting, you know."

"So you'll be the wicked witch? Or was that Medusa, with snakes for hair?"

"Be careful, or I'll turn you into stone with a single glance." Jenny punched him in the arm on her way to the back door. "I'm going out to play with the kids." The slam of the screened panel left him staring at Valerie across the kitchen.

"Do you want some tea?" She stood up and moved to the counter. "Jenny made it, so it's good."

"Sure." While she was so far away, he moved to the table and sat in a chair on the opposite side. She came close enough to slide his glass across the surface to him. Not close enough to touch.

"So how'd the rest of the cookout go?" he asked, when she sat down again. "Were the stars bright?"

"Beautiful." She nodded. "We saw Orion and the Pleiades Mars…everything we meant to find."

"Was dinner tasty?"

"Not too bad. It was a little chilly by then, so the stew felt good."

"Everybody returned safe and sound?"

"Most of them were asleep when we got back to school. Their parents carried them home and that was that."

He took a long draw on his tea. "How many phone calls have you taken this morning about…Ginny's stunt?"

"I think I've heard from every parent who wasn't there. I assured them that there was absolutely no danger because she hadn't brought ammunition."

"And concluded with the news that Ginny would not be coming back to the troop meetings."

Her shoulders slumped. "I don't see what else I can do, Rob. The safety of the other girls is paramount, and I—I really can't trust Ginny right now. I know she didn't intend to hurt anybody yesterday. But—"

"I understand. It was a stupid thing to do. We've talked about it some, but we'll talk some more. She's written a note for you and the troop." He took the folded sheet out of his pocket. "She really is sorry she caused a disturbance." At least, he was pretty sure she was sorry.

"Thanks." Valerie took the paper and creased the folds yet again. "Maybe later in the year, she can come back. Or next year…"

"Maybe." He got to his feet and carried his empty glass to the counter. "Ginny and I have some work to do before then."

"Sure." Valerie turned in her chair, watching him. "Rob, I know it's hard. I'm so sorry I have to—"

"Yeah, it's hard. And I'm the one who should apologize." His voice, tight and controlled, belonged to someone else. He kept his back to her, staring out the window, so she couldn't read his face.

"I don't understand."

"First, because I didn't see how much trouble Ginny was causing."

"Well—"

"Second, because I have to leave you without an assistant leader. Do you think you'll be able to find somebody to step in and help you out?"

Stupid, but she hadn't expected this. "I…I can find somebody, I'm sure." A knee-jerk reaction— Valerie wasn't the least bit sure…of anything.

She wanted to protest, to beg him not to leave the troop. To leave *her.* Which made no sense. If his daughter wasn't in the troop, why should he stay on as leader? "I wish this hadn't happened."

"Me, too. For a lot of reasons."

She thought she knew what he meant. But to say anything about what had happened between them personally would be like turning the knife in the wound.

And she, at least, couldn't stand the pain. "I appreciate all you've done already. You've given the girls a lot of fun and helped them learn at the same time."

When he turned, his half smile was doubtful. "I've had the advantage of a terrific example in leadership." For a long moment, he gazed at her across the kitchen. "You take care."

"Rob—" He paused on his way to the door, but didn't look back. "We'll still be neighbors. I mean… I guess we'll be staying with Jenny for a while, until I can find another house and get moved again."

"Sure." His shoulders lifted on a deep breath. "I imagine we'll run into each other all the time."

Meaning he wouldn't try to see her. "Of course."

And then the door slammed shut behind him. Through the screen, she could hear his deep voice and Jenny's lighter one, and the kids calling to the dog as she ran around the yard. Above the trees, the sky was a clear, sharp blue, the sunlight fresh and cool.

Just a peaceful Southern Sunday afternoon…on which her fragile longings for a future with Rob Warren had crumbled into dust.

HELP FOR THE TROOP came from an unexpected direction. After a horrendous Monday at the office, Valerie decided she and the kids would eat dinner at the diner, if only to give Jenny a night off after her weekend at work. There were other places to eat in New Skye, but nowhere quite as comfortable as Charlie's, nowhere else she felt so taken care of. Just seeing Abby's smile when they walked in improved her day one hundred percent…to merely awful.

"Y'all are early today." Abby led them to a booth beside the windows. "Sit down and relax. You want the usual to drink?"

"Soda for Grace and Connor," Valerie said. "But I think I'll have iced tea. Sweet."

"Got it."

While they waited, Valerie looked across the table to Grace. "How was your day? How'd that math test go?"

"Pretty good. I got a perfect score on my spelling test last Friday."

"Great. You're really settling into your subjects."

Grace nodded. "There was a lot of talk at school today about…the gun."

"I expect so."

"The boys kept bugging Ginny to tell them about it. Out on the playground, they kept following her around. And she couldn't get away because they're faster than she is. Finally…" She took a deep breath and hesitated.

"Yes?"

"Finally, she hit Corbin Lloyd with one of her crutches. He's such a jerk, and a big baby, besides. She just banged him across the knees, and he fell down and started crying. The teachers took them both away, and Ginny didn't come back for the rest of the day."

Poor Rob would have had to deal with all of that, on top of the traumas of the weekend. "Was Corbin hurt?"

Grace snorted. "No. He was bragging on the bus home that he'd done it just to get her in trouble."

"You heard him say that?" Grace nodded. "You should tell the principal tomorrow. It's not fair to blame Ginny for something she didn't do."

Grace thought for a minute. "You're right. Anna Padgett heard him, too. I'll get her to come with me."

Abby returned with their drinks and took orders for cheeseburgers and fries all around. Grace read her story for the next day in school and Valerie played tic-tac-toe with Connor while they waited for their food. When Abby brought the plates, she brought refills on the Manions' drinks and an extra glass for herself.

"Mind if I sit down a minute?" she asked. Grace scooted over and Abby dropped into the booth with a sigh.

"The dinner rush will begin in about fifteen minutes—I'd like to relax for the last time until eight o'clock."

"I don't know how you have the energy for all of this." Valerie played with her fries, not at all interested in really eating. "You work too hard."

"We all work hard, don't we? You, Rob…everybody. That's just the way it is. At least I don't have to wear a suit and stockings every day." She glanced down at her white shirt and khaki slacks. Her foot, in a white sneaker, sat toe-to-toe with Valerie's serviceable leather pump. "And shoes with heels—I couldn't stand that every day."

"I couldn't cook every day, all day," Valerie said. "I'd rather wear heels."

"I guess we're all in the right place, then, aren't we?" Abby sipped her glass of tea. "I saw Rob on Saturday. He was really upset."

"We all were."

"I guess Ginny's not coming back."

"Neither of them are."

"I was afraid of that." Abby shook her head. "I know how much he enjoyed the girls."

"I know how much easier he made my job. I don't know what to do without him. None of the other mothers will agree to be assistant leader."

"Even now?"

"I spoke with every family last night. They all had some excuse."

After a pause, Abby said, "Well…does the assistant leader have to have a daughter in the troop?"

"Not at all." Valerie smiled. "That's just the biggest

leverage I can use—you want your daughter to have this experience, you have to make it happen."

"So you could recruit somebody outside the troop, even outside the school."

"Sure. Did you have someone in mind who might be interested?"

Abby took a deep breath. "Me."

GO! REGULATIONS required paperwork to be submitted when leaders volunteered or resigned, when accidents happened, when girls were requested to leave the troop…a form had been created for any and all contingencies.

Predictably, the number and kind of reports Valerie had turned in during the last few weeks attracted attention from higher-ups, who summoned her to an interview at the district office.

Afterward, she consoled herself with lunch at the diner.

"Why the long face?" Abby set down a glass of iced tea—just what Valerie would have ordered, if asked.

"We've got a problem."

"The troop, you mean?" Abby slid into the seat at the table.

Valerie nodded. "Our big camping trip is ten days away. But headquarters may refuse to allow us to go."

"Because…?"

"We don't have the correctly trained personnel." She explained about camping training, first aid certification and the need to have two people separately qualified for one of the other. "I can't be everything. I have to be the camp person or the first aider."

"Couldn't a nurse or doctor do first aid?"

"That was my hope. But the parent in the troop who's a doctor is on call that weekend. Of the three nurses, one has three other kids under five years old and a husband who has to work. One's on duty that weekend, and the third hates camping and won't even allow her daughter to go on the trip with us."

"That's mean."

"It's definitely weird, considering she signed up for Girls Outdoors! You'd think she'd anticipate camping as part of the experience." Valerie propped her forehead on the heels of her hands. "If I don't find a qualified person, I'll have to cancel the trip. Not a tragedy, but—"

"But such a shame." Abby slid out of the booth. "What do you want for lunch, sweetie?"

"A tossed salad sounds okay." She couldn't think of a single food worth the trouble of eating these days, but she did have to eat.

"Right."

Abby went toward the kitchen and Valerie propped her head in her hands again. She thought she could just about fall asleep right here in the diner. Maybe Charlie would rent her the booth for an hour…

"Hey, Ms. Manion. How are you?" She was so close to sleep she thought she'd dreamed his voice. Then a warm hand shook her shoulder gently. "Valerie? You okay?"

Looking up, she found Rob standing beside her, a worried line between his sandy eyebrows.

"Sure." She blinked hard, and shook her head. "I'm fine. How are you?" Contrary to their assumptions, they hadn't seen each other at all in the last two weeks. Between rainy fall weather and her long hours at work, Connor and Grace hadn't had much opportunity to play outside and wander in Rob's direction. Or was that just her excuse?

"I'm great," he said, in answer to her question. "Working pretty hard these days, trying to keep Dad from doing too much."

"Is he feeling good?" Rob had lost some weight, she thought. And couldn't really afford it. He looked as tired as she felt. "Why don't you sit down with me? I'm getting a crick in my neck again."

His smile was strained. "Thanks." He took Abby's place. "The doctor's pretty pleased, overall, except we still can't get him to quit smoking."

Abby arrived with a tray. "Good to see you," she told Rob, setting down his glass of iced tea. "I'll get you a cheeseburger in just a minute." She put a dinner plate in front of Valerie. "You need more than just a salad, so I fixed a salad plate—tuna, chicken, pasta salads, plus the tossed. And some biscuits hot out of the oven." She nodded. "That'll get you going again." Before Valerie could protest, Abby had disappeared in the direction of the kitchen.

Rob was laughing. "Abby's mission in life is to keep us all well fed. Don't fight it—she always wins in the end."

"I know." Valerie sighed, then took a bite of tuna salad. "The great thing is that her food's so good, you get hungrier once you take a taste, and you want to eat everything."

"She's definitely got a talent." He took a drink of tea, then glanced out the window. "How's the troop doing? Are you and the girls getting ready for the big camping trip? Abby told me she's been helping you out at the meetings."

"We've had a couple of good meetings. Abby's a wonder with the girls—they all think of her as a big sister." But every meeting someone still asked when Mr. Warren would be back.

"Here you go. Enjoy." Abby slid Rob's plate in front of him and rushed away to a table across the room.

Rob picked up his burger. "I wonder when her batteries are gonna run down. The woman never rests. Is she going with you on the campout?"

Valerie shook her head. "Charlie can't spare her from work. She told me that before she volunteered to help with the meetings."

"So…who's going with you?"

"Keisha's mom, again. Anna's mom. Usually there are a few parents who will volunteer for everything, and a few who won't volunteer at all."

"Do you have a first aider?"

Valerie shook her head.

"A camping leader?"

She shrugged. "Me, I guess."

"How are you gonna go, if you don't have the required people?"

Using her fork, she pushed her chicken salad into a nice, neat dome. "I don't know," she said, still staring at her plate. "Unless…"

She looked up and pinned him with her gaze. "Unless you agree to come with me."

CHAPTER FOURTEEN

ROB PUT OFF giving her an answer at the diner, and by the Sunday before the campout arrived, Valerie still didn't know if he would help her salvage the trip. The weather had been dreary all day, with a chilly drizzle knocking some of the prettiest leaves off the trees. Valerie spent hours on the phone, calling about homes for rent and for sale, without much luck. Most of the houses she heard about didn't fit her budget, her family's needs or her ideas about where in New Skye she wanted to live.

Maybe the problem was simply that they were happy right where they were.

Rob left home in the middle of the afternoon to take a call from work and Jenny walked over to stay with her niece because Ginny refused to come play with Grace and Connor. Just before dusk, Buttercup needed to go out and Valerie went to stand on the porch to call the dog in as soon as possible. As she surveyed the yard, she noticed a splotch of red under the trees, near the back gate. In another minute, the splotch resolved into the red sweatshirt Ginny wore. To Valerie's amazement, the girl had propped her crutches against the fence and dragged one of Rob's metal chairs through to Jenny's side so she could sit down to pet Buttercup.

"Hello, out there." Valerie waved from the porch. "Aren't you getting wet?"

Ginny hesitated a long moment. "It's okay," she called back.

She was tempted to accept the brush-off, but decided to try once more. "I just made hot chocolate. Want some?"

Another pause. "Okay."

Buttercup came bounding over the grass, with Ginny following, and Valerie went quickly inside to get a mug of instant cocoa. She stepped out again just as Ginny slowly climbed the steps.

"It's a good thing your aunt Jenny put chairs out here," Valerie commented as she sat down. "Otherwise we'd have to sit on the steps in the rain." Panting with the pleasure of her run, Buttercup collapsed at her feet.

"I can't sit on steps. It hurts." Ginny reached for the mug and dropped into the other chair. "So everybody makes sure there are chairs for me."

"That's considerate of them."

She didn't respond, but sipped the cocoa with a sigh of pleasure.

As Valerie gazed through the mist hanging just beyond the edge of the porch roof, she decided to seize the chance which had presented itself. "You know, I asked your dad to come on the camping trip with the GO! troop."

"You did?" Ginny's wide eyes conveyed that Rob hadn't said anything to his daughter about the issue. "Are we...is he going?"

"He hasn't told me yet. Do you think he should?"

The shield came up again. "Whatever."

"No, not 'whatever.'" Valerie sat forward, bracing her forearms on her knees. "Tell me what you think, Ginny. I really do want to know."

"He probably wants to go," she said finally, quietly. "He likes the troop. And Grace and Connor. And…you." The last word was a whisper.

"We all like him."

Ginny hunched in her rocker, staring into her mug. Valerie reached over and put a hand on one bony knee. "We want to like you, too."

Without looking up, the girl shook her head. "Nobody likes me."

"There's a song that starts that way, you know."

Surprisingly, Ginny started to sing. "Nobody likes me, everybody hates me, think I'll eat some worms…"

Valerie laughed. "Right."

Ginny's dawning smile faded. "Well, it's true."

"Why is it true?"

"Because I'm…handicapped. They hate me 'cause I'm different."

"How are you handicapped?"

She looked up, startled. "I use crutches and braces. I can't play games. My fingers don't work."

"Those are challenges. But that's not your handicap."

Ginny lowered her eyebrows and scrunched up her forehead. "I don't understand."

"Your handicap is here." Valerie brushed two fingers over the little girl's temple. "And here." She put a hand over her own heart. "Your thoughts and feelings about yourself are your handicaps."

In the next instant, Ginny burst into tears.

WHEN ROB CAME HOME from rescuing a teenager and his date who'd locked themselves out of her dad's Cadillac, he found only Mat the Cat waiting for him on the couch.

"Hello?" He walked through the house, still wearing his jacket. "Anybody here?" No answer. A glance through the window showed him an empty backyard...but the gate to Jenny's house was open.

He trudged out into the rain again and crossed the leaf-littered grass. Just on the other side of the gate, Buttercup hit him with her muddy paws, leaving perfect prints on his jeans.

"Get down, silly dog. Down." He pushed her out of the way and then, in the next step, nearly tripped over his own lawn furniture. "What the...? Who moved my chair?"

As he emerged from under the tree cover, he found the answer to his question...and his missing person, gazing at him from Jenny's back porch.

"Search and rescue to base camp," he said, holding his hand up to his mouth and imitating the crackle of a walkie-talkie. "Suspects have been located." The two women sat in the rockers on the porch. Ginny had cuddled into Valerie's lap.

"What's going on?" he asked from the bottom of the steps. "Can I come up, or is this ladies only?"

"Make yourself at home," Jenny said. "We're admiring the weather."

"Liquid sunshine," Rob agreed. "Did you move that chair to this side of the fence, Gin?" She nodded without taking her head off Valerie's shoulder. While he loved seeing his daughter cradled in this woman's arms, he didn't understand. "Why?"

"I wanted to play with Buttercup. I can do that. I can move chairs by myself, too."

He nodded. "I guess you can."

"I take baths alone."

"You proved that to me."

"I walk a lot faster than most people think I do. I bet I could even run, if I wanted to."

Deep breath. "We can work on that."

She shook her head. "I can work on it."

Rob glanced at Valerie and got a nod in confirmation that confused him even more. "What does that mean?"

Ginny answered. "You have to stop taking…" She drew in a deep breath. "…taking such good care of me."

"That's my job, Ginny."

"But I want to grow up. You have to let me."

He looked from Valerie to Jenny and back again. "Did you tell her to say this?"

"No, Daddy." Again, his daughter answered. "We talked, but this is what I want. I don't want to be handicapped anymore."

"Honey, you—".

"I'm probably gonna be challenged my whole life. I'm not gonna be handicapped."

Understanding came to him very slowly. But by the

time he'd carried his daughter back across the wet lawns and into the house, by the time they'd warmed up and eaten their pizza supper and talked for a couple of hours, Rob had a handle on Ginny's new independence. She walked to her room that night—alone—and got herself ready for bed.

When she called, Rob came in. "You're all grown up," he said, noticing that she'd put her clothes in the basket, straightened her dresser and gotten her own glass of water before climbing under the covers. "I'm out of a job around here, I guess."

"Nope." She held out her arms. "You still get to kiss me good-night."

"Ah." He held her close, blinking back tears. "That's the kind of work I really, really like to do."

VALERIE DIDN'T SAY anything to the troop about Rob's agreement to join them for the camping trip. She had conceded that Ginny should come with him, but the rest of the girls didn't need to know in advance, not even Grace. She trusted absolutely in Rob's promise that Ginny wouldn't cause trouble this time. More significantly, she trusted Ginny herself. After more consultation, headquarters agreed with her assessment and gave their trip the go-ahead. The weather then turned gorgeous. At last, their GO! troop was on the move.

There were cheers in the school parking lot early Saturday morning when the girls in the troop realized Rob would be coming with them. A few of the girls ran up to Ginny's side of the black van and spoke to her, too. More than a couple of parents pulled Valerie over with questions, even protests, but she convinced them, through her own certainty, that there would be no unpleasant surprises from anyone this weekend.

Even Connor had sworn he would follow every rule. Rob's mother had planned to keep him, but at the last minute, Connor begged to come along and Valerie couldn't refuse. He really did like camping…and Rob Warren.

The morning went well as they unloaded sleeping bags and duffels from the cars, plus all the food and equipment they would need for cooking dinner and breakfast on Sunday morning. Their campsite belonged to the GO! organization and had been fitted with platform tents—heavy canvas covers erected on very sturdy wooden floors about three feet off the ground. The girls were delighted with the shelters.

"So far, so good," Rob commented, as they watched little girls flit in and out of each other's tents. "They seem fairly comfortable."

"I like this option for the girls—it's a good transition between sleeping in a house and sleeping on the ground."

"It's gotta be more comfortable than sleeping on the ground. I let Con have control of the setup in our tent. I think he's swept the floor twice, now."

"I don't know if he's more excited about sleeping outdoors, or sharing with you."

"I'm pretty happy to be here, myself." His gaze was warm, his smile tender. "Thanks."

"I'm the one who should be grateful."

"We're just a couple of really special people, then, aren't we?"

He always made her laugh. "You said it."

Midmorning, Rob led another hike along a wide, winding path that took them by easy stages to the river running through the property. He pointed out deer and possum tracks, discovered an old, long-shed snakeskin and a rock with a fossil fern imprinted on its surface. The girls wanted to find their own, of course, and they spent a peaceful hour by the water, then hiked back up to the site for the brown-bag lunches they'd brought with them.

Stick animals and spatter painting provided part of the afternoon craft project, along with leaf rubbings and nature stamps. About three o'clock, they set the girls free to play on their own for a while before dinner and everyone vanished into the magical tents. The other parent chaperones headed for their own tents to snatch a nap, leaving Rob and Valerie sitting on the logs around the fire pit.

The occasional muted scream and an avalanche of giggles filtered into the still air from the tents, the first of which were set a long distance away from the fire and any chance of floating sparks. "Good thing you came up and swept all the spiders out of the tents yesterday," Valerie commented. "We'd have some hysterical girls on our hands, otherwise."

"Isn't our GO! motto 'Forewarned Is Forearmed,' or something like that?"

She pretended to glare at him. "Think Ahead."

"Same thing." He ducked the stick she threw at him. "I haven't had a chance to talk to you about last weekend," he said after a pause. "Or, come to think of it, about anything at all for a really long time. I appreciate your help with Ginny."

"She did the hard part. I just listened."

"How's the house hunt going?"

"Not great. I can't seem to find anything I like."

"You will. Meantime, nobody's in a hurry for you to leave. Jen really likes having y'all around—you give her something to think about, people to talk to."

Valerie sighed. "I love being there, but—"

"I guess independence has its advantages, though. I gotta admit, I really like knowing that I'm the only one cooking, cleaning and doing laundry at my house most of the time." Picking up a nearby stick, he started breaking off little pieces of bark and throwing them into the fire pit, keeping his gaze fixed on the task. His expression gave nothing away—he might have been reading the label off a soup can.

"Rob…" She blew out a sharp breath. "You could have help with the chores."

He nodded. "Paying the bills. That's another pleasure I wouldn't want to share with anybody else."

"You're absurd."

"What I like best, though, is that great feeling of getting in between cold sheets every night. Or waking up at 3:00 a.m. with this wide spread of empty bed to roll around on. Oh, and not having to try to talk to anybody else when I'm worried, or stressed, or just plain mad. I hate having people get involved with me at times like that." More bark flicked into the charred center of the circle. His stick was nearly stripped clean.

"That's not what independence means," Valerie said,

keeping her voice low, her hands gripped tightly to-gether. "I want to be able to use my own judgment, choose according to my values. Independence is about respecting yourself as much as you respect other people, cooperating because you believe it's the right thing to do. Not because somebody has to win."

"I knew that." Rob looked up, and now he wasn't the least bit detached. In his eyes she read anger, impatience...and a desperate sadness. "I wasn't sure you did."

WHEN HER MOM HAD ASKED, Grace had said it would be okay to share a tent with Ginny. And she'd named some other girls, like Keisha, who would be nice about that.

Playing in the big, dim space was fun. They each picked a corner to sleep in—except for Ginny, who didn't come in after they finished the stick animals and leaf prints. Grace chose to set up her stuff in a corner near the back of the tent closest to the woods and moved Ginny's sleeping bag, body pillows and clothes duffel nearby. Nobody else had been able to bring as much gear as Ginny, but they couldn't expect her to sleep on the hard wood floor.

"Let's play Truth or Dare," Anna said. "C'mon—everybody sit in the middle of the floor. We each get a question, and we have to tell the truth or...or..."

"Walk barefoot outside after dark," Keisha said.

Grace shook her head. "That's against the rules."

"So what?" Anna rolled her eyes. "Nobody'll know. Unless you get bitten by a black widow spider...or a rattlesnake, or chased by a mountain lion."

Keisha shivered. "I don't want a spider bite."

"So you better tell the truth. Here's the first question: Have you ever kissed a boy?"

They all giggled, and Keisha said yes, and Anna made her tell them who.

"My turn," Keisha said. "Have you ever stolen anything?"

Tanya, the fourth girl in their tent, blushed a little. "Yeah…I stole a candy bar at the store last summer. Nobody ever caught me, so I did it a couple more times. Those clerks at the grocery store are sooo stupid."

She turned to Grace. "Okay, here's your question. Do you like Ginny Warren?"

Grace opened her mouth to answer, but Anna cut in. "Don't you think she's just the bitchiest, ugliest girl in school? I hate her—she never smiles, and she's always complaining."

"I know," Keisha said. "Sometimes I think about coming up behind her and kicking those stupid crutches out from under her, just to watch her fall."

Grace tried again. "I think she can be—"

"A pain in the butt," Tanya said, and the girls laughed. "I really like Mr. Warren, but I wish he could've left that little witch at home."

"Hey, maybe that's what she'll be for Halloween," Anna cried. "She can fly around on one of her crutches, instead of a broom!"

There was a sudden scuffling noise outside the tent.

Grace glimpsed Ginny's face in the crack between the tent flaps and then heard the clunky sound of crutches on the wooden steps.

"Ginny? Ginny, wait." She ran outside, but found the clearing in front of their tent empty. "You can't leave camp," she called. "Come back, Ginny. They didn't mean it." That was a lie, and she knew it as well as Ginny did.

"What are you yelling about?" Connor stood at the edge of the woods, near the tent he shared with Ginny's dad. "Ginny went that way." He pointed into the deep woods behind her tent.

Grace ran over and grabbed his hand. "Come on. We've got to bring her back."

He resisted her pull. "No. I'm not going anywhere with her."

For once, Grace was strong enough to make him do as she said. "You're coming with me. We're going after her. Now."

By the time they headed down the path, Ginny was far ahead of them, even with her crutches. Unlike the trail they'd walked in the morning, this one led steeply downhill. Worse, the dirt was damp and slippery, too heavily shaded by tall trees to dry out in the sun. Grace feared that the next minute would bring sounds of a fall from up ahead.

Instead, Connor tripped several times. She herself fell and scooted along on her bottom in the mud. Tears stung her eyes, but she finally stopped and found her footing.

Connor slid down to her. "Are you okay?"

Grace nodded and took off after Ginny again, with Connor close behind her. She could hear the other girl crashing through the bushes and vines as she tried to hurry over the bumpy ground.

"Ginny? Ginny, stop," she called. "You're gonna get

hurt." But the noise ahead of her continued, and she didn't seem to be catching up. How could somebody on crutches go so fast?

The path ended suddenly, and Grace had to skip to the side to keep from running right into Ginny where she stood at the edge of the trees. Connor, thank goodness, had time to stop.

"Look at that." Ginny pointed to a cabin just in front of them. "Do you think somebody lives there?"

"It looks like it's empty and locked to me." Grace tugged at the sleeve of Ginny's shirt. "Let's go back, Ginny. We're not supposed to leave camp without telling somebody."

"I want to look at this house." She started forward across the sandy space.

"We have to go back." Grace practically jumped up and down, she was so irritated, so worried. "They're going to start looking for us."

Ginny shook her head. "This place is awesome." She went to the side of the house and looked over the fence. "Wow. It's on the river."

Grace took a single peek and immediately felt dizzy as she saw the rush of water so far below them. "No, it's a long way above the river." Grace put a hand on Ginny's shoulder. "Come on. Please."

But Connor, the brat, had stepped onto the porch of the cabin and put his hand on the door handle. He looked over and grinned. "Wouldn't it be great if the door wasn't locked?"

At the word, he pushed on the panel itself…and the door creaked open.

"All right," he yelled, and vanished inside. Ginny shook off Grace's hand, wheeled around on her crutches, and followed as fast as she could to the porch.

"I'm going up to camp," Grace called. With her back to the cabin, she marched across the sandy clearing between the house and the trail. "You two can stay here and get in trouble. You oughta be used to it by now, anyway."

At the foot of the path, she stopped again. What would her mother expect? Should she stay here and watch out for Connor and Ginny? Or should she get help?

Connor stuck his head out the cabin door. "Grace, come in here! Tell us what this is—I've never seen anything like it!"

She tried, she really did, but her curiosity won out. With a last glance at the trail, Grace turned and ran toward the cabin.

The inside was dark, and she leaned back against the door as her eyes took a second to adjust. Along the right wall, a narrow wooden staircase led up into even more darkness. To her left, the room was pretty much empty—no furniture at all. Empty, except for the huge round stone in the middle of the room.

"What is it?" Ginny leaned on her crutches at one side of the rock. "What's this thing on top?"

Grace followed her pointing finger to the machinery above the stone. Made of metal, the top was a funnel with the narrow end forming a tube, which entered a hole in the center of the big stone. When she walked around the stone, she saw that a belt beneath the lower half would cause the bottom stone to rotate under the upper section. Anything which fell between the two stones would be ground to powder…

"A mill," she said. "This is a flour mill. You pour the wheat in up there." She pointed to the top of the funnel. "And it comes down between the stones to be crushed into flour." At the back window, she saw how the mill got its power. "See down below—the river works the water wheel, which turns these different belts and gears to change the direction of the force, so the final belt turns this lower stone to grind the grain."

"Awesome," Ginny repeated. "The farmers brought their wheat here and took home flour."

"They probably had to pay to have the wheat ground," Grace said, remembering some of the stories she'd read over the years. "And they might have to leave a sack of flour for the miller, too." She looked into the room again and found Connor climbing up onto the millstone. "That's a really bad idea," she told him. "Get down right now."

"I just want to see what's in here." He got to his feet on top of the stone and stood on tiptoe, trying to peer in the top. Before she knew what he was doing, he stuck his arm up into the funnel. "There's something up there—I can see it but I can't…quite…reach."

"It's probably a dead mouse," Ginny said with a laugh.

Connor gasped and looked at her. "Is not."

"Is too."

"You lie." But he wiggled, trying to jerk his arm out of the funnel. "Grace, come help me. I'm stuck."

"I told you so." With a pretend sigh, she climbed onto the stone with him, grasped his arm at the elbow and pulled. "What have you done now?"

"Ow! Stop!" Connor pushed at her with his free hand. "That hurts."

"Well, it wouldn't, if you'd listened to me." She pulled again, trying to be a little gentler. "Relax your hand, dummy. Don't make a fist."

"I'm not!" Still, the hand wouldn't come back through whatever hole now held it. Grace couldn't see because Connor's arm was in the way. "Help me, Grace. Get me out!"

"Stop yelling." She couldn't get her own hand far enough into the tube to help. "Just relax, okay? You probably made your hand swell, trying to pull it through. Let's rest a minute and then we'll try again."

But rest made no difference at all. Connor was completely trapped by the stupid mill machine.

Grace sat down on the stone. "Ginny, you've got to go back to camp and bring some adults down here. It's getting dark outside and they don't know where we are. I can't get Connor's hand out without help. Can you find your way back by yourself?"

"Yeah, I could." She was sitting on the stairs, her crutches put aside, and didn't make a move to get up.

"Well? Go."

"One problem," Ginny said.

"What?"

"When you came in, you closed the door. And now it's locked…from the outside."

KEEPING HIS RECENT lessons in mind, Rob had tried all day to worry less about Ginny, to let her operate independently as much as possible. Grace had helped get her gear to the tent this morning and been her buddy on the hike. Seeing them connect was a decent reward for his effort.

But when they called the girls to the fire circle to begin preparations for dinner, a cold fist grabbed his chest and wrung him out. He didn't see Ginny anywhere.

Then he noticed Valerie's wide eyes. She stepped closer to him. "Do you see Grace?"

"No. Nor…" he added, checking very carefully, "is there a trace of our third Musketeer. Where did they go?"

She held up a hand for quiet, and the girls settled down. "Does anybody know where Grace and Connor and Ginny are?"

Eyes wide, most of the girls shook their heads. Keisha and Anna just looked at each other. Rob crouched down in front of them. "Grace and Ginny are in your tent. When's the last time you saw them?"

Anna fidgeted with her shirttail. "Uh…we were just playing games."

"And?"

"Ginny was outside somewhere. Grace saw her and went out, too."

"Did you see where they were going?"

Both girls shook their heads. And though he wasn't sure they were telling the whole truth, he believed they didn't know exactly where Grace and Ginny had gone.

"I'll go look for them." Valerie went to the supply box for the portable first aid kit and a flashlight. "You're the camp certified person, so you should stay with the rest of the girls."

Rob took hold of her arm and turned her to face him. "You might need someone to carry a kid."

"I could carry any one of the three of them, Rob."

He couldn't stay behind. Simply could not. "I…I've done some tracking."

"Me, too." She put her hand over his. "I'd hate to be the one to stay here. Especially if Ginny was mine. I know you're worried. But the rest of these girls are just as important, and they're depending on you."

By sheer force of will, he loosened his fingers from around her arm and let his hand drop. "You're the boss. We'll get dinner going while you find those rascals and bring them back."

She gave him a wink and a smile. "Sounds good." Flashlight in one hand, first aid kit in the other, she headed for the perimeter of the camp.

"Valerie?" When she looked back, he smacked his right fist into his left palm. "Tell those three—from me—that it's gonna be at least a week before any of them sits down without a pillow under their butt!"

CHAPTER FIFTEEN

TRACKING GINNY, Grace and Connor didn't take much skill—the three of them had thundered down the slope behind the girls' tents like a herd of dizzy buffalo. The round holes made by the ends of the crutches were deep enough in the soft soil to use for setting fence posts, indicating a level of strength—or determination—Ginny rarely got credit for. Grace and Con had left clear prints with the bottoms of their sneakers. Valerie kept her flashlight trained on the trail, more to be sure she didn't trip than in fear of missing a vital change of direction.

The path bottomed out quickly to the clearing for the mill house. She'd known about the historic building and had intended to bring the troop down here tomorrow, to talk about using natural resources in conjunction with the water wheel. She couldn't help smiling as she crossed to the front porch. The girls and Connor had simply beat her to it.

"Hey, Grace! Ginny! Are you in there?"

"Mommy?" Grace's voice held a note of panic. "Mommy, get us out of here."

"Are Ginny and Connor with you?"

"Yes, yes. Oh, please, open the door."

Valerie stepped up onto the porch and reached for the door handle. "Why don't you—" She tugged, and then pulled hard. "Unlock the door, for heaven's sake. It's getting dark out here."

"It's darker in here." Ginny sounded calmer than Grace. "But the door won't unlock from the inside. We can't get out."

"That's ridiculous." Hands on her hips, Valerie stalked across the porch. "Can we open the window?"

"It's boarded up," Ginny pointed out, just about the time Valerie realized she couldn't see into the room on the other side of the glass. "I don't have anything to pry the nails out. My crutches are too thick."

"Don't use your crutches, sweetie." Valerie explored the end of the small building, but the wall there was solid. Nailed to the edge of the house was a heavy post which supported a chain-link fence. Far, far below, she could hear the water flow—much faster than at the spot on the river they'd visited this morning. She shivered at the thought of falling without ever having seen the drop-off.

Back at the door, she shone her light on the heavy black lock. "There's an iron box on this side, with a knob and a key hole." Gripping the ball, she turned. Hard. With both hands. "The stupid knob doesn't turn. What's on your side?"

"Nothing. Just wood."

Valerie suddenly realized she'd yet to hear Connor say a single word. "Connor is with you, right? Is he all right? Has he fallen asleep?"

"I'm right here, Mommy." She didn't need any psychic powers to detect the fear in his voice.

"What's wrong, Connor? Are you okay?"

"I'm okay."

"But…?"

"There's a—a mill in here," Grace said. "For grinding flour. Con got his hand caught."

"Under the stone?" The words felt like razor blades in her mouth.

"No, no," Ginny said. "In the funnel thing—where the grain comes down onto the stone. He's not bleeding or anything. But he's stuck and we're afraid to pull too hard without knowing what he's stuck on."

Valerie rested her head against the rough door panel. Relief made her dizzy. "Good…good thinking." After a minute, the world stopped spinning. "Okay. We've got to get you guys out. You have no tools in there at all?"

"None, unless we take the banister apart."

"Let's save that as a last resort. Maybe I can find a log to break the window, and then push in the boards." She started to turn toward the woods again, though how she would find anything when darkness had come on so fast, she didn't know.

"Mrs. Manion?" Ginny knocked on the door. "Mrs. Manion?"

"What's wrong?"

"I was just thinking," the girl said. "My dad might be able to help."

She blew out an irritated breath. "I believe I'm strong enough—"

"I know. Oh, I know. But…*he's* a locksmith."

ROB LOOKED UP from the loose shoelace he was tying for little Karen Rogers just as Valerie emerged from the woods. When he realized she'd returned alone, his fingers stiffened. Everything inside of him petrified in an instant.

She read his reaction from fifty yards away. "They're okay," she called, using her palms as a megaphone to be sure he heard.

Rob took a breath and felt his blood start to flow again. As Valerie came striding toward the fire circle, she dropped her hands. "They got locked inside the old mill house down by the river. The window is boarded up and there's no other way out."

She stopped a short distance away and shrugged, pretending to be at a loss. "Do you know anybody who's good at picking locks?"

"I just might." He patted Karen's head and pushed to his feet. "It'll cost you, though. After-hours service, traveling charges and mileage, special equipment…"

Valerie's dimple made an appearance. "I'll pay you twice what you usually get with this outfit."

"You've got yourself a deal."

In the end, while the other two moms stayed in camp to watch the fire and be sure their foil-wrapped dinners didn't burn, Valerie, Rob and all the girls headed down the path to the old mill. Whatever creatures might have been lurking in the woods that night were certainly driven away by the flare of twenty flashlights flickering through the brush, and the noise of twenty campers trooping through the woods in the dark, singing "She'll Be Coming 'Round the Mountain."

The girls played flashlight tag in the sandy clearing

in front of the porch while Rob studied the door, aided by the powerful lamp of the big worklight Valerie held high.

"An old rim lock," he murmured, running his fingers over the box. "These usually have a knob or a key inside to open the door. Are you sure you don't see a key in there anywhere, Ginny? Grace, can you check upstairs?"

"It's dark up there!"

When he frowned at Valerie, she nodded in response. The edge of panic in Grace's voice kept increasing. He could imagine how she felt, locked in a dark room she didn't know.

"That's okay, Grace. You and Con just sit tight. I'm gonna get this thing open in a jiffy." He turned to his tool kit on the porch beside him, and pulled out the skeleton key set. "Here goes."

Iron mechanism, near water, seldom used—a great recipe for an unpickable lock. Before Rob had even tried out all his keys, Grace had come to the door. "Mommy? Mommy, I gotta get out of here."

"I know, Gracie. You need to stay calm for me a few more minutes, okay? Mr. Warren's magic will work any second now. What's Con doing?"

As if on cue, a little boy's "Oooowwww!" split the night.

The girls playing tag rushed to the porch.

"Is somebody hurt?"

"What's wrong?"

"How long will this take?"

And from several places, "I'm hungry. Can we go back to camp?"

Valerie leaned on the door and put her ear against it. "Connor? Con, baby? Are you hurt? What happened?"

"He's okay," Ginny said calmly. "He tried to pull his hand out. We just need a light to see what to do." In a much softer voice, she said. "Soon would be really good, Daddy."

"I know, Gin. I'm doing everything I know how."

He sprayed lubricant into and around the lock, hoping to unstick the mechanism. He tried unscrewing the lock itself from the door, but the bolts were stripped and rusted, defeating his efforts. Frustrated, he stood up and stretched the kinks out of his back. Then, without even thinking about it, he kicked out sideways. The heel of his boot collided solidly with the black iron lock. The damn door didn't move.

"Mommy!" Fear had taken over Grace's tone. "Mommy, Con is bleeding!"

Valerie closed her eyes and drew a deep, shaking breath. "He probably cut himself on a piece of metal when he tried to pull his hand out. Con, are you okay?"

"It hurts," his voice quaked with tears.

"I'm sorry, honey." She pressed the flats of her hands against the door. "It won't be much longer now."

Teeth gritted, Rob set to work with yet another pick. The night got quiet…the girls in the troop were all sitting on the porch just behind him, watching intently, waiting for him to succeed.

No pressure here. And no freedom to swear. How was he supposed to pick a rusty old lock without swearing?

Rob closed his eyes, eased the pressure of his fingers on the pick and concentrated on the feel of the tumblers inside the lock. If he could just get the right angle, the perfect pressure...

With a sudden screech, the lock turned, the bolt pulled back. Almost before he realized what had happened, the door swung toward him. Open.

Valerie gasped, then flung her arms around his neck in a quick, violent hug. As she turned to go inside, Grace came rushing out. "Mommy! Mommy!" She threw herself into Valerie's arms.

Rob grabbed the work lamp and pulled the door open all the way. "Ginny? Con? You guys okay?"

The light showed him a small dusty room and the millstones in the center. Connor stood on top, his arm inside the hopper which fed grain into the stones. Beside him, Ginny had somehow managed to climb up and sit on the stone next to the little boy. She had her arm around his legs.

"Hey, Daddy. Boy, are we glad to see you."

He set the lamp on the stairs and then reached out to hug his daughter with shaking hands. "Same here." He really couldn't think of anything funny to say. "Let me help you down, honey, and then I'll help my man out of his predicament."

Ginny came willingly into his hold. "Grace stayed by him a long time, but when it got dark, she was nervous. So I said I would sit with him."

"I'm impressed you got up there." Rob put her down next to her crutches and steadied her until she had her balance. "You look mighty uncomfortable," he told Con as he climbed onto the stone. "Let's get you outa here."

The little boy gazed up at him, his pale cheeks streaked with dirt and tears. "Please?"

Valerie came in at that moment, holding Grace close to her side. "Oh, baby. What a fix you're in." She reached for her son's ankles and held on tight.

The other girls in the troop had poured into the mill behind them, and now twenty flashlights explored the corners, discovering spiders and dead bugs. Footsteps trooped up the stairs to the attic, down again to the main room, and all the while they chattered about the exciting events of the evening.

Rob smiled wryly and caught Valerie's eye. "They'll sleep well tonight."

"Thank God," she said fervently. "Can you get him out?"

"Sure." He peered into the funnel from the top, using his small flashlight. "Yeah, I see. There's a little trapdoor on hinges," he told Connor, "which you've pushed open. But when you try to pull your hand down, you pull the door down, too. It cut your wrist just a little. All I have to do is hold the door, like this…" He reached his fingers in and caught the edge against Connor's skin. "And you can pull yourself out."

Connor tugged his hand free and collapsed in a heap on the stone. His mother scooped him up and went to sit on the stairs with her son in her lap. "It's just a little cut," she crooned over his sobs. "I'll get you cleaned up and bandaged and this will all be over."

Ginny looked up at Rob as he started to hop down. "Connor said he saw something up there, and when he tried to reach it, he got stuck. What did he see?"

Rob straightened up and went back to the hopper, reaching his hand in from the top so he wouldn't get stuck. His fingers closed around a piece of metal that felt different from the rest of the mechanism, and he pulled it out.

"A key, stuck in the trap." An old iron key. He jumped off the stones and crossed to the door. "What do you want to bet…?"

When he fitted the key into the lock, the bolt shot out as it should, then retreated to open the door. "How about that? My man Connor had the key all the time!"

With the door securely fastened and the key in the pocket of Rob's jeans, they all started their hike back to the campsite. Valerie carried Connor and Rob carried Grace, who was almost as worn out by their ordeal as her brother. Ginny's eyes were heavy, but she got herself back up that trail under her own steam. Rob had never been prouder.

Dinner had been removed from the coals at just the right moment, and the hamburger stew inside was delicious. They washed dishes in the dark—not the best hygiene, Valerie commented, but great for discipline and morale. And then they all sat around the campfire to make s'mores and sing.

"We've got a slight problem," Valerie told Rob once the girls started settling in their tents.

"Another one?" He winked.

"No tools required for this." She managed a tired smile. "Grace and Connor both want to sleep with me. And Grace wants Ginny with her, too. There's not room for two extras in the girls' tent. I hesitate to subject the moms to the kids, especially since they're mine—I mean, mine and yours." She felt her cheeks flame. "But the only spare tent is yours and Connor's."

Rob didn't appear to have noticed her mistake. "No problem. I'll sleep in my van, and y'all can have the tent."

"You'll be awfully cramped."

"Nope. I can recline the seat and move it back and be more comfortable, probably, than on the ground. And I can turn on the radio. I call that a real luxury."

She put her hand on his arm and looked up at him in the dark. "You really are something special, you know. I've never, ever met a man like you."

For once, he didn't turn away her compliment. "You'll have to decide what to do about that," he said seriously, and set his warm palm over her fingers for a second. "The choice is yours to make."

She didn't know how to answer, but he didn't give her the chance, anyway. He went to help Ginny and Grace move their gear to his tent, then moved his own stuff to the van. By the time Valerie got her sleeping bag and duffel relocated, Rob had vanished, not to reappear until morning.

And the morning was hectic, with breakfast to cook and clean up, yet another hike down to the mill and then on through the woods, identifying trees by their bark, plus the process of packing up to leave again. Lunch was peanut butter and jelly sandwiches, expanded by leftovers from all the previous meals. The last activity before getting in the cars to return home was a quiet moment in the fire circle.

"You've all done a good job this weekend," Valerie told the girls. "Most of you followed the rules, did your jobs, and paid attention to safety. We did have a little problem last night…"

She glanced at Grace and Ginny and Connor, sitting side-by-side. A ripple of laughter ran around the rest of the circle.

"…but I think we all handled that pretty well, too. Though no one should have left camp without telling an adult, at least nobody left without a buddy, and the buddies all took care of each other."

Now for the hard part. In the dark last night, after the other two had fallen asleep, Grace had shared the unhappy events of yesterday afternoon which led to Ginny's flight.

"I want to remind you all, while we're here together enjoying the sunshine on this beautiful day, what being a GO! troop really means. It's not just about having fun, or even about learning new skills and facts.

"Being a troop means that we're all friends. We're looking out for the other person's safety as much as we are our own. And we care about the other person's feelings as much as we do our own." Valerie looked straight at Anna, Keisha and Tanya to make her point. "How you treat other people says more about what kind of person you are than what kind of person they are. And in GO! we're trying to be the best.

"So before you say mean things about someone else—especially another GO! girl—think about what your words will say about you. Think about her feelings, and put yourself in her place. I believe you'll discover you'd much rather say something nice, or not say anything at all."

Glancing around the circle, she saw guilt in several other faces—including Ginny's. Valerie nodded, and smiled. Everybody bore some responsibility for the trouble that had surfaced yesterday. They all could take something from this lesson, even Rob and herself.

She got to her feet. "Let's make our friendship circle, sing a closing song and then we'll head back home." They all joined hands, arms crossed, and began to sing. Ginny put her crutches aside and crossed her arms to hold Rob's hand and Grace's. And when the time came to turn out by uncrossing arms, Rob and Grace kept Ginny on her feet.

That, Valerie thought, smiling, *is the way it's supposed to work.*

"THIS IS awesome." Standing on the back porch, Grace looked out over Jenny's yard and could hardly believe her eyes. "Your family does this every year?"

Orange pumpkin lights had been hung along the four sides of the yard. Strings of white skeleton lights crossed from corner to corner. Twenty different jack-o'-lanterns grinned at her from tables set near the fences. And in the middle of the wildness danced at least a hundred costumed people. Most of them, to her amazement, were adults.

Beside her, Ginny nodded. "My dad has pictures of me dressed as a bunny when I was just a year old, and they'd been having Halloween parties a long time before that." She wrinkled her face in the way she did when she was thinking. "I guess they skipped the year I was born, since my mom had just died."

"What's your favorite costume you ever wore?" Grace fingered her own outfit, a dress like Jo would have worn in *Little Women*. She even had her hair in a snood, a kind of hairnet with a velvet bow at the top, which was the neatest thing of all. Instead of a mask, she wore real makeup—eye shadow and blush and lipstick and everything. How cool was that?

"I like this year's best," Ginny said. "I can't believe Mr. Rhys actually let me wear one of his medals." In a black velvet riding hat, red jacket and tan breeches, with tall black boots taking the place of her braces, Ginny looked just like the photographs of Mr. Lewellyn when he rode at the Olympics. "I just wish I could have brought a horse, too." She smiled, because that was impossible, of course.

Connor and his new friend, Daniel, raced by in their space warrior costumes, pretending to shoot at each other with laser pistols that flashed blue-and-green lights. "Boys." Ginny rolled her eyes. "They always have to be something from the movies."

"I know. It looks like they get better when they grow up, though. Your Uncle Trent is dressed as a cowboy, right? And there's Mr. and Mrs. Bell—he's Lancelot and she's Guinevere. Your grandparents came as some kind of farmers. Ma and Pa Kettle, whoever that is."

"And Mr. DeVries is Abraham Lincoln. But his beard keeps falling off."

"I don't see your dad, though. What's he wearing?"

"He wouldn't tell me. Said it was a secret. And he

said he'd be late." Ginny shrugged. "Your mom is here, so I know he'll come sooner or later."

Grace turned away from the party and leaned back on the porch rail. "Do you think they're going to get married?"

"I think my dad wants to."

"I think my mom does." Suddenly doubtful, she looked at Ginny out of the corners of her eyes. "And I told her there was no problem as far as we were concerned. Right?"

Her friend grinned, and for a second she looked a lot like her dad. "Definitely right. Whatever the problem is between those two, nobody can blame it on you and me!"

ROB USUALLY AVOIDED creatures of evil for his Halloween costume, not to mention the ones who probably didn't really exist—werewolves, Frankenstein and the like. He'd always worried about giving Ginny nightmares.

But this year, with the number of nights he'd been spending roaming the house—not sleeping but drinking too much of a thick black brew that might as well be blood, and staring at the moon—he figured he was already halfway to being a vampire.

So he smoothed his hair back, donned a tux and a red-lined cape, inserted a set of false canine teeth and stepped into the dark as a creature of the night.

Jen's party was in full swing when he came through the gate. Crowded, as usual, with kids and with grownups. He saw Ginny and Grace together on the porch, like an old-fashioned portrait of the lady and the horse-man. Connor and Daniel fought right beside him with-out even recognizing his face—must have had something to do with the white greasepaint and red lip-stick. Rob couldn't believe women went around with this taste on their mouths every day.

Now dancing with Trent, Jenny had dressed as Sa-lome in veils and tinkling jewelry and shoes with long, pointed toes that had bells on the ends. Cute. Rhys and Jacquie had come in matching horse costumes, driven as a pair by their children, who seemed to get a great pleasure from using the "whip."

Of Valerie, he saw no sign, but he didn't know what her costume would be, so how could he find her? Ginny had said she didn't know, and he hadn't seen the woman herself since Sunday's campout, except for an hour at the GO! meeting, so he hadn't asked. They could be here together all night long and never know it.

At the thought, Rob actually felt the urge to bite something. Or somebody. Before he could choose a victim, he felt a tap on the shoulder.

"I vant to drink your blood," declared a fake Tran-sylvanian accent.

Turning, he stared into another vampire face—sleek dark hair, white makeup and lipstick, fake teeth. "Count Valerie, I presume?"

She executed an elegant bow. "The pleasure is mine, Count Varren. Vould you like to dance?"

He relaxed for the first time in days. "Vy not?"

There were no slow songs at the Halloween party, so they bounced around with everybody else, talking to friends between records, getting something to eat while the DJ took his break. He danced with Ginny and Grace, engaged in a brief space duel with Connor and discovered that vampires can be killed with laser bullets.

And all the while he was tired…tired of trying, tired of waiting, tired of holding up and hanging on. After one more dance with Valerie, he stepped back and made her a bow.

"It's been a pleasure, Count Valerie." He used the ridiculous accent they'd been teasing with all night. "I feel the sun coming up, however, and must return to my coffin." *Keep it light. You can fall apart when you're alone.*

She stared up at him in the darkness, her smile fading. "Understandable." Another flourishing bow. "Sleep vell."

If she wasn't going to detain him… "Thanks." He made his way through the crowd, shaking hands, slapping backs, producing fake smiles around his fake teeth. Those came out as soon as he reached the shelter of the trees.

When he looked across to his own house, though, a white face floated in the blackness on the other side of the gate. White hands gripped the pickets of the fence.

"That's eerie," he told her. "I could almost believe I'm in trouble, here."

"You are." She opened the gate and stepped back to let him through. "Come and meet your fate."

He followed her through the trees into his own yard, where things had definitely changed. Soft music—Sinatra—beat back the lingering noises from the party. Lighted candles of all sizes sat on the porch rails, the steps and his lawn tables. A bottle of harvest wine rested in a bucket of ice, with two glasses waiting nearby.

Most amazing of all, a new piece of furniture had been added to his collection—a double chair, meant to allow a couple to sit side by side, newly sanded and painted a soft turquoise. Like his car.

"Where did you find that?" He stepped close, running his hands along the arms, tracing the fretwork in the back panel. "It's terrific."

Valerie joined him. "My dad kept it. My grandparents always had chairs and tables sitting out in the grass at their house, but I hadn't seen them for a long time. So I called, and this is the only piece left. He shipped it down and Trent refinished it for me this week."

"I've looked for one of these..." He ran a hand through his sticky hair, and tried to pull himself together. "Thanks, Valerie. As Ginny might say, it's awesome."

But what did it mean?

Valerie saw the uncertainty in Rob's face, and the weariness. She'd felt the same way herself until the chair arrived and she saw its heart-shaped back panel. In that moment, everything in her life had fallen into place, with a sweet click like the sound of a well-oiled lock and the perfect key.

"Let's sit down," she suggested. "Want some wine?"

"Sure." As she'd hoped, he sat on the double chair and bounced a little, trying it out. She brought him a glass of wine and smiled at his surprise when she sat down beside him.

"The ultimate test, right?"

"Right." He shifted a little away from her, putting his back into the corner of the chair. His free arm went along the edge behind her shoulders.

"I've been giving the house situation some consideration this week." She started out as casually as she could. "And I've decided there are two houses I could live in."

"That's…good." He pulled his arm back a little.

"The problem is, they're both still occupied."

"Unfortunate."

"Mr. Bowdrey has turned the screws to get me out of my contract on the other house."

Rob nodded. "That's only fair."

"So I'm wondering if I can offer these people enough to let me have the house I want."

His forehead creased. "Valerie, I gotta say that sounds pretty impossible. I mean, if you walked up to my front door and held out a bucket with enough cash in it to pay twice or three times what this house is worth, I wouldn't sell. Home matters more than money."

Setting her wineglass on the table beside her, she turned to face him in the chair. Her throat felt tight, and the breath she took was shaky. "Really? Is there anything in the world I can offer you to let me live in your house?"

He sat motionless, but his eyes widened and his jaw dropped a little.

Valerie held out her hands, palms up. "I've got a little girl who thinks you're the best man on the planet. And a little boy who's come back to himself since you started giving him the manly attention he needs." She moved close, so her knees touched his thighs. "I can give you sex—great sex, in my opinion. A good paycheck. Health benefits, so you wouldn't be tied to the job with your dad. If you wanted to go out on your own in the security business, you wouldn't have to worry about Ginny's doctors' bills. Maybe you could simply use that as leverage with your dad—if you don't have to stay, he might be more willing to open his mind to your ideas."

Rob nodded, as if he were considering her offer. The twinkle had come back to his eyes. "That's it?"

Valerie barely suppressed her smile. "You want more?"

"What else have you got?"

She took his glass away. "I'm digging deep, now. A woman who loves you."

He squeezed his eyes shut for a second. "Go on," he said in a rough voice.

"A woman who wants to work with you and live with you for as long as you both shall live."

"What about the whole independence thing?" His hands came to her waist, lifted her onto his lap.

"Independence is good." She nodded, smoothing the silky cape over his shoulders. "But in my opinion, there are some aspects which have been highly overrated. Household chores, for instance, get done faster if two people cooperate."

"True." He stroked her back, her arms, cupped her shoulders, and she started to melt.

"Finances are more secure with two people paying

the bills," she said a little breathlessly. "Especially if you have kids who'll go to college one day."

"Good point."

"And…" She leaned forward, touched his cheek with her lips. "Yuck. You taste like makeup."

"You think?" He swiped the sleeve of his tux over his mouth, leaving a smear of red.

Grinning, Valerie did the same. "Now, where was I? Oh, yes…the sleeping alone in a big bed part. I happen to have cold feet. So I'm convinced that having another person in the bed, keeping it warm, is really a better idea." She brushed her mouth lightly across his. "What do you think?"

Rob took a sharp breath. "Think? What's that?"

In another instant, neither of them were thinking, only feeling, as they kissed and touched, sighed and shivered. He forgot the taste of lipstick and makeup, forgot all the obstacles as he breathed and tasted Valerie again, held her against him and felt his heart come back to life. He could have gone on without her, of course— he'd done that before.

Thank God, thank God he didn't have to this time.

"I love you," he told her, skimming her face with his fingers. Most of the white makeup was, by now, smeared across the shoulders of his cape. "I do love you. If you want to take another job, on the other side of the planet… I figure they'll need locksmiths there, too."

"Thank you," she said simply. "Thank you for being the man I wanted…and the man I needed." She sighed and rested her head on his chest. "Can it get any better than this?"

"You bet it can," he assured her.

And proceeded to prove the point.

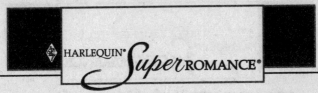

HARLEQUIN *Super*ROMANCE®

A *new six-book series from Harlequin Superromance.*

WOMEN *in Blue*

Six female cops battling crime and corruption on the streets of Houston. Together they can fight the blue wall of silence. But divided will they fall?

The Partner by Kay David
(Harlequin Superromance #1230, October 2004)

Tackling the brotherhood of the badge isn't easy, but Risa Taylor can do it, because of the five friends she made at the academy. And after one horrible night, when her partner is killed and Internal Affairs investigator Grady Wilson comes knocking on her door, she knows how much she needs them.

The Children's Cop by Sherry Lewis
(Harlequin Superromance #1237, November 2004)

Finding missing children is all in a day's work for Lucy Montalvo. Though Lucy would love to marry and have a family of her own, her drive to protect the children of Houston has her convinced that a traditional family isn't in the cards for her. Until she finds herself working on a case with Jackson Davis—a man who is as dedicated to the children of others as she is.

Watch for:
The Witness by Linda Style (#1243, December)
Her Little Secret by Anna Adams (#1248, January)
She Walks the Line by Roz Denny Fox (#1254, February)
A Mother's Vow by K.N. Casper (#1260, March)

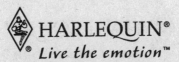

HARLEQUIN®
® *Live the emotion*™

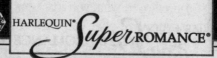

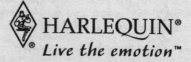

If you enjoyed what you just read,
then we've got an offer you can't resist!

Take 2 bestselling love stories FREE!

Plus get a FREE surprise gift!

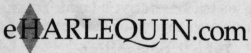

Receive a FREE hardcover book from

HARLEQUIN ROMANCE®

in September!

Harlequin Romance celebrates the launch of the line's new cover design by offering you this exclusive offer valid only in September, only in Harlequin Romance.

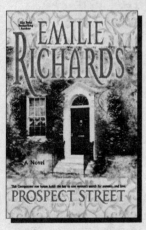

To receive your FREE HARDCOVER BOOK written by bestselling author Emilie Richards, send us four proofs of purchase from any September 2004 Harlequin Romance books. Further details and proofs of purchase can be found in all September 2004 Harlequin Romance books.

Must be postmarked no later than October 31.

Don't forget to be one of the first to pick up a copy of the new-look Harlequin Romance novels in September!

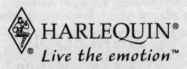

HARLEQUIN®
Live the emotion™

Visit us at www.eHarlequin.com

HRPOP0904

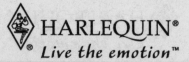